THE ZOO

ANDREW PHELPS

Copyright © 2021 by Andrew Phelps

All rights reserved.

No part of this book may be reproduced in any form or by any electronic or mechanical means, including information storage and retrieval systems, without written permission from the author, except for the use of brief quotations in a book review.

ISBN: 979-8-478960-74-2 (paperback)

Cover Artwork by Richie Cumberlidge at More Visual Ltd.

Fo' Leifo. Of course.

CONTENTS

1. WEDNESDAY, 25th AUGUST   1
   Dorothy
2. TUESDAY, 24th AUGUST   23
   Munchkinland
3. MONDAY, 23rd AUGUST   57
   The Scarecrow
4. SUNDAY, 22nd AUGUST   83
   The Tin Man
5. SATURDAY, 21st AUGUST   119
   The Cowardly Lion
6. FRIDAY, 20th AUGUST   155
   The Yellow Brick Road
7. THURSDAY, 19th AUGUST   193
   Emerald City
8. WEDNESDAY, 18th AUGUST   229
   No Place Like Home

Acknowledgements   259

WEDNESDAY, 25TH AUGUST

Dorothy

*T*rapped within a bramble thicket by a thousand spiny barbs, Dorothy's eyes flicked open.

Somehow it was daytime. In a fraction of a moment the darkness had disappeared, replaced instead by the thin light of a new day. Succulent blackberries hung all around her face, while a fiery headache raged.

This made no sense. She closed her eyes again.

The babble of songbirds. Occasional growls of traffic. She was still outside, still in the countryside. A mattress of spines jabbed at her hands and legs and the back of her head. Dorothy tried to move an arm, which shifted inside the damp sleeve of a jacket snared by the same talons. Still it made no sense. Dorothy scoured her memory for a clue. She knew that West had almost caught her, and she'd fallen off the road. And there were lights in the sky. But nothing that looked like an explanation.

This was meant to be the end of her journey. Dorothy turned her head gingerly towards the low morning sun, dragging sharp hooks across her cheek.

The pale rays reached across the rural landscape and caressed her face. She began to shake. At first imperceptibly – tiny spasms in her arms and neck – but as her heartrate quickened the twitches multiplied. Her limbs trembled inside her snagged clothing, rubbing against sticky layers of sweat, as the pain in her head swelled until it had burned a path across her temples and back past her ears. The thicket strengthened its hold.

With each involuntary shudder she shook off a little more of the paralysis, and the barbs bit harder into her flesh. Even though she barely had the strength to shiver, a thaw was under way. Her teeth started to rattle wildly against each other as her shaking intensified, and still the brambles' grip tightened. The convulsions grew until they had become an uncontrollable fit, flaying Dorothy's limbs about in every direction in a random dance, jabbing at the branches for signs of weakness. The spines tore fine rips in her clothing and gouged at her legs and hands, sending razor-sharp bursts of pain into her blazing head that she was powerless to stop. The seizure intensified into a frenzy as her panic surged. Dorothy tried to turn over, to tear herself loose, carving ever deeper channels of blood.

And with a final twist she broke free, tumbling onto the earth below.

Rising to her knees, Dorothy guzzled at the air, catching her breath, her dirty blonde hair trailing behind her into the depths of the briar. She knelt there as her breathing slowed and her shaking subsided, willing the disorientation in her brain to clear.

Although Dorothy was often mistaken for being younger than her nineteen years, it was impossible to even guess at her age beneath all the dirt and the network of scratches that scored her face. She was still wearing her filthy orange puffer jacket, zipped all the way up to her neck, above a pair of rainbow-coloured leggings, but both of these had been irreparably damaged by her escape. Her left trainer, which had started off life in dazzling white, now sported a generous spattering of dried blood underneath the mud.

In the morning light, Dorothy tried to gather her bearings. Even through the overwhelming pain in her head, she could feel the stinging from her lacerated hands, and a cramping nausea. She couldn't tell whether her headache was caused by hunger, or if she was feeling sick because of the torment in her brain, but it had been well over a day since she'd eaten anything. Whichever, she was certain that she was running a fever, and the woolliness that dulled her thoughts was probably not going to get much better.

Dorothy's gaze darted anxiously from side to side, trying to make sense of her surroundings. She was kneeling at the base of a steep embankment, from the top of which came the intermittent sounds of traffic. In every other direction a chequerboard landscape of fields taunted her for as far as she could see. The shivers returned. She was a long way from the comforting familiarity of the city. Even after all this time, all this effort and pain and sacrifice, she was still only one step ahead of West and all the other people who wanted to drag her back to the Zoo. None of this was happening in the way it was supposed to happen. None of this had been part of the plan.

As she attempted to climb to her feet, a fresh explosion of pain flared inside her head. She retched, pressing her bloodied hands to her ears to quieten the agony. Finding no respite, she started to attack an aggravating spot on her left forearm. Digging her nails through the padding of her jacket, she scratched away at an unseen wound, prodding and punching, squeezing and wincing, unaware of the tears that leaked down her cheeks along two clean tracks.

Some way ahead on the road above her, a car slammed on

its brakes, screeching across the tarmac, and the driver leaned heavily on his horn. Snapped back into the moment, Dorothy instinctively ducked below the bramble thicket and listened nervously. She could hear the driver shouting, but she couldn't pick out any meaning from his muffled ranting. A door slammed and an ugly silence descended. Dorothy tensed, desperately surveying the nearby terrain for her best opportunity of escape, until finally she heard the car pull away to resume its journey.

Whatever had just taken place, it was a reminder of just how exposed and vulnerable she was. She needed to get moving again.

BEHIND HER, an unharvested crop of shimmering yellow rapeseed had grown to waist height, and vibrated with the sounds of honeybees. After waiting impatiently for a lull in the traffic, Dorothy launched herself into a sprint that would take her away from the road, crossing the field towards the cover of a hedgerow that grew along the far boundary. She had only taken two steps when a dull pain in her right knee slowed her to a stumble, and a mounting trepidation followed her as she limped the rest of the way to safety across the unprotected terrain. By the time she had reached the distant thicket and squeezed through a gap, Dorothy had convinced herself that she must have been spotted by a passing motorist. Maybe not by West, maybe not even by the police, but by someone who knew she shouldn't be there. She curled up into a ball and screwed her eyes closed, breathing in the foetid odour of slept-in clothing and dried urine, resigned to her fate.

The sun rose higher into the clear August sky, cosseting Dorothy with its comforting warmth. Eventually she dared to look up again, but when she found herself completely surrounded by unpredictable nature, the jitters returned and she retreated once more into the sanctuary of her huddle. With her head pressed against her knees, she became aware of the steady thump of her heartbeat, felt how it modulated the suffering in her brain with every stroke. The closer she listened, the quieter became the gossip of hidden insects and the tussle of leaves in the breeze. She could hear her breath rattling in her throat, each gasp longer and deeper than the last. Slowly her focus drifted away from the anguish and fear back to the reassuring misery throughout her body. And with it came the confidence to continue her journey.

The plan had changed, but then the plan was always changing. This was not going to be the end of her story.

WITH A STAGGER, Dorothy set off, keeping out of sight on the far side of the hedgerow as she followed a parallel course to the road. At no time since the start of her journey had she felt so unprotected, and with so few opportunities for escape. The pain in her head came in surges, a rising swell that seemed to build from the knots in her stomach before crashing down in a violent deluge. These moments made Dorothy wail in distress, as she pressed her hands to her ears, or buried her eyes into the dark crook of her elbow. Slowly the misery would ebb away, allowing her an opportunity for a frenzied scratching session on her forearm as she waited for the torment to regroup.

All the while she continued her faltering advance, sometimes purposefully, more often lurching from one step to the next. As her path took her to the edge of one field and into the next, she saw that each was planted with the same yellow crop. She struggled across gates and stiles, and climbed over wire fences when she had no choice, only to be offered another identical view ahead – arbitrary perimeters on an otherwise unbroken golden carpet. Only the occasional appearance of faraway tractors convinced her she was actually making any progress.

She was midway across a field when a burst of excited barking disturbed her momentum. Dorothy turned around in time to see a border collie squeezing itself through the metal bars of a gate. Although still a couple of hundred yards away, the dog was staring directly at her. In an instant, she was ejected from her meditations on pain and self-pity. All she could think about was what would happen to her if she got caught. Not for the first time, she cursed the absence of a crowd to disappear into, or a corner to hide behind. With limited options, she plunged into the forest of rapeseed and crawled rapidly away on her elbows, deeper and deeper into the jungle. The barking intensified as the dog raced along the edge of the crop, clamouring from the sidelines as the woman crushed a passage through the leafy stalks. From the direction of the gate a shrill whistle sounded. Dorothy froze. The barking stopped momentarily while the dog considered its options before resuming its bluster.

'Christ's sake! Come around, lad!'

The distant command rippled through the screen of swaying crops. The dog paused again, then with a final bark scurried off to join its master. Dorothy remained completely still for the briefest of moments before the terrified shaking set in again, agitating the stalks in sympathy.

Close your eyes. Breathe. Think only about your breathing, nothing else. As Dorothy gulped air into her lungs, she poked her head up above the flowery canopy. On the far side of the field her would-be captor was walking away, but even at this distance she could make out the back of the familiar long-sleeved grey uniform. They were getting close. But they hadn't found her yet.

∼

Eventually, Dorothy's trek across the fields brought her to a line of trees, which stretched from the edge of the road into the far distance. She clumsily negotiated the barbed wire fence and allowed herself to be swallowed up by the dense woodland. By the time she emerged on the other side, with fresh wounds and tears in her clothing, the sun was high in the sky. After the recent shade, the fresh assault of daylight brought another searing rush of pain to her head. Dorothy clamped her hands over her eyes, peering through the gaps between her fingers to consider her new environment. The unexpected heat caused her lips to sting, but when she went to lick them she found that her tongue was completely dry, bumping uselessly across the burred skin. She tried to suck some saliva into her mouth, but all she managed to produce was a renewed wave of nausea. It was going to be painful progress underneath the blazing sun, even though she still felt cold inside her thick jacket.

In contrast with the tended landscape that she had left behind, the world on the far side of the forest had long been left to fend for itself. Abandoned and disowned, overgrown and disordered. A neglected track ran along the edge of the woodland, wide enough for a car or tractor, but it didn't look as if any vehicles had passed this way for a long while. Random piles of rusting metal grew amongst the dense weeds, with fossilised tyre tracks exposed in barren patches.

Somehow, it seemed familiar – a flashback to something that Dorothy barely remembered, if indeed she remembered it at all. There was nothing distinct, no obvious landmarks, but it felt as if she was looking at somewhere she ought to know, like the view from a window after a heavy snowfall. Dropping her hands, she tottered into the sunshine, weaving amongst the corroded artefacts, desperately trying to recall something just on the cusp of her memory.

When she finally spotted it, it knocked all the air from her body. She staggered backwards and clutched at her forearm, swaying chaotically, gawping. Hidden in a clump of nettles were the decaying remains of a girl's bicycle. Designed for a five-year-old, it sported wire baskets on the front and back, with rusted slots around the rear wheel where she had once proudly watched her stabilisers being removed. Two lengths of dirty rainbow-coloured ribbon had been tied to the handlebars.

This couldn't be right. This wasteland was too different to the sunshine-filled memories from her childhood. If she wanted any proper answers, she needed to get to the house. Her house. She needed to find her father.

PERCHED a little way back from the crest of a small incline and obscured behind a row of ancient oak trees, the farmhouse was the perfect place for a well-intentioned couple to escape from soulless suburbia and re-establish themselves amongst nature. A rustic idyll promising exciting new opportunities away from all the stresses and uncertainties of modern life. It was a chance to tend to the earth, with patience and diligence and love; to rediscover a slower and more meaningful existence. Just a few acres, somewhere to keep chickens and maybe even a goat, but still close enough to the city to go out to a restaurant from time to time, or maybe even the theatre.

After all this time, after all the walking and the deceit and betrayal, Dorothy was finally at the end of her journey. She had less than a mile left to travel. Suddenly her hobble wasn't fast enough, and her impatience soon turned to desperation. The ache in her knee was more debilitating, her hunger more acute, her fever more muddling. In another thousand yards her father would be able to see her approaching, and he'd run out to catch her before she collapsed. He'd take her inside and give her food and a bed, and hide her from all the people who were chasing her. Yet at no time since setting off a week earlier had she felt more like lying down and giving up than she did now.

As Dorothy stumbled around the line of oaks, her first sight of her childhood home forced her to a stop. She teetered on the spot, her mouth agape. The farmhouse, along with whatever dreams her father might have once had for a brighter future, had been long abandoned. Without anyone around to address the violations caused by time and weather, the building had fallen into a state of terminal disrepair. Although the main walls were still standing, the roof had almost completely collapsed, and piles of shattered slate ringed the house. A malignant ivy had claimed one corner of the property, devouring empty window frames and uninspired graffiti.

The appearance of the dilapidated farmhouse, exactly where she had left it all those years before, seemed as unexpected as it was inevitable, but this moment was entirely at odds with the fantasy that had sustained Dorothy for the past seven days. A profound sense of confusion pushed away any feelings of terror or despair. She had never actually planned past this point, anyway – even if her father had still been living there, she had no idea what to do next. But somehow the need to figure out how she could have got everything so wrong outweighed any concern for her wellbeing. For the first time since starting the journey, she felt completely lost.

The front door hung ajar on broken hinges, leaving a gap wide enough to allow Dorothy to squeeze her body through. Inside, daylight flooded through sizeable holes in the upstairs floor, illuminating shattered bottles and old mattresses from long-departed squatters. And everything adrift on a sea of broken slate. On the other side of a stone archway, the space opened out into the room where all the business of the house would once have been conducted, its centre dominated by a dining table so thick and robust that it had managed to resist any efforts to repurpose it into firewood. Unluckier fragments of furniture were piled beside a deep fireplace, along with a stack of books that must have served as kindling. A rotting wooden staircase climbed towards the precarious remainder of the first floor, and patches of thick black mould marked where kitchen appliances had once stood.

With so much of the ceiling missing, from this vantage point it was possible to look into every crumbling nook in the entire building. It was completely empty.

Dorothy limped through the stone archway and lingered on the threshold. For the past week, every step she had taken had moved her forward, brought her closer to safety and the prospect of seeing her father again. After they had dumped the stolen car in the middle of nowhere, or while they searched the backstreets in the city, or when she was running from the police, this was the one thought that had sustained her, kept her resolute. Every step was a step in the right direction. And now this next one wasn't.

She had nothing left in the tank. Her damaged knee buckled under the realisation, and she lurched forward. Dorothy grabbed the edge of the dining table to stop herself from falling, and lowered herself awkwardly onto the surround by the fireplace. Finding herself drained of purpose, her headache raged unchecked, but she was too exhausted to even feel sorry for herself. Without the mission to focus her thoughts, her overheating brain had begun to simmer, and she cautiously pressed her burning face against the cool mosaic tiles on the wall. The bloodstain that covered her left trainer was now completely concealed by mud. It was the last thing she had to remind her of Henry, all that was left of him, and it too was lost forever. It was another sign of what she had had to sacrifice to get there. If she didn't get rid of some of this heat quickly, it threatened to boil over into a lonely meltdown.

It took a moment to register, hidden near the bottom of the pile of fireside paperbacks. Reaching down, Dorothy pulled a book from the stack, scattering the surplus kindling. It was a picture book telling the story of *The Wizard of Oz*, handsomely illustrated throughout with drawings of the characters from the film and printed on thick childproof paper. This wasn't just her favourite story; this *was* her story. She thought of all the times as a little girl when she had pleaded to be whisked away, far from the stresses and the people that wished bad things on her. Only her story didn't have the unhappy ending. In her story she never clicked her heels together. She got to stay in the colourful land of Oz with her friends forever. She wiped a sleeve over the sooty cover and opened the first page, where its previous owner had painstakingly scrawled her name. She traced the word with her finger and whispered, 'Dorothy.'

Hearing her name spoken out loud, the dam finally broke.

She had no idea how long ago she had built the defensive barriers inside her head, but she could almost hear them bursting apart. A deluge of long-forgotten memories flooded through the fractures. Not just shiny static snapshots, but real moments. Moving pictures. Emotions. Choices and consequences, triumphs and failures. Times when she had played happily in the house, and times when she had to hide. Flashbacks to the adventures she had when it was just her and her father, and memories of what happened after The Woman came to live with them. Happy and sad; carefree and frightened; everything arriving in a confused jumble that made it impossible to associate feelings with events. The floodwaters had broken through, sucking Dorothy into the tangled wreckage of her childhood. And she was drowning.

It's the Munchkin, isn't it?

It was a whisper, almost lost in the maelstrom. Something escaping through the cracks that should never have been set free. It wasn't even a voice, more a passing moment of sense amongst the noise and clamour. And then it was gone, swallowed back into the morass.

It hit Dorothy like a punch from an unseen assailant.

Her head snapped around, scouring the room for something – anything – to offer an explanation, trying to hear above the tumult that surged through the empty farmhouse.

It's the Munchkin, isn't it? What has she done now?

Dorothy's head lolled. No one ever called her Munchkin. No one except her father. She shouldn't be here. She shouldn't have come back, she knew that now. Dorothy tried to stand, but her damaged knee buckled under her weight and she fell forward onto the floor. The breach widened. The voice became stronger.

What's going on? Is everything OK?

From her position on her hands and knees, the room around her looked so big, so overwhelming. She probably couldn't see over the top of the table, even if she stretched up as high as she could reach. There was no way she could make it to the door without being spotted.

It must be nice to live in your fairy castle.

A different speaker. This voice was louder. Clearer. Shrill and angry. And disappointed, always disappointed. Just hearing it triggered a discharge of adrenaline, followed by an urgent nausea. Dorothy heaved until green bile fouled her taste buds and dribbled from her mouth, the sound of her gagging lost in the discord that filled the silent room.

I swear she's trying to drive me mad.

It was The Woman. The Woman her father had brought home with him one day, and who then never left. Dorothy lifted her hands to her face, covering her eyes, but the chaotic battering of images and memories continued. She pounded on her forehead, desperately trying to empty her head of thoughts.

But sweetheart, she's only seven.

Dorothy froze. This voice came from behind her, from the archway leading into the room. Her breath lodged in her throat and her eyes bulged. He was in the room with her. She could feel her father's presence; his height; how he smelled after a day of digging up the garden. If she only dared to turn her head, she would certainly be able to see him, but a paralysis had infected her muscles. A cold draught passed through her hair and lingered on the nape of her neck.

I knew it was pointless trying to talk to you.

Ahead of her the shadows gathered. An indefinite form slowly parted from the gloom and emerged into the half-light of the dining room, but bringing most of the darkness with it. It was impossible to see where the figure ended and the shade started. Against the mottled greens of the ivy that crept in through the broken windows and the caustic orange of Dorothy's coat, the figure seemed to be completely devoid of colour.

'You don't have to deal with her shit all day,' it growled.

'I know. I'm sorry,' the voice of Dorothy's father replied, as a second hazy presence drifted into view from behind where she crouched. Taller, but stooped. Older. A strange melancholia clung to the shadowy silhouette. It glided between shafts of daylight, but the rays passed through the grey profile without seeming to touch the person beneath.

'It's not forever,' it reassured the agitated apparition.

Still Dorothy stayed locked in place, immobile. She could have shut her eyes, but the more she concentrated on the unfolding drama, the better she could endure the confused turmoil of memories and the pain that blazed through her head. The illusion bobbed in front of her like driftwood on a turbulent sea, and she grabbed at it. It wasn't real. It might not even be the truth. But at that moment it was the only thing in the farmhouse that made any sense.

In front of her, the conversation continued regardless. The Woman floated across to intercept the shadow of her father. 'No. Something needs to change,' she barked. 'The child is a mess. She's certifiable. You saw what she did to her dog.'

Dorothy's father opened his arms, stretching loose wisps of darkness through the gloom. 'When we get her back into school...' he began, but his conciliatory tone seemed to have the opposite effect.

'What school?' The Woman interrupted. 'Come on! What school is going to take her? There's nowhere left. There's something broken in her head.'

'Sweetheart – she's a kid. She's just a little kid.' By now, the colourless figures had drifted together. Seen side by side, Dorothy's father didn't look as tall as he once had. The Woman's hands had moved to her hips as she squared up to the other apparition, which slumped forward to meet her. They were going to have an argument, whether he wanted one or not.

'You don't spend all day with her. You don't understand her,' The Woman explained calmly, as if moving through a conversation she had already rehearsed. 'That's why it's not your choice any more.'

Even as Dorothy stared up at them, she knew she shouldn't be listening to this. Their words were never meant for her to hear. But this was important. This was about her. *Don't run away. Hide, Dorothy. Hide where they can't see you.*

'But she's my daughter!' pleaded her father, his words choked by a sudden desperation. 'Of course I have a say in this! She's my daughter, not yours!'

The figure of The Woman shook her head contemptuously. 'Don't give me that wicked stepmother shit,' she snarled.

There were a thousand places to hide in the farmhouse, and Dorothy knew every single one of them. She knew how long it took to scamper between them, and how to time her runs to avoid being caught. She knew which hiding places had already been discovered, and which were still safe. She could even get upstairs without touching a creaky stair. And it was at the top of the staircase that Dorothy should be right now, two steps down, just before she reached the landing. There she could press her body against the lumpy stone wall and study the whole of the dining room without fear of detection, quietly disappearing should someone approach. It was only a matter of time before one of the grown-ups spotted her on the floor, anyway, and she was amazed she'd gotten away with it for as long as she had. The figures, however, were more concerned with their altercation, and The Woman still had something to say.

'We're not helping Dorothy if she stays with us,' she explained, the sinister detachment returning to her voice.

Her father's shadowy form rocked backwards, and he stood upright for the first time. Another chilling draught crept through the room, and it looked like he had felt it too.

'What have you done?' he croaked.

'The people from social services came by this morning.

They could see it straight away. Soon as they met Dorothy, they could see it.'

Dorothy's father let out a low moan and his apparition started to sway erratically. Only when his wailing had developed into grief-stricken sobs did The Woman carry on. 'The formal evaluation is next week, but they already know she needs expert care,' she announced without a trace of emotion. 'Care she can't get if she's living here. Whether that means moving to a unit, or some specialist foster home, they don't know yet.'

'Oh God,' Dorothy's father spluttered. 'What have you done? What have you done?'

'Only what you lack the balls to do yourself.'

'But she's my daughter!' Dorothy's father howled. 'She's my daughter!'

'Yeah?' The Woman replied, staring him down. 'Well, now it's just you and me.'

And with those words, Dorothy snapped.

Her reaction came as just as much of a surprise to her as it did to the hazy grey figures in front of her. For the first time since falling inside her long-forgotten memory, Dorothy's perspective on the debate was no longer within her control. A raw fury had exploded through her exhausted body, vaporising all traces of confusion and anguish. Before she could question where this unexpected rage had come from, it had propelled her to her feet and launched her towards the startled combatants. She had suddenly become part of the drama, a passenger in events she was now powerless to alter.

Her father turned towards the onrushing girl, finally acknowledging her presence in the room. 'Munchkin!' he bawled, crouching down, his arms outstretched, preparing to catch Dorothy in a protective hug.

But she had her mind on other matters. Sidestepping his

embrace, she ran at The Woman, roaring and flailing her arms. The apparition braced herself against Dorothy's onslaught, but the girl's wild offensive passed ineffectually through the mirage, finding only air. Caught off balance, Dorothy collapsed awkwardly onto the dining room floor, her hands breaking her fall on a carpet of broken glass and jagged slate. Spasms of pain screamed out above the fracas, but vanished just as quickly as she was engulfed once again in the melee.

The grown-ups spun around as one to confront the fallen girl. Holding his hand out, her father advanced towards his daughter as if trying to corner a frightened cat. 'Munchkin! Calm down!' he blurted between sobs. 'I'm not going to let anything happen to you!'

Dorothy turned to the shadowy form of her father as he approached through the gloom. He crouched down, leaning towards the tiny girl on the floor until he was finally close enough for her to stare into his face.

Although somehow it was Thatcher that gazed down at her.

Even through the noise and confusion, the sight of her old travelling companion made Dorothy gasp in dismay. This was definitely *not* her father. This was not even close. It had been so long ago that she had almost no memory of what her father actually looked like, but this was still a cruel trick for her subconscious to play. This man was someone who had promised to help her, and then had tried to hurt her. Thatcher's long grey hair looked even more silvery than usual, the furrows along his forehead deeper. She raised a bloodied hand to ward him off.

'It's for your own good, Dorothy. It'll help you feel better,' countered The Woman. 'It's not going to be forever.'

Around her, the impossible inhabitants of the dining room were becoming clearer, drifting into focus. Now that Dorothy had allowed Thatcher into the drama, other actors were stepping in to fill the remaining roles. Her stepmother's abrasive whine sounded lower, even more gruff, and when the colourless figure shuffled into view behind her father with her arms crossed, Dorothy was not surprised to see Crane's pallid face sneering down at her. Another companion, another friend she had lost along the journey. Even though Crane was male, the instinctive contempt he shared with The Woman made it difficult for Dorothy to tell which one of them was actually speaking to her.

It was only when she spotted the enormous figure of Parsley on the other side of the room that Dorothy finally knew she would be safe. This was the one person that would always keep her out of danger, always protect her, whatever it took. Barely visible behind broken bannisters, sitting two steps down from the top of the staircase, he waited motionless, impassive, watching the scene play out below him as he clutched Dorothy's *Wizard of Oz* picture book to his chest. She felt an urgent need to go to her friend, to huddle beneath his substantial shelter while she dealt with this rage and turmoil.

Dorothy pressed her hands against the floor in an effort to stand up, but a sharp pain shot along her arm, causing her to topple backwards again. Over the course of her inelegant tumble, a sizeable shard of glass from a broken wine bottle had wedged itself in one of her palms, and she had just shoved the fragment further in, burying it deep into her flesh. Although the initial discomfort had barely even registered over the turbulence in her head, it was coming through more clearly now she'd seen the wound. For a moment, Dorothy felt a panic try to assert itself through the chaos – an instinctive reaction to an injury that she knew she couldn't deal with alone – but it was quickly replaced by a curious sense of reassurance. She was still part of the real world, despite all evidence to the contrary.

As the stab of pain subsided, Dorothy found herself back in the abandoned farmhouse, sitting alone on the floor amongst the jagged debris. The apparitions had faded away, becoming just echoes in the room.

'You can be better, can't you, baby?' urged Thatcher's despairing voice. 'If we help you?'

But before Dorothy had a chance to question her new reality, The Woman had reappeared, leaning over her. 'You're not allowed to blame me for this,' she cautioned Dorothy in Crane's voice. 'You've left us no choice.'

And then her father was back as well, competing to fill Dorothy's field of view. 'Just tell us you want to try, Munchkin,' he beseeched her.

Tell us you want to try. The terrified desperation in her father's appeal cut a swathe through the tumult, and in that instant Dorothy realised why she had been brought back to this moment in time, why she was reliving this particular conversation. The sentence had acted like a key, unlocking something deep within her troubled psyche. Something that had gone on to shape the person she had become. Even as a frightened child, Dorothy had recognised that whatever she said next, whatever promises she made or assurances she gave, her father couldn't protect her from what was already under way. And this was the one person who professed to love her, who told her he would always forgive her despite everything she did that was wrong or bad.

It was the epiphany that had marked her last moment of childhood.

In the hush that followed, the warring apparitions leant in to hear her answer. When Dorothy finally spoke, there was no bitterness in her voice.

'I can be better,' she whispered.

It was not a commitment; it was a challenge to her subjugated father. It might take her ten years, maybe even twenty. But she would do it. She would be better, and then she would come back and show him. Show him that he had given up on her way too easily. Show him that he was stupid to have let The Woman come and stay with them. Show him that he had made the wrong choice when he picked someone else as his favourite.

A curious calm began to permeate through Dorothy's consciousness. She turned her attention away from the ongoing play towards the dull ache in her hand. Her last manoeuvre had pushed the broken glass so far into her palm that she could see a bump under the skin on the top of her hand, where the tip of the shard was threatening to break through. Blood was dribbling from around the wound into a pool on the floor next to where she sat. This should really hurt, Dorothy thought, surprised by her indifference. She usually hated the sight of blood, especially when it was her own, but where she would normally expect to be feeling faint, she instead found herself marvelling at how fragile her body was. And how, after so much abuse and suffering, it could still withstand something as obviously horrific as this. Or maybe she'd just got used to it after carrying Henry's blood around on her trainer all week.

Dorothy reached across and gave the shard a tug, expecting it to come free with the same ease with which it had entered her hand. The action created a twinge of discomfort, but the splintered glass was firmly wedged in place. This was going to require slightly more heft to remove, and maybe a bit of a wiggle as well. She clutched the glass, trying to find the best grip.

No longer the focus of the girl's attention, the voices had retreated into the gloom, bickering with each other again rather than addressing her directly. But then Crane and Thatcher were always arguing.

'It's not too late!' claimed one.

'You should have done this years ago,' replied the other.

Annoyingly, a session of methodically twisting the exposed glass didn't help it come out after all. All it did was make the blood flow faster. The trickle had become a rhythmic pump, squirting dashes of red across the debris like a child's painting. But actually, it was probably OK to leave it in there. It didn't hurt, really, and her arm was getting awfully heavy.

'But she's my little girl!' protested a voice somewhere in the distance, straining to be heard above the gentle murmur of the world outside and the steady thump of a beating heart.

I'm going to miss her too, you know?

And with that, Dorothy was alone.

Outside the farmhouse, the sun had reached its zenith, lovingly caressing the countryside under a cloudless sky. Inside, a beam of sunlight had found its way through one of the gaps in the roof and ceiling, spotlighting a column of dust that stretched all the way from the floor and up to the heavens beyond. Dorothy sat watching the motes gently swirl and rise; so many graceful trajectories slotting perfectly together without ever colliding.

Had she felt the need to take stock of her circumstances, she would have been pleasantly surprised. Her debilitating headache was all but forgotten, and even the insatiable itch on her forearm had blossomed into a teasing tingle, like the playful breeze of a lover's breath. Dorothy neither questioned nor acknowledged these things, she just accepted them.

So much so, that when Henry drifted towards her from out of the darkness, she knew right away that it was meant to be him. He wasn't playing a role in someone else's story. He was missing all of his colour as well, but there was no mistaking his grin – the special smile that he only ever used when he was around Dorothy. She knew that Henry was already gone, and he couldn't be there. But there he was, illuminated in the spotlight, his silly hair with too many curls, beaming so hard that she wondered what kind of mischief he had planned. The corners of her mouth flicked up into the widest smile she could muster.

'Henry,' she breathed at the approaching figure.

And then he was beside her, taking her in his arms, cradling her from the vagaries of the outside world and keeping her hair from falling into her face. Dorothy closed her eyes and rested her head on her lover's shoulder, knowing he was about to say something that would make her laugh.

'Shame on you, Princess. Keeping me waiting like that.'

She giggled softly and nuzzled her head against his neck. A delicate tranquillity rose up to welcome her, whispering sweet promises about their future together on some colourful journey, free from all obstacles and the concerns of others. The rhythmic thump of her heart slowed, shrinking the world around her until only the two of them were left. Dorothy breathed in Henry's musk for the last time before allowing herself to be swallowed by the comforting darkness.

TUESDAY, 24TH AUGUST

Munchkinland

*H*uddled into the corner of a child's wooden den, surrounded by outdoor toys and empty chocolate wrappers, Dorothy's eyes flicked open.

Although she hadn't been there for years, her first view of the inside of the hut in daylight triggered an unexpected swell of nostalgia. For a fleeting instant Dorothy was aware of all the other lives she could have lived since she was last there, and with this came a painful longing for the chance to go back and choose a different path. The den wasn't somewhere that she particularly cherished from her childhood, and the urgency of her reaction caught her completely off-guard. This morning she wasn't going to be given an opportunity to prepare herself for the new day.

There had been something in her last dream. Dorothy cast her mind back through the few surviving fragments before they vanished. She had been running from someone, she remembered that, and she had hidden in a caravan (at least, she assumed it was a caravan, even though she had never actually seen inside one before). And Henry had been there with her. A clammy layer of sweat had made the inside sleeves of her puffer jacket damp, but even though the orange coat was zipped up all the way to her neck, she still felt cold. Maybe Crane had been right after all. Maybe she was getting sick, running a fever. It would certainly explain why she was being plagued by these strange thoughts and emotions when she should really be focusing on the mission at hand. Dorothy couldn't stop a pang of anguish from interrupting her contemplative mood. She wished she had a little more time so she could get back to missing Henry properly.

Outside, the world was busy with the sounds of a Tuesday already in full swing. Every type of garden bird was awake and chattering, gossiping over the distant commotion of excited children and city traffic. On either side of the den's undersized door, two small rectangular holes had been cut out for windows, keeping the inside of the hut dark and cool. Dorothy was aware of an unpleasant stench in the stagnant air, and it seemed to be coming from her. It was probably later in the day than she was expecting, and she wondered how she'd managed to stay asleep so long through this racket.

The garden den had clearly been built to last: it was an absurdly over-engineered construction that resembled a miniature Alpine log cabin, intended to outlast the play needs of countless children. It was a little too short to allow Dorothy to stretch out, forcing her to spend the night curled in a foetal position on the hard floor amongst unfamiliar toys. Sitting up, she rolled out the knots in her back and shoulders as well as the space allowed, while leaves and twigs tumbled from her clothes and swung unnoticed in her hair. Even though she had devoured her stockpile of chocolate bars the evening before, she still felt hungry, and the headache, which had started last night, felt even worse in the daylight. Even in the subdued glow she had to screw up her eyes to protect against the brightness.

Over the cacophony of birdsong came the sound of a door latch, followed by the gabble of children. Dorothy stole a cautious glance through one of the windows in the den, which opened out across a long garden strewn with plastic toys and balls. On the far side, past the miniature goalposts, children poured through the side door of a large semi-detached house. Three – no, four – kids, each with an identical backpack: makeshift siblings in foster care with a mix of hair colours and skin tones, continuing a noisy game of tag that must have started inside the house.

Then Aunt Ruby appeared through the same door.

Dorothy reeled backwards, into the safety of the unlit den, as an unexpected anxiety swept through her. The sensitive spot on her forearm flared into an obstinate itch, which she pawed at through her puffer jacket. There were suddenly too many things to think about. Voices telling her to get out and make a run for it, no matter that this would take her right past Ruby; other voices reminding her that, if she did that, she would never be able to find out how to get to her father's farm; another voice telling her to breathe, to think only about each breath, to stay where she was until there was no one around to see her.

And then there was Ruby's voice, floating across the garden and reverberating through the wooden shelter. 'Wait up! Don't go running off!'

Dorothy froze. What kind of witchcraft could read her thoughts from all that way, and in the dark as well? The irritation on her forearm screamed for attention, but she couldn't risk moving a single muscle, barely even drawing breath into her lungs. Ruby continued, 'Jack! Kwame! Not near the road! How many times?'

During her stay as a guest in the house when she was younger, Dorothy had witnessed plenty of examples of Ruby's 'in trouble' voice. When she had done something that made Ruby not angry but disappointed, and other times when Ruby had actually just been angry. And this was not that voice. No, this was a tired mantra spoken by an overloaded foster-parent. The panic loosened its grip as Dorothy dared to believe her plan might still be in play. She craned her neck to chance another peek through the window.

Although Ruby's warning had done little to calm the disorderly children, her attention was now focused on someone loitering inside the house. Ruby squatted down and extended one of her hands to the unseen figure. At this angle, she looked much more like the kind-hearted soul that Dorothy had hoped she would be when they had met all those years ago. Slightly too old, frequently overwhelmed, but always trying to be someone's mum.

Ruby called back into the house in her lilting West Country burr. 'C'mon, my lovely girl. Can't go lurking in there all day.'

A hesitant young girl stepped out into the garden. She must have been about eight years old, with long blonde hair and wide soulful eyes that looked as if they had already seen too much. The girl had picked out an ensemble of bright but clashing colours, and her hands were clasped around a book. Ruby flashed her an encouraging smile as she reached past to pull the door shut.

From her vantage point, Dorothy felt a strange pull towards the girl, although she had no idea why. She had an inexplicable urge to run up to her and hold her hand, to smell her hair, to be the one that answered the all stupid questions that grown-ups ask and to listen to her when she was reading. She worried that no one would ever take the time to try to properly understand what the girl was thinking, and what made her do the things she did. In acknowledgement, the girl turned her sombre gaze down the garden towards the darkened window in the wooden den, and stared directly at Dorothy.

Dorothy let out an involuntary gasp as their eyes met, but she didn't move, didn't break away from the contact. Whatever was happening, whatever this was, she somehow knew that this was not going to be the moment when all her meticulous planning fell apart. This was something very different – reassuring but unsettling nonetheless.

'Francie?' Ruby called back to the girl, her attention focused on keeping her more boisterous charges out of the path of traffic. 'Francie girl?'

Francie's eyes lingered an instant longer before she turned away. Ruby stole a glance towards the den before holding her hand out. 'Were you after something from the garden?' she asked the young girl. Dorothy's muscles tightened, aware that the wrong answer would surely mark the end of her journey, but instead Francie's gaze drifted off towards the other children who had already bounded away up the road.

'Oh, you are being a dotty daisy this morning,' Ruby cheerfully admonished her as the two of them shuffled off in pursuit.

In the den, Dorothy collected her thoughts. As the empathy and adrenaline subsided, her headache returned with a vengeance, and with it a need for food and something to drink. She plucked at her nagging forearm, trying to make sense of what had just passed. It was clear that she now had another responsibility to deal with when her mission was complete, and she would someday have to come back to this place. But that was for a later time. Right now, she had a job to do.

Getting the back door open was easy – all she needed was a long garden toy. In through the cat-flap, a nudge upwards on the handle to unlock it, then a sharp tug down to open the door. It was a manoeuvre that Dorothy had practised so often as a child that she even knew the angle at which the locking mechanism made the most noise, enabling her to get in and out of the house at all hours of the night without waking anyone. Inside, Ruby's kitchen looked almost identical to how she remembered it. The floor was scattered with someone else's toys, and the fridge plastered with different artwork, but otherwise very little had changed. The same stack of dirty bowls and cups surrounded the sink, and the same pile of muddy shoes lined the back door.

The plan had always been to get in, find her father's address, then get out again as quickly as possible. But as she passed through the kitchen she found herself slowing down, mesmerised by the familiarity of the sounds: the drone from the old fridge; the two-note melody of water dripping from the taps and hitting the metal sink; the percussion of the old cuckoo clock. She was back listening to the music of her childhood.

It was the clock that fascinated Dorothy more than anything else, but then it always had. She walked over to examine it up close, pulling a dining chair with her to stand on before realising she was now tall enough to reach it unassisted. After a lifetime of being over-wound by eager children, the clock's once nondescript tick had been stressed into a twang that sounded like it was repeatedly asking the room's occupants, 'Why?'

Dorothy placed a finger against the minute hand and rotated it through to the hour mark, ignoring the protests from the cogs and springs. As it clicked into place, a silent cuckoo popped out through missing doors and immediately ducked back inside. On its third outing, Dorothy caught the tiny bird between her thumb and forefinger and inspected it more closely. Satisfied, she released it back into the belly of the clock for another hour of nagging questions.

The kitchen symphony played on. The power that these childhood memories still held had caught Dorothy by surprise, and she let out an involuntary shiver. She should get on with what she was there to do, and then leave as quickly as she could. And maybe also see if there was something to eat in the fridge on the way out.

CHILDREN WERE NEVER TECHNICALLY FORBIDDEN from going into Ruby's office; the house was, after all, a refuge, and they were all guests. However, they were certainly discouraged from letting their activities spill across its threshold. Toys left inside the room had a habit of getting trodden on and broken, and all play had to be completely quiet when Aunt Ruby was working behind the big desk. In the end, it was usually easier to just set up in a less contentious spot. Because of this, the office was where the thrall of the house was at its weakest.

But Dorothy still felt a moment of disquiet as she entered the room. This was the place where every important piece of paper was carefully sorted and filed, an activity that had looked to the younger version of herself to be both essential and utterly incomprehensible. She remembered the imposing rows of lever-arch files and numbered cardboard folders on the shelves behind the desk. While once these only highlighted the fact that there was more fun to be had elsewhere in the house, now these were gatekeepers to the secrets that Ruby had kept hidden from her all these years. But what had given

Dorothy her sense of foreboding was the one object that was strictly off-limits to everybody.

Sitting on a dedicated table, shielded from sight and away from temptation, was Aunt Ruby's old dollhouse.

Not even Ruby herself was sure exactly how old the dollhouse was, but it was a matter of record that her great-grandmother had been presented with this curio on her tenth birthday by her doting father. Even after being passed down from mother to daughter through the generations, it had somehow managed to remain immaculate inside and out. Peering through the missing façade at the decor inside provided an exquisite snapshot of domestic Victorian life: rosewood cabinets stacked with Sunday china, bed-warmers, dress-making mannequins and ornate modesty guards. And not a single scale-model Victorian in there to clutter the place up.

Guests usually received instructions about the dollhouse on their first day. They were delivered in a regretful, yet friendly, manner, along the lines of: 'Although it looks like a toy, it's very, very old, and because of this the house and all its contents are too fragile to touch.' Even a strong breeze would apparently be enough to bring about the collapse of the house, and the office door had to be opened with care in case it created a catastrophic waft. And then there was the story, shared amongst the children during late-night whispered conversations, of the young boy who had stolen a sideboard from inside the dollhouse, and when he was caught by the police he had to immediately go back to live with his homicidal parents. And no one ever heard from him again.

So, the forbidden plaything passed from curiosity to cautionary tale and eventually indifference, forgotten amongst all the sanctioned opportunities for entertainment. Being in the same room as the dollhouse again, Dorothy was overwhelmed by the childish nervousness that she had felt as a teenager. Only now she could get as close to it as she wanted. She could peer into every chamber, maybe even move some of the furniture around – and there was nothing Ruby could do to stop her. The prospect was utterly thrilling, and she needed to take a moment to remind herself why she was really there.

She hadn't spent much time imagining how the filing system worked during her stay in Ruby's house, so Dorothy knew only that a piece of paper with her father's address would be kept somewhere in that room. That said, she didn't remember there being quite so many places where it could hide. Against her better judgement, she felt a twinge of regret that Crane wasn't there to help. His plan had focused on what they needed to do to physically get there, into the office, and Dorothy assumed that he had a separate plan for how to efficiently search through Aunt Ruby's archives once they were inside. Even if he didn't, at least he could have started at the other end of the shelves and cut the workload in half. Dorothy cut her introspection short and berated herself for thinking about her former companion. She was doing fine under her own steam.

Even so, the task ahead was daunting. The realisation made Dorothy feel woozy, and she had to clutch the desk to steady herself. She scanned the names of the files for a clue, hoping to find inspiration in Ruby's careful scrawl. Folders marked *Schools* or *Legislation*, each followed by a specific year, seemed to be the most popular; elsewhere *Letters*, *Training* and *Court Info* each had their own binder; and stretching along the whole bottom shelf, a series labelled *UKFN Misc. 1* to *12*. But nothing called *Addresses*.

She seemingly had no choice. She had to start at the beginning, and make sure she didn't miss anything that might be important. Her head throbbed with pain, and she reeled for a second time. Still, faint heart never fucked a goat, as Henry used to say before embracing a new task. Dorothy pulled the left-most lever-arch file from the bottom shelf, *UKFN Misc. 1*, laid it gently on the desk and opened it. The file was heavy with a stack of irregularly sized letters and pamphlets, piled so deep that the restraining clamp could barely secure the paperwork in place.

Tracing her finger down the top page, she began to read the first document.

Dear carer

A number of our members have recently reported an increase in 'phishing' emails, and I would like to take this opportunity to remind you all of a few simple rules to stay safe online and avoid identity theft.

Dorothy paused. Now that she was compelled to concentrate on something, she could properly appreciate how groggy this fever was making her. Nothing seemed to be going in. She went back and reread the opening sentence. No – this wasn't going to tell her anything about her father. She turned to the next document: a glossy leaflet containing more information on the best ways to avoid identify theft.

This didn't look relevant either. And then her patience with the process ran out. There had to be an easier way. She wrapped her fingers under the last page and riffled through all the contents in one breezy motion, staring intently at each fleetingly exposed sheet. This was, if anything, even less productive than her first idea. She shoved the file onto the floor and pulled the second one down from the shelf: *UKFN Misc. 2*.

The front door slammed.

Dorothy stopped and stood stock-still, wide-eyed with trepidation. She had no choice – the only door from the office opened out into the hall, which would bring her face to face with whoever had just entered the house. File in hand, she strained to listen for other noises over the frenzied thumping of her heart.

Footsteps from the hall. Shuffling, distracted. Getting louder.

The handle turned and the office door swung open. Ruby ambled into the room, engrossed in sorting through a stack of mail. Up close, she still bore a resemblance to the loving surrogate parent that Dorothy remembered from when she moved into Ruby's house all those years ago, who had told Dorothy that she'd keep her safe and support her for as long as she needed. Even then her aunt had been in her late fifties, with a careworn countenance that she bore with a martyr's zeal. Soon after her arrival, Dorothy had noticed that her aunt behaved differently when she thought someone was watching her, adopting a tortured grimace and slowing every action down as if to emphasise that whatever was about to follow was for someone else's benefit, despite all her aches and pains.

Today, it was only from her aunt's cheerful expression and casual stride that Dorothy knew she hadn't been spotted. Lost in concentration, Ruby sauntered across the room directly towards her. Dorothy's mounting unease was only a couple of steps away from maturing into a full-blown panic attack when her aunt stopped in her tracks and sniffed at the air, a confused expression on her face. The older woman glanced up, and found herself staring directly at her frightened visitor. She let out a shriek, staggered backwards, and fell onto the floor in a blizzard of envelopes.

The two women gaped at each other in silence for the longest moment. It was Ruby who eventually managed to regain enough composure to break the tension.

'Dotty?' she enquired uncertainly. 'Dotty-girl? How are you...?'

Getting caught was not a scenario that Dorothy had thought about. She found herself floundering, struggling to figure out what to do next. Her loudest voices demanded flight, and with Ruby helpless on the floor, Dorothy was pretty confident that she could slip past and escape. Her unease receded slightly. What was certain, though, was that there was now nothing she could do to stop herself from being in trouble. At that moment she was a small child again, caught in the act of torturing the wooden cuckoo.

'Mother of mine, Dotty! You nearly knocked the devil himself out of me!' Slowly, Ruby pushed herself off the floor and started to climb back to her feet. 'Should you be here, my lovely? I'm not sure you should.'

It had only needed Ruby to open her mouth to remind Dorothy that this was not the compassionate spirit everyone else claimed her to be. No, this was the same harridan who had spent so much time not listening to what Dorothy had to say. This was the same old woman who had wasted all that energy trying to assert her will and control over everything Dorothy did, until she gave up as well and sent her away just like her stepmother had done. Without really understanding why, Dorothy was becoming more and more outraged, angry that her aunt had put her in this situation. She'd been doing just fine on her own, but Ruby couldn't help herself. She had to get in the way all over again.

'You lied,' Dorothy hissed at her former foster-parent. 'You lied to me.'

Ruby looked apprehensively around the room. 'Are you here on your own?' Her gaze hesitated on the dollhouse before returning to the indignant girl behind the desk. 'Are those friends of yours in the house?'

'You need to listen,' Dorothy insisted, keeping a fragile check on her rising temper. 'I know you lied to me.'

'Dotty-girl – you have to tell me this,' Ruby said, sounding increasingly concerned. 'Is there anyone else here?'

Dorothy glanced at her feet as a flash of remorse displaced her resentment. 'My friends ... my friends are all gone,' she mumbled sadly.

Ruby exhaled in relief. 'Well then, why don't you come through to the kitchen? I'll make us a cup of tea. You can tell me all about it.'

Seeing Ruby try to back away towards the door reignited Dorothy's irritation. She slammed the file onto the desk. 'You know where he is,' she snarled. 'You know, and I know you know.'

The older woman's nervous expression gave way to a sudden realisation. 'Oh, Dotty! Is this about your father again?' she asked incredulously. 'I thought we'd put done to all that. The Agency don't tell me their business. It's not mine to know. I told you all this.'

It was the same old story, the same old lies. All the effort she'd made, all the bridges she'd burned, just to get into that room, and still her aunt couldn't show her any respect. Dorothy opened the lever-arch file she was clutching. 'Is he in here?' she demanded. She tore the top sheet out of the file and gave it a cursory glance. 'Is this it?' Dorothy tossed the sheet to one side and moved to rip out the second page in the file. 'Or this?'

'Dorothy Gale, you stop that!' Ruby warned her. 'You stop that right now!'

That was just two sheets of paper. It was going to take forever if Dorothy wanted to yank every page out of every file – almost as long as it would have taken her to actually read them. She grabbed a thick wad of pages and tried to detach them all in one swift tug, but when they refused to rip she found herself ineffectually waving the file about in one hand. She threw it to the ground in disgust and turned to pull the next one from the shelf. 'Is he in this one?' she asked, letting it fall to the floor. She moved down the row, dragging the folders off one by one. 'Are you listening to me now?'

'Stop it! Dotty – that's enough!' This was definitely Aunt Ruby's 'in trouble' voice, and Dorothy instinctively halted in her tracks. Ruby strode over and snatched the file from her former ward's hands.

'You don't understand, and you can't ever be told.' Ruby snorted. 'Your head is like some fairy castle, full of stuff you thought up and wanted to be true.' Placing the file carefully on the desk, she opened a drawer and pulled out a pen and a jotter pad. 'You never did trust it to me to do what's best,' she muttered. 'And you won't be told, will you? Oh no. Even though I'm the grown-up. Can't tell Dorothy Gale anything she hasn't already decided.' Ruby scribbled something on the top sheet and dramatically tore it off the pad. 'Don't know the name of the farm – never did. All someone ever mentioned was the road. It goes all the way out of the city. The farm could be anywhere. Can't see how he'd still be there anyway, but it's your time for wasting.'

Ruby brandished the scrap of paper, and Dorothy accepted it in stunned disbelief. Even though she'd been caught red-handed, somehow she'd just managed to expose years of deception by her aunt, and all she'd had to do was throw a few files about. Against all the odds, her mission was back on track. A strange détente descended between the two women. The rapid de-escalation of tension had taken Dorothy completely by surprise – it wasn't clear whether she was even in trouble any more.

Ruby was first to speak. 'Goodness to grace. All this silly

bickering,' she started. 'Such a dippy way to spend the day. Why don't I leave you to fix up this jumble you've done and I'll go put the kettle on? Maybe get you cleaned up a bit, because you really don't smell the freshest. And then you can tell me how you managed to get all the way down here.' Placing her hands on her hips, Ruby perused the limited carnage on the office floor, tutting quietly to herself, before heading out of the room. She pulled the door shut behind her, leaving Dorothy to stare aimlessly at her piece of paper.

The journey that had brought Dorothy to Aunt Ruby's house had proved to be unfathomably complicated when held up against Crane's original plan. Now this part of the quest had ended, a whole new one was opening up ahead of her, but this time she'd have to figure it out for herself without any help. She was so lost in contemplation that it took a few seconds after hearing the key turn in the office door lock before she realised its implications.

Dorothy lurched across the room and twisted the door handle. Nothing happened. A sick feeling slammed her in the depths of her empty stomach. She was being punished. She was being given some 'sorry' time to consider the consequences of her actions. She hammered on the door as a primal rush of shame bubbled through her, calling out to her captor, 'Aunt Ruby! Aunt Ruby! Open the door! Please open the door!'

'You stay put right there,' replied Ruby from the other side of the door. 'You're not meant to be here, are you? I don't think anyone would be happy if they knew you were here.'

'Please! Auntie Ruby! I'm sorry!' Dorothy wailed. But her desperate tone of voice carried much more despair than she actually felt. Even though her distress had flared up in a Pavlovian outburst, she was surprised to feel it quickly ebb away to something much more rational. She was acting out a reaction that had been instilled over the course of many years, but that had all been a long time ago, and she wasn't nearly as terror stricken now by the 'sorry'-time ordeal as she had been as an impressionable ten-year-old. In any case, being shut in the office was nothing like as bad as being crammed into the dark space under the stairs. But she still needed to get out. Regardless of how the next phase in her journey was going to play out, if she stayed locked up too long it might not even start at all. There was no way she could fit through the window; she had to get out the same way she got in. Dorothy glanced around the room for a tool to help unlock the door.

And there it was. The perfect bargaining chip, sitting on its own dedicated table, shielded from sight and away from temptation.

At that instant, Dorothy felt the dizziness lift from her brain. Despite her illness and the relentless headache, she found herself completely lucid for the first time that day.

'Aunt Ruby?' she called, all traces of distress replaced by a composed authority. 'Open the door, or I'll blow your dollhouse down.'

From outside the room, Dorothy heard someone squirm. But Ruby didn't answer.

'I will. I really will. Just listen,' Dorothy continued.

Even under these extenuating circumstances, approaching the dollhouse still felt very wrong. This was as close as Dorothy had ever got to the cherished heirloom, and she took a moment to properly examine it for the first time. Everything inside the house had been prepared with incredible patience and precision: the dining table was laid with plates, cutlery and wineglasses for four people; vases of miniature cut flowers adorned the sideboard and coffee table; and a fresh piece of paper had been fixed to the blotter on the bureau, alongside a pen in an ink well and a picture of a woman in an intricate silver frame.

Finding herself wavering, Dorothy wished that she had more of an instinct for vandalism. Wantonly damaging something so delicate felt horribly inappropriate, and she cast around to find the object in the house least likely to be noticed by its absence. As soon as Ruby realised that she was completely serious, Dorothy fully expected to be allowed to go on her way with the minimum of fuss. She gingerly reached into the dress-making room and pulled out a mahogany rocking chair.

'Are you still there?' she called out into the hall beyond. 'Are you still listening?'

If the older woman was there, she refused to answer. Dorothy gently tapped the rocking chair on a door panel. 'It's a little chair. A chair with curves on the legs.'

On the other side of the door, Ruby let out a moan. 'Don't,' she hissed. 'Don't you fucking dare.'

'Are you going to let me out?' Dorothy pleaded. 'I only want you to let me out.' She stood expectantly while a moment of silence passed without the rattle of a key in the keyhole. Her heart sank. The opportunity for a stay of execution had expired, and now she was obliged to make good on her threat. Dorothy hooked her fingers around the wooden armrests and pulled them apart with the gentlest of tugs, slowing ratcheting up the pressure, and all the while hoping that her aunt would relent before any real damage was done.

In the end it took a surprisingly forceful heave to separate the rocking chair into two parts, and then it was with a disappointingly placid pop rather than the dramatic snap that Dorothy was hoping for. This wasn't going to serve as an instructive threat if Ruby couldn't hear it.

'Oh – did you hear that?' she shouted through the door. 'Sorry. Hold on.' Dorothy bent each part in turn, trying for a louder fracture, eventually managing a series of reassuring cracks from the upright spindles in the back of the chair. Whatever the story being told to the guests in Ruby's house, the furniture in the dollhouse was anything but fragile.

From outside the room, everything stayed silent until the third snap, then came a gurgling roar, quickly followed by the stumbling patter of footsteps disappearing off in the direction of the kitchen. Now caught up in the destruction ritual, Dorothy kept on noisily splintering whatever parts remained to be broken on the chair, even though her audience had left. She called out to her unseen jailer, 'Aunt Ruby? Are you still listening? Were you listening to that?'

This wasn't working. She'd need to raise the stakes, maybe find a piece of furniture that was more integral to the house, something more disruptive to the Victorian feng shui. She fished an imposing grandfather clock out from the living room.

'I've got the tall clock now,' she called back through the door. 'Are you going to let me out?'

This seemed to do the job. The key twisted in the lock and the door swung open. Ruby barged into the room, holding the longest and nastiest-looking kitchen knife in her collection, and clutching a cordless telephone in her other hand. With the knife thrust out towards Dorothy, she edged across to install herself between the dollhouse and the wrecking ball.

'You step away from that, you worthless little bitch,' Ruby snarled, forcing the girl to back away from the serrated blade. Having regained some control over the situation, Ruby glanced towards the telephone and thumbed repeatedly at the nine button. Keeping the knife raised, she lifted the telephone to her ear. 'Oh. The police, if you'd be so kind.'

Dorothy felt her blood physically chill as it pumped through her arteries, and her dizziness returned in a rush that caused her to sway awkwardly. The police would ruin everything. When news of her arrest made its way back to the Zoo, there would be nothing Dorothy could do to stop West and her minions from swooping in to claim her. There was no one left to stop West from pumping her poison into Dorothy's veins until she'd killed her too. Despite their long history of distrust, and all current evidence to the contrary, Dorothy didn't believe that her aunt would knowingly put her life in danger. Given enough time, she might have been able to make her see reason. But not at the end of a knife, and not with the imminent threat of capture. Dorothy scanned the room for options, but all she had to hand was the grandfather clock. Long and pointed at one end, just like her aunt's weapon. She raised it towards Ruby, mimicking her threat. 'Stop. Stop that talking,' she mumbled through her daze.

Her aunt paused. After a moment of deliberation, she returned to her phone call. 'I'm sorry, can you please hold back there one extra mo?'

What Ruby did next took Dorothy by surprise. After weighing the phone and the kitchen knife in her hands, her aunt carefully laid the receiver on the table next to the dollhouse. Then, with the knife thrust out in front of her, she advanced across the room towards Dorothy. The girl backed away from the blade until she bumped into her aunt's desk; still Ruby crept towards her. As Dorothy leant backwards, away from what threatened to be a slow-motion shanking, the older woman wrapped her talons around the clock and snatched at it.

Dorothy's attempt to intimidate her aunt was about to fail. It was only a matter of time before the police arrived, and everything she had achieved would be wasted. She tugged on the clock, trying desperately to keep hold of her last bargaining chip, but the older woman wasn't about to give up her firm grasp. The effort, however, did twist her aunt away from the door, and for a moment the pathway to freedom was left unguarded. Without hesitating, Dorothy bolted. Ruby, however, quickly regained her balance and lurched to intercept her before she could reach the doorway, swinging at Dorothy with the kitchen knife, unleashing a shriek from her snarling mouth. The two women collided in a heavy shoulder-barge that knocked Dorothy to the floor and spun Ruby backwards.

Backwards. And into the table under the old dollhouse.

Frantically reaching behind her for something to break the fall, the older woman and the table collapsed to the floor in tandem. The foundations were ripped out from underneath her great-grandmother's favoured plaything, spewing chairs, dressers and dining-ware through the absent wall. For a moment it looked as if her aunt was going to be able to catch some of the contents, to limit the damage, but then the back of her skull slammed into the edge of the broken table and rebounded with a sickening crack. Ruby crumpled to the floor as Victorian furniture rained around her, before the frame of the dollhouse landed square on her contorted face, splintering and buckling around her head.

Under the carcass of the broken dollhouse, and amongst the debris of the miniature household, Ruby's eyes stared out, unblinking, her neck bent at an impractical angle. A hideous silence descended.

To anyone watching, Dorothy's immediate reaction to the accident would have seemed cold, impassive, but inside her head an eruption was under way. A clamour of screaming voices had suddenly ignited, burning through the silence in the room with an unintelligible hubbub. Adrenaline flooded her body, replacing her concern for Ruby's wellbeing with something less rational and more overbearing: a desperation made all the more terrifying by its refusal to focus on anything. All Dorothy was able to do was to sit perfectly still amongst the discarded lever-arch files and allow the wildfires to rage unchecked.

From somewhere in the thunderous tumult, a tiny voice was struggling to make itself heard. 'Madam? Madam? Are you there? We heard a sound. Are you OK? We can see that the line is still open. Are you able to hear us?'

Although the small voice should have been completely smothered by the blaze that roared through Dorothy's brain, it somehow felt different to the rest of the incoherent babble; something substantive amongst the paralysing pandemonium. The longer it talked, the more confident Dorothy became that the words were actually coming from somewhere outside her head, drawing her attention away from the inferno. It was coming from the direction of her motionless aunt, and her first instinct was that she was being addressed by a diminutive Victorian whose house had just been demolished. The voice continued. 'We're despatching a car to your location now as a precaution. We have your address as 39 East Close. If you can hear us but are unable to respond, please hold tight. Help is on its way. If you are able to open the front door for the police when they arrive, that may reduce the need for any property damage.'

It was the word 'police' that finally barged its way through Dorothy's bewilderment, but this time the trigger was different. The frantic screaming in her head returned, but now everyone was hollering with one voice. *Go*, they said. *Go now and figure everything else out later. Run. Survive.* A powerful manic energy coursed through her, feeding off her certainty, stoking her fear. Doing nothing guaranteed the end of her journey, and with it her probable death. This at least was a course of action. Dorothy jumped to her feet and careened through the door without a backwards glance.

In the hallway, sat halfway up the stairs like a prisoner

behind bars of bannisters, the young girl that Dorothy had spotted earlier from the den peered down, her hands still clasped around the book. Their eyes locked for a second time. Dorothy stumbled to a halt. In spite of the frenzy that urged her forward, she had once again been blindsided by this mysterious connection. The young girl's expressionless stare said nothing about what she might have seen or heard, but Dorothy sensed that this shared trauma would bring them even closer together, reinforce their bizarre bond. It would be stronger, but also uglier. Whatever the young girl needed Dorothy to do to rescue her from her tribulations, Dorothy couldn't be the one to help. She didn't even have time to listen to her story. This shared moment was all they would be granted, and it was up to her to break the spell.

Dorothy lifted her arm towards the young girl, desperately searching for something coherent in her jumble of thoughts. Eventually she just whispered, 'I'm sorry.'

It didn't even scratch the surface of all the things she needed to say. But it was enough. Dorothy allowed her gaze to linger a second longer before hurrying to the front door.

∿

DESPITE THE URGENT commotion that rampaged through her head, and lungs ill-prepared for exercise, Dorothy ran. She needed to get to where there were large numbers of people – to escape into the comforting anonymity of a crowd – and she intuitively weaved her way along side streets and across estates while her brain continued to bellow in anguish. Only when she had been absorbed back into the distracted masses could she feel like she was no longer being watched, when she could pass unnoticed amongst all the other faceless people who were preoccupied with their own stories and journeys. And only once she had become invisible could she allow herself to stop running, to try to pick out some sense from within the fiery mess.

If the quiet voices that had guided her through the city yesterday were speaking now, they were lost in the ruckus. Even so, Dorothy felt herself being steered by some arcane instinct, and she gratefully ceded control so she could better concentrate on beating back the feelings of despair. These were streets that she recognised, even after all these years, although she was seeing many of them in daylight for the first time. These were the same streets she had explored as a much younger child, when she would sneak out of the back door of Ruby's house after everyone had gone to sleep. Then she had been focused on finding the way back to her father's farm, but now this knowledge was keeping her one step ahead of the police and out of West's murderous clutches.

As she fled deeper into the city on autopilot, she became increasingly distracted by the sight of poorly remembered landmarks, or when she passed one of the metal poles onto which she had once scratched her initial with Aunt Ruby's kitchen scissors. These childish tags stretched out from her aunt's house in every direction, and had at one time allowed Dorothy to more efficiently pick up her search where she had left off the night before. But despite all her efforts, she had never managed to spot anything in the suburban darkness that resembled the muddy track that led to her father's house, or the intimidating forest that bordered his land. Ushered along by these long-forgotten markers, Dorothy had no idea where she was going, only that, wherever it was, she knew how to get there.

The trail eventually brought Dorothy to a covered passageway that led from the car park behind an old church onto a busy cobbled street. At the sight of shoppers and pedestrians, she finally allowed herself to stop stumbling forward and to let the maelstrom howl uninterrupted. In the passageway, a stone cattle-trough from the earliest days of the city welcomed visitors to the historic town centre, its plughole now clogged with old shopping bags and loose straw, trapping an inch of stagnant rainwater in its hollows. As Dorothy gasped for air and fought back waves of nausea, she spotted the liquid and was overcome by an inexplicable thirst. Before she could question her actions, she had plunged her hands into the putrid water and was cupping greedy mouthfuls to her lips to quench her insatiable thirst.

Her laboured breathing slowly settled. Dorothy unzipped her puffer jacket to reveal a filthy beige T-shirt beneath, ripped from the collar to the navel, and exposing her once-white bra. She struggled to peel back the coat, to cool her arms and chest, but she only managed to drag one of the shoulders away from the clammy glue that held it in place before she had to vomit. Leaning forward, she struggled with her coat between dry heaves, until she was rewarded with a sour-tasting green discharge that splattered indelicately onto her sleeves and mixed into the bloodstains on her trainer. The elasticated wrists of the damp jacket refused to release her hands, but she finally succeeded in uncovering her arms by turning the coat inside out. Propping herself against the wall, she slid to the ground.

On Dorothy's left forearm, a long history of needle punctures was spelled out in scars and scabs. Amongst the tracks, an inflamed wound stood out – swollen, red, burning hot and with blue-black tendrils creeping out from its centre. A green pus had bubbled up, unlanced and demanding attention. It was only when she glanced down and noticed the infection that she felt a compelling need to scratch it; with her hands still pinned inside her coat, she eventually had to settle on savagely rubbing her forearm against her filthy leggings.

As she slowly cooled down, Dorothy was surprised to find a fragile rationality returning to her thinking. She was only twenty yards away from safety, where she could conceal herself in plain sight, disguised amongst the indifferent masses. Whatever Ruby told the police when she woke up, they wouldn't be able to find her here, no matter how upset her aunt was about her dollhouse or her broken neck. Teasing snippets of coherent thought were beginning to emerge, assuring her that all the answers she needed were right there. A resolution to her quest surely lay hidden just below the surface – if only she knew how to quieten the chaos.

Glancing down at the long tear in her T-shirt, Dorothy was hit by a sudden dread. For the second time that day, she found her thoughts turning to Crane, and again she had to stop herself from wishing that he were there with her. At least he didn't know where she was going. Crane had almost certainly been caught by now – if he hadn't actually gone and turned himself in – and Dorothy knew that he would be doing everything he could to help West to catch her. Just thinking about West brought on another flash of panic, which left Dorothy's brain feeling even more skittish and set off another furious attack on her infected forearm. Thank God Crane's sense of direction was so bad. He might even still be wandering around, lost.

After the events of the last week, her father was the only person left who cared for her enough to help fix everything, who knew enough to keep her safe. Thatcher and Crane and Ruby could then just become other stories that she'd never have to think about again. And her father was close by. Dorothy had always known this, even though all her night-time adventures through the city had failed to find him. He was always just 'down the road', which had served as a comfort in her early days as a guest in Ruby's house, and later as a source of confusion and anger when he never reappeared to rescue her. But all she needed to do was to find the right road, then follow it until she got there. If she could keep it together long enough, and not get caught by West or the police, she stood a chance.

Because for the first time, she knew what the road was called.

∼

From a hidden vantage point behind a row of industrial wheelie-bins, Dorothy had been surreptitiously watching the woman who drove the taxi for about ten minutes. Even though she was screened from view, Dorothy felt more exposed now than she had done when she cooled off in the bustling city centre, and a restless unease had joined the discord in her head. The taxi driver would know where all the roads were, and even the ones she didn't know would be on one of her maps. All Dorothy had to do was ask. But there was something that nagged at her, something she really needed to know, and it was stubbornly refusing to present itself as an intelligible thought. Whenever she felt that she had grasped one end of the message, her focus drifted again and the meaning slipped away from her. She'd been staring at the woman all this time, waiting for a break in the noise, and still she wasn't sure what she was expecting to see.

On the other side of the street, the taxi driver sat in the front seat of her car, eating sandwiches, focused on a sudoku puzzle that she had propped up against the steering wheel. Up to now the woman had done nothing untoward, nothing that might raise suspicion, but Dorothy was far from reassured. As soon as she had opened herself up to the possibility that the driver may have been stationed there to watch out for her, Dorothy's mind had somersaulted off into deranged fantasies about whatever retributions might be visited onto her back at the Zoo. Between these delusions, brief snippets of clarity reminded Dorothy that she needed to keep moving; that the only way out of trouble was to stay ahead of the threat until she found her father; that she wasn't going anywhere until she knew where she was going. That there was nothing to see here, nothing that should stop her from being brave. Dorothy broke cover, scampering across the tarmac to talk to the driver.

Pulling open the rear door of the taxi, Dorothy hastened inside and slammed it shut behind her. She poked an apprehensive head above the parcel shelf to check whether anyone was following. The manoeuvre had taken the driver by surprise – after letting out a startled gasp through a mouthful of bread, she was now dealing with a violent coughing fit. Satisfied that she had made it to the car unseen, Dorothy pushed her father's address into the driver's line of sight. When the convulsing from the front seat didn't stop, Dorothy shook the piece of paper until the choking woman took it from her.

The driver hacked out the last of the blockage before turning to face the young girl. 'Sorry 'bout that, my pretty,' she spluttered. 'You gave me quite a start.'

The blood drained from Dorothy's head in an icy rush. It was West.

There was a tiny moment of perfect silence as her brain inhaled, then the desperate commotion screamed out again. But louder, more jumbled. With it, Dorothy lost control over her limbs, and she lolled about, punch-drunk, on the back seat. She tried to speak, but all she could muster was an airless gurgle.

'Are we alright back there?' West asked the dazed girl. A

look of distaste crossed her face as she sniffed the air. 'Good God. Has something happened to you?'

After all that effort to stay ahead of the chase, Dorothy had just given herself up. Whatever fate was now coming to her, she had no one else to blame. She must have been duped by the bobble hat that West was wearing to hide her perfect shiny brown hair.

'What's this you've given me? Is this where you want to go?'

The initial shock subsided. Dorothy regained some mobility. She scrabbled at the door in a frantic attempt to escape. West glared down at her with a concerned expression. 'Whoa! Hold your horses, my pretty! I'll come and sort you.'

The woman slid out of the front seat and gingerly opened the rear door from the outside. Dorothy barged against the side panel and tumbled out of the vehicle into an unruly pile on the ground. When she looked at the car from the outside, it was so obviously West's Lexus, with the malevolent squinting eyes and the grille that looked like an enormous moustache. Just painting over the granite-grey finish and sticking a triangular TAXI light on the roof wasn't going to fool anyone. Dorothy wriggled away across the tarmac, a fresh riot under way in her head, fighting the urge to get up and run.

'We should get you up and out of the road,' West suggested anxiously. 'We don't want to cause an accident, do we?'

The woman took a couple of careful steps towards Dorothy, who scurried backwards on her hands and heels, further and further into the path of possible traffic. Eventually West stopped and held up her arms in submission; in one hand, Ruby's piece of paper fluttered in the breeze. She followed Dorothy's eyeline. 'This road? You want to go there, do you?' Dorothy stared up at her from her precarious position on the ground. West continued, 'If you can get yourself up and out of the way of the cars, I can help you. Please?'

There was absolutely no way that Dorothy was going to get back into West's car. When she opened her mouth to speak, she found that a brick of air was blocking the breath from leaving her lungs. She needed to tighten all the muscles in her chest just to push a single hoarse word past her lips.

'Which...?'

Hearing the girl speak for the first time, West seemed to be strangely relieved. 'So, you can understand what I'm saying, then?'

Dorothy continued to monitor the woman, poised to jump to her feet and escape back into the sea of people at the slightest provocation, struggling to ignore the deafening racket in her brain.

'And there's someplace on this road you want me to take you?'

Dorothy shook her head forcefully.

West tried again. 'You want to get there on your own?'

When Dorothy refused to answer, the woman glanced anxiously up the street before offering her a deal. 'If I tell you the way, do you promise to get onto the pavement so you don't get run over?'

Dorothy nodded cautiously. West glanced at the piece of paper again. 'You know this is a really long road, don't you? All the way out of the city? I'm not sure what's on it that you want to get to, and it's certainly not made for walking.'

Dorothy stared up at her expectantly, until West turned away to gesture in the opposite direction. 'Alright. See up there? Up this road? See the traffic lights? You turn right when you get to them. That takes you to a big roundabout after about a mile, mile and a half. Ignore all the other roads off to the side. When you get to the roundabout, go right again. And that's your road out of town. But really, it's not the kind of—'

Her sentence was cut short by the growl of an over-revved

engine hastening towards them from around a blind corner. Swearing under her breath, West stepped past the girl on the ground and braced herself for the arrival of the unseen motorist by waving her arms above her head. A red hatchback sped into view and bore down on the two women without reducing its speed. West glanced down at the young girl. For the first time, Dorothy saw a glimmer of fear appear in the woman's eyes. But before she had a chance to process what this might mean, her thoughts were interrupted by the sound of screaming tyres and hammering from the vehicle's anti-lock brakes. The car slid to a reluctant halt ten feet away from West before its strained suspension relaxed and the bonnet sprang back to its correct height.

After a brief period of silence, the motorist vented his relief on the car's horn. A teenager with an immaculate haircut leant out of the side window and bellowed, 'What you doing? Take it out the road, you dozy cow!'

Still holding her arms above her head, West cautiously approached the hatchback, looking more like she was negotiating the release of a hostage than calming an angry adolescent. 'I am sorry about this, young man,' she said between gulps of air. 'That poor girl is not the full fruit-basket. Just give me a couple of moments...'

With the other woman blocking her view, Dorothy hadn't registered how close she had just come to being run over. Seen from the back, the bits of West's bob-length hair that poked out from underneath the bobble hat appeared considerably longer and less glossy than normal, as they brushed against the dirty collar of her jacket. Although Dorothy couldn't make out any of her words, West was clearly getting into it with the driver of the other car, and their unheard conversation further fuelled her paranoia. That was, until a voice called out through the confusion.

Go.

This was her last opportunity. She had to seize it before it was lost forever.

Dorothy jumped to her feet with unexpected agility and launched herself towards the distant traffic lights. Behind her, West was still trying to placate the legitimate indignation coming from inside the hatchback. By the time that the woman turned around and found the young girl missing, Dorothy was already far enough away to be someone else's problem.

∽

WHEN DOROTHY ARRIVED at the big roundabout and started on the road out of the city, she quickly lost track of time passed and distance travelled. Now she just needed to get to where she was going. At some point the day flipped over into night; the view switched from houses and shops to fields and distant hills; the raised pavement became a grass verge alongside the road. Still she walked.

The number of cars thinned out as well. More often than not, they flashed their lights or sounded their horn when their headlights caught the reflected orange glow from Dorothy's puffer jacket. A harsh wind had picked up, buffeting Dorothy to the left and right with more random movement for the motorists to avoid.

The fiery turmoil that had raged inside Dorothy's head had largely burned itself out, leaving only a few troubled embers that occasionally sparked into life, but then just as quickly extinguished themselves again. From time to time, the image of Aunt Ruby lying beneath the debris of her treasured dollhouse appeared in the ashes, quietly pleading with Dorothy to make her way back to her old foster home and apologise.

Whatever had happened after she'd left, the police would certainly know all about her by now. Whether she got caught by them, or by West, or by one of her minions, the outcome was likely to be the same. But with every stride she took, she consoled herself that she was being carried closer to her father and further away from the carnage. Before too long any residual shame was swallowed up by an endless flow of nonsense words, the sound of her subconscious idling, attentive only to the next step on the road.

As her mind slowly cooled, Dorothy was reminded again about just how much discomfort she was in. She realised that she had probably had the same headache all day, but had just been too busy to notice it. Her knees ached with the exertion of walking, and twinged every time the wind knocked her too far off course. A painful cramp had lodged in her stomach and she could taste the metallic remnants of bile; Dorothy couldn't tell whether she was still feeling sick or just hungry, but her mouth felt too dry to chew anything anyway.

And she was exhausted. There was so much she needed to tell her father, about all the crazy things that had happened to her during the time they had spent apart, but the first thing she was going to do when she finally got to his house was sleep. And while she was asleep he was going to fix all these other problems, so that when she woke up they could just carry on from where they had left off without having to worry about anything else. Dorothy kept moving, concentrating on the happily-ever-after.

Because the sky was so dark, and because it had been such a long while since she was last blinded by the headlights of a passing car, Dorothy noticed the glow: dim flickers of blue reflecting off the leaves on the trees that lined the road. Unsure of exactly what this heralded, Dorothy turned around to see distant blue flashing lights heading noiselessly towards her at great speed. Before she had the chance to contemplate her options, she had already leapt off the verge and down the steep embankment, running at first but quickly tumbling, rolling head over heels through the grass and scrub into the bramble bushes at the bottom of the slope.

As she lay snared in the clutches of the thicket, she watched the flashing lights briefly illuminate the low clouds in the night sky as the police car passed above her, oblivious to her presence. In the fall, Dorothy had jarred a knee and grazed her thigh, but she was surprised by just how comfortable it felt to be lying down again, even if it was on a bed of prickly thorns.

Only once the hum from the engine had disappeared beneath the noise of the wind did Dorothy begin to extract herself from the brambles. The process took an eternity, partly because she was hooked all over by invisible creepers that tugged at her clothes and hair, and partly because she felt sapped of all her energy. Her knee protested whenever she shifted her weight onto it, and when she finally broke free of the brambles, she only managed a small hop before collapsing backwards into the same bush.

As she lay on her oddly welcoming mattress, collecting her breath, Dorothy reflected on her situation. The police were out looking for her, and almost certainly they'd come back. They weren't going to give up just because she'd outwitted them this time. Even if she'd felt able to clamber back up the embankment, walking on the road was not an option any more. She knew she'd be better off following a path through the fields and hedges, where she could advance without being seen.

She'd come this far, and she was probably really close to her father's house. But first she just needed a few minutes' rest.

MONDAY, 23RD AUGUST

The Scarecrow

*P*ropped up on a plastic chair in the corner of a railway station waiting room, underneath a poster advising travellers to be on the lookout for anyone acting suspiciously, Dorothy's eyes flicked open.

Someone had just spoken her name, summoning her out from a chaotic nightmare. Whoever it was had been close enough to whisper in her ear, and had woken her up midway through an anxiety attack. In her dream she had been alone in a dark room, and every time she went to look for someone, the room got bigger and harder to search. Or was she the one who was trying to hide? The vision was fast evaporating from her brain, leaving behind only a lingering restlessness. Something had been spawned deep in her subconscious, something grotesque and threatening, and Dorothy dreaded that it might still be in there. She had no idea how she'd managed to calm down long enough to fall asleep anyway.

She was alone in the waiting room, but outside the station was filling up with smartly dressed commuters lost in their smartphone screens, and older men in coloured Lycra walking their bicycles along the platform. Through a wall of acrylic windows, Dorothy gazed out at the scene as if she was watching a drama unfold on television, until she counted too many concerned looks being sent in her direction and realised that she was actually the exhibit.

Crane wasn't there. He wasn't in the room, as he'd promised he would be. He had stayed glued to her side after all the trauma of the previous evening, being extra vigilant and extra attentive, and this was before they had even got on the train. He had been with her when they had arrived at their destination in the middle of the night, and he had assured her that he'd keep lookout in the waiting room while she tried to get some sleep. Dorothy began to prowl around her cage, piecing together the events of the previous evening for clues. As she stood up, she realised that she must have wet herself during the night, but after the ordeal of the evening before, soiling herself actually seemed like a sensible idea. Her uneasiness grew, and with it her forearm started to itch again. She embarked on a savage offensive against the wound hidden underneath the zipped puffer jacket, marching wet footprints up and down the concrete floor.

Crane was the smart one – the brains of the outfit, as he liked to label himself. He was the one that had come up with the plan and, because it kept changing all the time, Dorothy had given up trying to stay on top of it. Crane knew exactly what was going on, so that Dorothy didn't need to. She let her apprehension grow, pacing faster, muttering his name under her breath. 'Crane? Where are you, Crane?' Before too long she'd developed enough speed to escape, launching her through the doors of the waiting room and out onto the station platform.

'Crane?' she called over the sea of heads. 'Crane? Are you here?'

Again, the voice whispered her name. Dorothy wheeled around, searching the faces of the startled travellers for a clue. The crowds parted in front of her as Dorothy moved down the platform. A middle-aged woman glanced up from her paperback, directly into Dorothy's eyeline, and held her stare for a moment too long. Dorothy hastened over to her.

'Have you seen Crane?' she demanded. 'Was he here? Was he talking to me? Did you see who was talking to me?'

'No. Sorry,' the woman stammered. 'Who?' she added, then maybe wished she hadn't.

'Crane!' Dorothy insisted. 'He was here!'

'Doz? Doz! What you doing?' A different voice, a man's voice, behind her, uttering her name through clenched teeth. Dorothy turned to face him, giving the paperback reader time to gather up her bags and retreat. With a cardboard coffee cup in his hand, Crane limped towards Dorothy, leaning to one side as he held an elbow against his ribs. By now Dorothy had been quarantined in every direction by the nervous commuters. The man broke through the cordon.

Crane was only ten years older than Dorothy, but he already had a patina of well-established wrinkles around his eyes and forehead. Although his head appeared to have been transplanted onto his compact frame from a much taller man, it was also disconcertingly narrow; from the upturned collar on his jacket to the slight hunch in his shoulders, he virtually demanded distrust. It wasn't even that his eyes were too close together, more that his whole face was too close together. It didn't help his cause that he was also covered in bruises and cuts. When they had boarded the train last night, the skin around his injuries was red and tender, but overnight his face had ballooned, sprouting patches of purple and amber that he prodded at absent-mindedly, even though every touch caused him to wince.

At the sight of her friend, Dorothy's unease was replaced by a feeling of suspicion that left her just as unsettled. 'Where have you been? What did you want? Why did you leave me?'

Without breaking stride, Crane caught her by an arm and gently guided her away from the throng of passengers towards the relative privacy of the rear of the platform. 'Hey!' he hissed through one side of his mouth. 'Calm it down! We don't want any attention, remember?' He pushed Dorothy against a wall and checked all around to see whether they were still being scrutinised, but most people were just happy to have one less thing to trouble their morning meditations.

Satisfied, he turned back to Dorothy. 'Chill it, Dozza! I'm not going anywhere. Not leaving, OK?' He rattled the cardboard cup in front of her face. 'Just getting us some coffee. Here.' Crane took a long pull through the spout in the plastic lid, sucked some cooling air across the liquid in his mouth, then went in again for a second gulp. He shook the cup to estimate its contents. Satisfied, he offered it to Dorothy. 'Have some.'

Dorothy took the cup. She hated the taste of coffee – she even hated the smell of someone's breath after they had been drinking coffee – but she liked the tingling sensation on her fingers from holding something slightly too hot. His explanation didn't sound plausible, despite the evidence in her hands. There was something he wasn't telling her.

Crane looked the anxious girl up and down. 'Are you OK, Doz? Are you feeling alright this morning?'

Dorothy nodded uncertainly. 'Did you see what happened to your face? In the night?' she asked.

Crane raised his eyebrows and stared at her for the longest moment. 'Yeah. You're feeling alright,' he finally responded. 'Listen, why don't we get out of here? Go for a walk? Go get some breakfast? Figure out what we should be doing?'

'We need to go and see my aunt,' Dorothy said. 'We should do that now. Before anything goes wrong.'

'Yeah – got that. We just need to work out a plan.'

Dorothy's restiveness started to return. She felt the insatiable itch on her forearm flaring up again, and was drawn back into a frenzied scratching session. 'But we have a plan,' she insisted. 'Your plan. Why isn't that good any more?'

'Yeah, sure, we have a plan,' Crane reassured her without conviction. 'Of course I have a plan. But this is a big place. Isn't it? You know how to get there?'

'We need to go and find Aunt Ruby!' Dorothy barked, causing Crane to jerk his head backwards in astonishment. 'Now!'

Crane flapped his arms frantically to quieten the agitated girl, checking over his shoulder to see whether they had attracted any unwelcome attention. 'Jesus Christ! Can you keep your voice down, please?' he implored through gritted teeth. He reached over and caught her fist as she pummelled her itchy forearm. 'Here, let me see that,' he demanded. Without waiting for permission, he rolled up the sleeve of her puffer jacket, exposing the tracks of old scars before uncovering the troublesome needle wound.

When Crane finally got a glimpse of the source of Dorothy's irritation, he recoiled in dismay. 'Euugh!' he proclaimed. 'Oh wow, Doz ... this isn't good.'

Dorothy pulled at her arm but Crane held it tightly, gaping, fascinated by the slender black tendrils that snaked outwards from the glowing puncture hole.

'It's good. It's OK,' she ventured.

'It really isn't. That's not good at all. It's infected,' Crane explained slowly, still mesmerised by the wound. 'Icky. You need medicine. We need to find a chemist. It's going to get worse otherwise. More icky.'

Dorothy hadn't checked her arm for a couple of days. If she was being honest, she was also a little unnerved by how it looked. But this was something that her father could deal with once she and Crane made it to his house, and it certainly wasn't bad enough to justify messing about with the plan. Then again, it was quite itchy. She weighed up the options in her mind.

'On the way,' she finally decided. 'OK, but only if we find some medicine on the way.'

∼

As the self-appointed leader of the party, Crane guided her out of the station and then stumbled onwards in the same direction. He was moving awkwardly, obviously still in quite a lot of pain. Already Dorothy could tell that this place was significantly larger than the seaside town from which they had just escaped, and she was struggling to get her bearings. At the rate that Crane was walking, they might be pottering about in the city all day without ever getting as far as Ruby's house.

Dorothy fell in behind Crane, unable to shake off a sense of misgiving about her friend's intentions. She couldn't even put her finger on what Crane had done to provoke her scepticism, but she certainly felt more comfortable when she could keep an eye on him. She didn't really want to speak to him, anyway. He'd only want to talk about what had happened the night before. He'd already bombarded her with questions all the way on the train, and made her think about things she really didn't want to have to think about. Just looking at the bruises on his face was enough of an unwelcome reminder. In any case, this was the time that she should be thinking about Henry. What had happened with him was much worse than anything that Thatcher could ever do to her and, as far as she could tell, she was dealing with that OK. Other than infrequent flashbacks to some moment they'd shared together, or the occasional glimpse of him in the distance, Henry wasn't making her as sad as he used to. Maybe she'd miss him more if she didn't have so much to do.

Walking around the city again after all these years was proving to be a frustrating experience. There were times when a bit of the city looked vaguely familiar, but Dorothy had yet to spot anywhere that she definitely recognised from her childhood. She couldn't be sure whether these hazy recollections were genuine memories, or whether this place just looked like every other city. But the more they walked, the more Dorothy became aware of another viewpoint, some ill-defined opinion that lurked just below her conscious thought. It wasn't loud enough to be called a voice, or articulate enough to be a guide, but it seemed to know more about the city than she or Crane did.

Crane led them through a maze of underpasses, around roundabouts and across a bridge. He took them past a pub garden where people were already smoking and nurturing pints of beer in silence; he took them past opaque shop fronts offering tattoos and piercings; he took them through a pool of shattered glass by the boarded-up window of a corner shop. All the while, the opinion murmured in her ear.

The hints were so subtle that Dorothy worried that she might miss an instruction if she didn't concentrate properly, their form so intangible that the slightest lapse in attention might disperse them forever. She was trying to listen to a whisper that was almost too soft to hear. And it questioned Crane's choices at every turn he made. The circuitous path he was taking, the lack of urgency in his pace – it was looking less and less like ineffective leadership and more and more like he was doing it on purpose. Dorothy had no idea where they were headed, but she was certain that it wasn't to her aunt's house. Her elusive accomplice agreed. She already knew how Crane could be, even before they'd started the journey. She knew how he liked to disguise the things he wanted to do when he thought no one else wanted to do them. How she could never be completely sure of his agenda. How he could scheme and plot and deceive. There was something going on right now that she didn't understand, and she wasn't the only one who was suspicious.

Dorothy's distrust built with every stride, until finally it became too much to ignore. Without a word, she pushed past Crane and set off on her own path with resolve. Her travelling companion called after her – 'Doz! Oi! Dozza!' – but she stayed focused, staring at the road ahead, unwilling to give him the opportunity to mislead her with more disinformation. Before too long, his grumbling had dried up, replaced by a heavy wheezing as he struggled to keep up. Although Dorothy couldn't say for sure whether they were close to Ruby's house, or even whether they were walking in the right direction, the opinion was definitely the best information she had. She just needed to make sure that she kept tuning in.

The journey took them through a small industrial district, past car parks full of yellow diggers and warehouses advertising new tyres and exhausts, before they reached the end of a high street. Ahead of them, the commercial centre of the city was coming to life, preparing itself for another Monday. Uniformed shop workers wandered sluggishly to work through discarded litter and broken glass; other people queued outside a coffee shop, next to rough sleepers laid out in sleeping bags. The sound of metal shutters mixed with the beeps of reversing trucks and the stale odour left by a weekend in the city. Without pausing to acknowledge the change in scenery,

Dorothy set off down the street at the same brisk pace, while Crane hustled to keep up.

'Hey, do you know where we are? Do you recognise this?' he called after her.

Dorothy marched on without answering. Crane threw up his hands in despair and lurched forward to catch up with his speeding friend. He wormed his fingers into the crook of her elbow and spun her around with a sharp tug.

'Doz!' he exclaimed between gasps. 'What the actual fuck? Where are we going?'

When Crane caught her arm, Dorothy had been so focused on listening for the next instruction that she had actually forgotten that he was still behind her. Now that she was facing her companion, she could see that he was confused and more than a little concerned. Since she had started following her own route through the city, Dorothy's misapprehensions about Crane's ulterior motives had died away, and for a moment she toyed with the idea of trying to explain what was going on inside her head. But there was no point. Crane wouldn't be able to help – in fact, all he would do was distract her. He would have questions, and almost certainly a whole bunch of theories, and she really just needed him to shut up and leave her alone until they arrived at Ruby's house. She glowered at him and growled, 'Let me go!'

Crane dropped her arm and hastened backwards out of striking range. 'Wow, Doz. Shit!' he blurted nervously. 'Look. Over there.'

On the other side of the road, a pharmacy was already open. Two green crosses framed the owner's name – 'S. POINTING' – above a patchwork of medical posters and displays of stacked boxes. Dorothy turned to follow Crane's direction, leaving her indignant expression in place while she tried to figure out what he was showing her.

'Dozza? Are you OK? It's a chemist. Remember?'

Of course Dorothy remembered their earlier conversation. She just wasn't sure whether that justified the interruption, when everything had been progressing so smoothly. It had been an abrupt landing back into the real world, and Dorothy's senses were suddenly full of the bustle and noise of the city centre. The fragile murmurings were now completely inaudible, drowned out by her exasperation, and she didn't know whether she'd scared them off permanently. However, Dorothy was also aware that she was unintentionally scratching away at the needle wound with no small amount of vigour, and this had probably cost her the right to be annoyed. Her face softened. Crane exhaled audibly. 'Are we...?' he asked, making an elaborate series of gestures with his index fingers to denote enduring friendship. When Dorothy didn't react, he continued, 'Are you feeling alright? Doz? Do I need to be worried about you?'

After a moment's pause, Dorothy shook her head. Crane cracked a smile, glanced across at the pharmacy, then back to catch Dorothy's gaze. 'Listen. Why don't I go inside and have a chat with the doctor? OK?'

With a grudging nod, Dorothy muttered, 'OK. Let's be quick,' and moved to cross the cobbled road towards the pharmacist. It came as a surprise when Crane caught her arm again.

'No! Doz. You need to wait here. I'll go.'

In an instant, all her earlier misgivings started to bubble up again. Crane persevered. 'You ... you really don't smell too good. Seriously. I'll only be a minute. Just one minute, OK?'

Crane released her arm and took an experimental step backwards. Dorothy continued to stare at him. He raised his palm towards her and stole another step in the direction of the shop. By the time he finally turned around and hurried across the road, Dorothy was back on high alert. Crane was making the same mistake he often made: underestimating her intelligence, misinterpreting submission for stupidity. There was a reason he didn't want her inside the shop, and it wasn't because of the way she smelled. Dorothy followed his progress as he reached the front door. Crane turned to check that she was still doing what she had been told, and then scurried inside.

The ringing of the bell above the door brought a bald man in a white coat with an almost perfectly circular face out of hiding. Crane walked up to the counter before engaging the pharmacist in conversation, leaning inwards conspiratorially. The pharmacist in turn bent in to listen until their heads were almost touching, the consultation becoming intimate, secretive. After a lengthy dialogue, Crane twisted around to look for Dorothy, and appeared surprised to see her staring back at him. He returned to the conversation, gesturing awkwardly towards the young girl. The pharmacist leant around Crane to steal a look at Dorothy, nodded sympathetically, then tottered towards a phone mounted on the wall behind him. He picked up the handset and began to punch in a number.

Dorothy ran.

Without direction, without the whisper to guide her, without even realising that she was already primed for flight, she ran. The quest to find her father had been swept aside by her need to vanish, to make sure she wasn't about to get drawn into whatever double-dealing Crane had set up. Her companion blundered out of the shop and lumbered painfully after the fleeing girl.

'Hey! Doz!' he bellowed. 'Doz! Wait up!'

Running away was a tactic that Dorothy had relied on plenty of times in her past: just go, don't look back, try not to stop until you've found someplace where whoever is after you can't see you. Put enough distance between yourself and the threat before they have a chance to react, and chances are they won't even bother trying to chase you. And then when you're safe, you can take all the time you need to figure out what you really should have done instead. It seemed, however, that Crane wasn't prepared to let her disappear into the city without him. Although Dorothy had a sizeable head start, her escape route along the high street was clogged up by early morning shoppers and tardy shop assistants. Unused to the demands of an actual pursuit, she was spending too much time looking over her shoulder to properly avoid the crowds ahead. Dorothy danced around obstacles where she saw them, bounced off the ones she didn't, and slowed at every turn. In spite of his injuries, it didn't take long for Crane to catch up with her, to grab her dirty jacket and drag her to a halt.

'Hey! Stop! Where you going?' he demanded, gulping air into his lungs.

Dorothy spun round to confront her captor, pinned to the spot by his tight clasp. Even the short distance had left her out of breath, and she greedily sucked in air through her nose, giving her the appearance of a snorting bull lining up to make a charge. There was no good answer to Crane's question, other than 'away', and she glared at the man, waiting to see what he would do next. It was another question.

'What's going on, Doz?' he demanded.

This one she did have an answer for. 'You're trying,' she accused between pants, 'to get me caught.'

'What? Stop acting mad!' Crane protested. 'Doz, please. I'm here to help you.'

'No! You're here to...' Dorothy trailed off. What *did* she imagine Crane was doing there? The whole thing had been his idea, but now that she came to question his motives, she couldn't figure out what he actually stood to gain. Crane had never met her father, and he might not even be allowed to stay in her father's house after they finally got there. This was

Dorothy's journey, and Crane was simply the architect. If he wasn't there to help, there was only one other possible reason.

'To watch me.' The girl haltingly finished her sentence as the answer revealed itself. 'You're just like West. You want to watch me. See how I fall apart.'

Crane looked at his young friend. A reassuring grin began to form at the corners of his mouth, although the smile failed to register in his eyes. He lessened his grip, and Dorothy relaxed her shoulders.

'No,' he answered, slowly and assuredly. 'I'm here to help you find your father, remember? You need to take a moment and think, OK? Calm down a little bit. Stop being all paranoid.'

And there was the other trigger. If Crane had paid her slightly more attention in all the years they had been friends, he would know that. Don't treat her like she's stupid, and don't ever tell her she's acting crazy. Dorothy's eagerness to slip away again crumbled beneath a sudden rage, a peculiarly precise fury that drove away all the noise and burnished her thoughts into crystal clarity. She pushed herself free of Crane's grip, eyes ablaze with rational resentment. 'You think I haven't figured you out?' she spat at the man, a guttural rasp that built from the depths of her throat. 'You think I'm too stupid to understand you? To understand what you do?'

Crane took a nervous step backwards. 'Whoa! Chill yourself down! OK?'

'No – *you* chill yourself,' Dorothy hissed, advancing on her companion, closing down the gap as fast as he could create it. 'Why is it only you that's left? Why aren't Bill and Parsley still here? Was that part of your plan?'

Crane halted his retreat and pushed his bruised face towards Dorothy. 'Thatcher?' he replied incredulously. 'That Bill? You have got to be kidding me, Doz.'

'Bill used to make sure I was safe from you,' Dorothy barked. 'And then you changed that. How did you do that?'

'Come on, just have a think about what you're saying for a minute.' Crane had adopted that tone again: slow and deliberate, condescending and arrogant. '*I* make sure you're OK. *I'm* here to look after you.'

It was impossible to tell whether Crane was self-delusional or just being wantonly hypocritical, but either way Dorothy had had enough. With a single stride she closed the space between them and lunged forward. Sensing an impending collision of heads, Crane raised his arms to protect his swollen face, giving Dorothy the space to thrust her hands into the outside pockets of his jacket and burgle their unguarded contents. It was high time to see whether he'd been telling the truth. She stepped backwards, dragging whatever she could grasp with her, and a shower of crumpled banknotes, coins, train tickets and sweet wrappers burst over the cobbled street.

'Hey! What are you...' exclaimed Crane as he dropped to the ground, scrambling after his scattered possessions.

Above him, Dorothy sieved crudely through the two handfuls of stuff she had retained, discarding paper money and coins, spilling more debris around the frantic man below. 'Looking after me. Here to look after me,' she muttered as she picked her way through his possessions.

Crane attempted to trap a banknote as it got caught by the breeze, while awkwardly fishing coins out of the cracks between cobbles. 'Christ, Dozza! Don't you remember what we had to go through to get this money?' he whined. Dorothy glared disdainfully at the back of his head as he scuttled about. It was a view of her travelling companion with which she was becoming familiar.

Having finished her inspection, she plucked a single object from the haul and released everything else in a fresh downpour. Without looking up, Crane voiced his displeasure. 'Really, Doz? For fuck's sake!'

It was a small plastic pot, half-full of pills. Dorothy held it up to more closely examine the contents, but there were no labels or markings. This didn't come from West's stash. This was all Crane. Even though he'd specifically promised not to bring any drugs with him. She rattled the jar, and his frantic movements stopped. When she glanced down, she found her companion staring directly at her, wide-eyed with apprehension.

'Hey! No! Those aren't...' he spluttered. 'Give them back. Can I have them back, please?'

Without breaking eye contact, Dorothy unscrewed the lid from the jar. Crane staggered to his feet, leaving discarded banknotes to dance away in the wind. The game was over, and his frustration had become a desperate anger. 'Give them back!' he screeched. 'Give them back to me!'

'Looking after me?' Dorothy enquired, her resentment still burning. With a dramatic flick of her wrist, she launched the contents of the pot into the air, distributing the tablets across the high street where they landed with a string of delicate pitter-patters.

Crane's momentary flash of rage collapsed into shock. 'What are you doing?' He twisted away from her as if he was about to chase the discarded pills, before abandoning it as a fool's errand. He turned back to Dorothy despondently.

With her point proven, Dorothy allowed her animosity to taper off. 'You think I don't see you?' she challenged Crane. 'You think I don't understand? You're not as smart. Not as much as you think you are.'

Crane bent down and plucked a note out of the detritus on the ground, before petulantly kicking at the remaining litter, firing coins in all directions to ricochet off the cobbled paving.

When he spoke again, all emotion had been washed away, replaced by a cold condescension. 'Well. That's just fucking brilliant. You stupid. Fucking. Idiot. All this way. We made it all this way, and now we have to go all the way back again.'

There it was. Dorothy finally had her proof – her friend had no interest in helping her make her way home. He probably didn't even care if she found out whether she was going to die or not. Even though she hated being on her own, Dorothy knew that this was where she needed to part ways with her last travelling companion. 'Go back,' she muttered, even though she knew that continuing the journey without Crane meant finding her way without a plan. A rush of anguish set off the itch in her infected forearm, and she attacked it while considering her next steps. He had brought her this far, but this was the only option left to them both. With more conviction, she declared, 'Go back. You can't stay with me.'

Crane shot her a look of pure theatrical sarcasm that must have caused his bruised face to ache slightly. 'Yeah. Right,' he replied. 'You don't think I'm just gonna leave you here, do you?'

But Dorothy's mind was made up. She backed away from Crane, unsure what his reaction would be. He held out his arms, his palms upturned, unconvinced. 'Where do you think you're going?' he called after the departing girl, but he made no attempt to follow her.

Dorothy continued to edge away until there was enough distance between them to justify making a run for it. She paused and gently shook her head, a sombre farewell to a friend she could no longer trust. And with that she was gone, hightailing it through what remained of the milling crowd.

'You stupid fuck! You stupid fucking fuck!' Behind her Crane bellowed his dismay, but he remained rooted to the spot. 'How are you going to manage?'

As Dorothy clumsily weaved through the shoppers, Crane's voice grew quieter and more expansive, until it stopped sounding like it was coming from one place and instead echoed his contempt from every building. Ahead of her a flight of steps led up into a shopping centre, with all its swarming humanity and opportunities to hide. She glanced backwards just in time to witness Crane's final lament.

'You can't leave me,' he implored, but before she could answer Dorothy was through the doors and invisible.

∼

EVEN WHEN SHE was out of sight, Dorothy kept moving for another ten minutes before she finally let herself believe that she was safe, squatting at the back of an amusement arcade behind a row of air-hockey tables. As soon as she allowed herself to relax and collect her thoughts, she was overwhelmed by an uneasiness about where recent events had left her: on her own in a city that she no longer recognised, and with no obvious means of finding her aunt's house. A chill set in. She started to tremble, even though her puffer jacket was zipped all the way up to her neck, and a strange nausea lodged in her gut. She unleashed her anxiety into an all-out assault on her itchy forearm and tried to focus instead on her breathing.

It took Dorothy longer than normal to properly dampen her jitters, breathing in through her nose and out through her mouth, thinking only about counting and the delicate breeze that tickled the hairs at the front of her nostrils. But before too long she found herself settling into a deep meditative state, and with it came an unnerving sensation of falling backwards into unseen dangers, the tips of her toes desperately clutching for the floor below her feet. When Dorothy eventually broke her mind free, she had little sense of how much time had passed, although there had been a significant increase in the number of customers in the arcade. Her jacket felt cold against her clammy skin, and she had trouble disentangling all the muddle from her thoughts, even after she'd talked herself down from her day-mare. She clearly had more processing to do before she could claim to have dealt with the events of the previous evening. Looking around, Dorothy could see that she had drawn the attention of two red-shirted employees, both of whom were glancing over in her direction and chatting furtively. She had outstayed her welcome here.

Getting out of the shopping centre proved to be more challenging than getting in, especially finding an exit that didn't open onto the high street. It would do her no favours if she ran into Crane again, now that he'd had all this extra time to come up with a more convincing argument. Without her constant vigilance, he would certainly get picked up by West before she did, and the sooner she got back on her mission and far away from that bit of the city, the safer she'd be. Eventually, Dorothy managed to access a stairwell through the carpet section of a large department store, and from there the car park and the city beyond. Still nothing looked familiar. With no obvious course to follow, she picked a direction at random and set off at her earlier brisk pace, hoping that recreating the same conditions would lure the whispering opinion back again.

But it didn't return. Even with her fingers in her ears to cut out the noise of the city; even when she started making random turns and heading aimlessly down anonymous side streets; even when she tried to conjure a false sense of fear and suspicion. A lingering irritation soon set in, loosely aimed at Crane for having interrupted her with no good reason. It turned out to be impossible to clear this sense of annoyance, even though Dorothy knew it was probably blocking access to her whispering guide. Eventually she stopped at a local shop and swapped all the change in her pockets for an assortment of chocolate bars, in the hope that fixing her blood-sugar levels and quelling the rumbling in her stomach would help. Dorothy left before the shopkeeper had counted his way through her shrapnel, despite the protestations that followed her out of the store. She suspected that she might have done slightly better out of the deal than he did.

After a couple more hours, Dorothy found herself on a long, straight road alongside an airport, at which point her frustration came dangerously close to flaring up into a full-on tantrum. She sat down on the bonnet of a parked car for a while as she tried to compose herself with chocolate, before swinging around and heading off on a perpendicular tack. She didn't remember having to endure the incessant whine of jet engines during her childhood. It was bad enough being lost, but worse still to be lost in the wrong place.

~

It was late in the afternoon before she finally had a breakthrough. After trudging up a narrow side road behind a boarded-up pub, she spotted her first 'd'.

Near the top of a metal pole that held a street sign in place, Dorothy had found a mark that she had once carved by torchlight, half a lifetime ago, on one of her nocturnal rambles: a lower-case 'd', complete with cursive flourishes and a looped stalk. It was her specific brand, hacked out of the paint by a pair of blunt scissors, that let her know she had already passed this way. The discovery of her childhood mark triggered a renewed sense of determination that swept her resentment away. Now everything had changed. She had found an outer marker, and she awarded herself a quiet pat on the back for the systematic nature of her search. If she could just map out how her letters were distributed in the nearby streets, she might be able to figure out a direction to the centre of the circle.

Despite her concerns about how she would manage without Crane there to make the plans, Dorothy had just uncovered a decade-old breadcrumb all by herself.

~

BY COMPARISON, finding Ruby's house from there on was a breeze, even though Dorothy was initially only able to narrow down the options to a choice between turning left or right on a radial road. After half an hour of walking, she convinced herself that her fifty-fifty guess at the start had been wrong, and turned around; after another hour walking in the opposite direction, she wound up at the airport again, and re-convinced herself that her first guess had been right all along. The sun was already lodged firmly over to one side of the sky when Dorothy finally began to recognise some landmarks from her childhood forays, and from there the quiet voice that had earlier guided her through the city returned, getting louder and more confident with every step.

The closer Dorothy got to Ruby's house, and the more she remembered, the more apprehensive she became. Spending the day annoyed at Crane had kept her from considering a more dangerous possibility, and she was becoming increasingly nervous that she might be heading into a trap. Although she was convinced that Crane wouldn't be able to find his way to her aunt's house without her, West was much better equipped. She had a car and maps, and a crew; she could probably even get hold of Ruby's address if she wanted to. The only thing that West didn't know was where Dorothy was heading, and it wouldn't take her long to cajole it out of Crane if she caught him. She wondered what her old companion was up to at that moment. The thought entered her mind that maybe he had just been inept after all, that everything that had passed between them had been a massive misunderstanding. She shook off the idea before it could develop into remorse. If she couldn't trust him, then he had to go, whether her doubts were justified or not.

Before too long, Dorothy found herself standing at the end of Ruby's road, and her dogged restlessness was back in control. Key to the success of Crane's original plan was to be inconspicuous at all times, but here she was a long way away from the sheltering crowds and the bustle of the city centre. She must have only passed four or five people in the last twenty minutes, and she was acutely aware that she was now very visible indeed – it was still daylight, after all, and she was dressed in a bright orange jacket. However, it wasn't until her first glimpse of Ruby's house, about a hundred yards down on the other side of the road, that Dorothy realised how mentally unprepared she was for the shock of seeing her childhood home again. Without warning, a barrage of shame-filled memories assaulted her – all her failures and her wrongdoings, and the hours she'd spent locked under the stairs. She stumbled to a halt, struggling to concentrate hard enough to figure out what her next move should be.

Dorothy's uneasy reverie was interrupted by the appearance of a child on the empty driveway of Ruby's house, excitedly rushing in no particular direction to evade capture by another breathless child who materialised soon afterwards. Their chaotic game quickly spilled onto the pavement, then into the driveway of the neighbouring house, and Dorothy found herself staring at them, trying to work out the rules. Before too long came the muffled sounds of scolding. Although Dorothy was too far away to make out what was being said, just hearing her aunt's angry voice was enough to cut through the mental chatter and bring about an instant terror. She dropped out of sight onto her hands and knees behind a car just as the old woman appeared.

Ruby limped out onto the pavement to catch the children by their arms before gruffly reprimanding them and releasing them to continue their game in the back garden. Leaving the displeased look on her face, she glanced up and down the road before following the kids back inside.

Still perched on all fours, Dorothy shivered at the close encounter and nervously scratched at her forearm while she forced herself to consider her options. Her situation was already extremely precarious, and now she had an extra person to avoid. She needed to bide quite a bit of time, and this was very definitely not a safe vantage point.

∽

Being allowed to go to the nearby playground was a rite of passage for guests in Ruby's house. When a child turned eight, they were permitted to walk to the park unaccompanied, provided they could demonstrate that they could be trusted to safely cross a couple of minor roads on the way. When they turned eleven, they could take responsibility for a younger sibling or two. In all her time at the foster home, Dorothy had never been considered suitably dependable as a chaperone, which was a source of quiet annoyance given how many bigger roads she'd had to negotiate on her solo night-time walks through the city. As a result, she had so often walked the route between Ruby's house and the park in a huff that she still felt the ghost of teenage umbrage when she passed through the gates all these years later.

Pride of place in the middle of the fenced-off play area was the slide. Although it looked smaller than it had when Dorothy was a child, it was still an impressive edifice, constructed on a wide triangular platform of wooden logs. A series of rectangular foot- and hand-holds were nailed onto one side, and the stainless-steel chute ran down the other, but that was really only for very young children. For everyone else, hanging out on the summit cemented your place in the local hierarchy. How you climbed up there was up to you, but it rarely involved using the designated holds.

Sitting on the top also offered you the best views. You could keep an eye on any younger charges playing in the kids' area, or see over the hedge that grew along the perimeter of the park to watch the road on the other side. When she was much younger, Dorothy had had a grandstand view when a local tramp tottered off the pavement in front of an approaching car, and was noisily bounced off the bonnet before coming to rest some way down the street. The traumatised motorist, who lived nearby, had parked his car on his driveway and never got behind the wheel again, and Dorothy and her pseudo-siblings would excitedly check out the unrepaired dent every time they passed his house. The tramp, they never saw again. In the middle distance, you could also see the upper two storeys of Ruby's house. Dodging her way through animated children, Dorothy scrambled up to resume her rightful position on the wooden roost, and began a quiet vigil.

Late afternoon turned into evening, and the swarm of younger children in the play area gradually dissipated. After a couple of abortive conversations initiated by concerned parents, Dorothy was surprised to find that she pretty much had the entire slide to herself, with the local kids being directed upwind towards other playthings in the park. By the time it became too dark to recognise colours properly, she was on her own, incrementally swallowed into the blackness; first a statue, then a silhouette, and finally a memory.

Ahead, the lights in Ruby's house switched on and off as children moved through the rooms on the upper floors, and ultimately into bed. Eventually, the whole house was in darkness except for a single dimmed light on the top storey, where her aunt had her bedroom. While the original idea had involved sneaking into Ruby's office after she'd gone to sleep and quietly riffling through her files, Dorothy was now feeling increasingly uncomfortable about her ability to complete the task without waking anybody. It would be much less risky if she could get in and dig out her father's address when the house was empty.

However, it had also become clear that she couldn't stay in the park until then. About a hundred feet away from the children's play area, a group of five teenagers had lumbered in and sat down, gathered around the flame from a garden torch. They were laughing and jabbering loudly to each other, taking long swigs from a plastic bottle and passing cigarettes around the circle. Dorothy remembered well enough the rules of the park. This was now their territory.

But they hadn't spotted her yet. She maintained her surveillance, grateful to be finally hearing voices that didn't want to talk to her, while the scene below became progressively more boisterous. One of the teenagers, who was dressed in a dark green camouflage jacket and vibrant blue trousers, kicked repeatedly at the feet of his friend opposite; in the thin light from the torch flame, his upper half was almost completely invisible, leaving only a pair of animated legs. 'Just stop being a wanker and give me some cider.'

'Every time! Get your own fucking cider,' the second teenager jeered.

'Yeah? Like you don't just nick it from your mum's boyfriend's stash. The shit he gets from the gypsies.'

'Tastes alright, though,' the second teenager replied, before raising the bottle to his lips and taking a long draw. With his eyes closed in mock rapture, he breathed an orgasmic, 'Ah! Lovely!'

'Tell you what, you keep drinking that shit and you're going to end up like your mum's pikey boyfriend,' ventured the half-hidden teenager. 'You know your whole house stinks of his balls now? Seriously, that's all I can smell when I come round. You must be tasting the smell of his balls all day. You keep drinking his pikey cider made by his pikey mates – bet they all washed their nut-sacks in it first.'

The other teenagers laughed and whooped, much to the chagrin of the wannabe pikey. 'Fuck you!' he countered. 'Have a taste of these balls, dickhead.' He took a long pull on the bottle until his mouth was full and his cheeks distended, before spitting the contents towards his friend. His tormentor leant forward, his mouth open wide as the deluge hit him square in the face.

A shocked silence fell over the party. The wet teenager shook his head like a sodden dog, craned his head back and gargled a few notes through second-hand cider before gulping down the contents of his mouth. He grinned at his friend opposite. 'Know what?' he asked. 'That actually does taste alright.'

Hysterical laughter immediately consumed the teenagers. One of the girls fell over onto her back, so convulsed with hilarity that she was finding it hard to breathe, gasping for air between howls of mirth. Sounds of irresistible glee rang around the quiet park until the boy with the cider bottle glanced in Dorothy's direction. A moment passed as he stared into the darkness, a confused grin on his face, before he leapt to his feet.

'Fuck!'

The others followed his gaze, searching for the source of his concern.

'Shut up!' the frightened boy ordered. 'Look! On the slide!'

One by one his friends stood up, all amusement forgotten. An ashen-faced girl breathed a sober, 'Jesus. What is that?'

'What the hell?' said the frightened boy. 'Can you see it?'

'Is … is it a person?' the wet boy stammered. He called over to Dorothy. 'Hey, mister. Are you alright? Can you hear me?'

But Dorothy didn't answer. She didn't move. All her attention was focused on the distant light in Ruby's room.

'Get a stick,' one of the girls demanded. 'Go and give him a prod.'

Across the small park, on the other side of the dangerous road, shielded from anyone not watching from the top of the slide, the light in an attic window switched off. In one movement Dorothy stood up and stepped cautiously down the chute. In front of her, the five kids dispersed in terror into the night, leaving their burning torch behind, as Dorothy strode across the grass to her next hideout.

SUNDAY, 22ND AUGUST
The Tin Man

Wedged against the wall of a beach hut, lying on her orange puffer jacket and shrouded under sandy towels for warmth, Dorothy's eyes flicked open.

Above the tranquil sound of breaking waves and the wails of seagulls, an argument was already under way. Although Crane and Thatcher seemed to be trying their best to keep their voices down, their bickering had already become too heated to be conducted in hushed tones. In the light that spilled through every imperfect wooden join and knot, this was also Dorothy's first view of the inside of the beach hut. She had awakened in an unusually jumbled state, and she knew that it would take her a couple of moments to untangle her thoughts. She lay still while the conversation raged around her.

'You are showing absolutely no regard for my feelings,' Thatcher hissed. 'Can you please afford me a little consideration? I'd be grateful if you could at least try to understand how difficult this has all been for me.'

'Jesus Christ, I'd be grateful if you could stop being such an extraordinary twat,' Crane countered, less quietly. 'How hard can it be? You're a junkie. You hang out with junkies, you recognise other junkies. Simple as.'

'That was someone else! That was a completely different person.'

Dorothy heard the distinctive click-clack of the rosary beads on Thatcher's necklace, which he only ever played with when he was upset. 'In any case, they're almost certainly going to think I'm with the drug squad.'

Despite her muddled logic, Dorothy understood that this was her cue to enter the conversation. She sat up. A painful red swelling had developed on her left forearm sometime during the night that demanded scratching, and she attacked it with her dirty fingernails without looking down.

'No drugs,' she interjected. 'We said no drugs.'

Crane was close by, mired in shadow, his back to Dorothy. When she spoke, he lurched forward in surprise. 'Fuck! You're awake!' he exclaimed, clutching his chest.

At the far end of the hut, Thatcher crouched amongst the shards of sunlight that crept around the door. He looked even bigger than he normally did, as if cramming his tall frame into the undersized space added some kind of false perspective. Bigger and older. His long grey hair hung loosely around his face, the tips brushing the shoulders of his black coat as he moved his head. Dorothy knew that her friend was a lot older than the rest of them, and although Thatcher had never confirmed or denied Crane's various estimates, the consensus put him safely into his fifties and probably even older still. This morning, the daylight revelled unkindly in the wrinkles and lines on his handsome, but perpetually melancholic, face, etched into place by a lifetime of taking everything to heart. When Dorothy sat up, he moved from fiddling with his necklace to scraping his hair back into a ponytail.

'Hey, sweetheart.' He smiled unconvincingly. 'Did you sleep OK?'

'What are you talking about, Bill?' Dorothy demanded, keen to resolve the dispute and restore some peace to the beach hut so she could wake up properly. 'What are you and Crane saying?'

Composed again after his scare, Crane shifted his position so he could address both of them directly. 'We were just thinking. Looking at options.'

Thatcher twisted his torso to relieve some discomfort in his spine; being taller than the beach hut was long, he must have had to fold himself uncomfortably for whatever sleep he could get. 'You know, this really feels like the end of the line,' he declared sadly to Dorothy. 'Shouldn't we be considering getting back?'

'Bollocks,' Crane retorted. 'We've still got a plan.'

'And we need to get Parsley back,' Dorothy insisted, a little miffed that they'd interrupted her sleep to argue about a decision that had already been made. 'Remember? We all agreed.'

'Yeah, yeah.' Crane held up a hand. 'Absolutely. We've got to at least *try* and get Parsley back. But we still need money. Money for food. Money for the train. There's no way of getting to your aunt otherwise.'

'Please don't go troubling Dorothy with your ridiculous notions, Mr Crane,' Thatcher implored. 'She isn't going to go along with—'

Crane spun towards Thatcher and wagged his finger aggressively. 'Just shut up for a second!'

Silence hung in the air like one of the dust motes caught in a beam of daylight. Crane stared at Thatcher for a moment longer before lowering his finger and returning to Dorothy. 'Doz, we're a little bit screwed,' he confessed. 'Low on options.

You should probably check the kitty, but I think we've only got about eight quid left. No credit cards. Nothing.'

Dorothy redoubled the assault on her inflamed forearm, looking to Thatcher for confirmation.

'We've gone as far as we can,' the tall man answered, shaking his head sadly.

'What did I just say?' Crane rounded on Thatcher again, before resuming his dialogue with Dorothy. 'Doz, I think we may have figured a way to get out of this town. Today.'

'We?' interrupted Thatcher. 'This plan has absolutely nothing to do with me.'

'So, we totally need to go spring Parsley,' Crane persisted. 'You and me, like we said we would, right? But while we're doing that, why doesn't Billy-boy here go sell the drugs we stole from West? Go back to the pub. Get us some money, money, money. And then we all meet up at the station later, go find your dad together.'

'I'm sorry, but that is not an option,' Thatcher announced.

'Two choices!' Crane explained, raising his voice. Dorothy turned to look at him, and he held her gaze with an earnest expression on his face. Leaning in, he continued, 'One – we do what Snatcher wants and go hand ourselves in. Or...' He started to nod. 'Or we can get some money. Get the fuck out of this town. Keep going with the mission. Like we planned.'

The further they got into the journey, the less Dorothy understood what made Thatcher tick. Sure, they'd become becalmed in this shitty seaside town for longer than she had hoped, but that didn't change anything. Crane was doing that thing again of assuming that she wouldn't bother questioning his ideas just because he was smarter than her, but it didn't always mean that he was wrong. If she didn't get the opportunity to speak to her father, there was a very real chance she'd be dead before too long. And somehow Thatcher seemed to be

OK with that possibility, even though he always claimed to have her best interests at heart.

Dorothy turned to address her tall friend. 'Do you want to come with me and get Parsley back instead? Then Crane can go sell the pills.'

'No fucking way,' Crane interjected. 'Doz, this is what Thatch does. He knows what he's doing.'

Thatcher gave a dejected sigh. 'Sweetheart, the police aren't going to let Parsley go. Not after what he did.'

'So, go sell the drugs while Crane and I go and get him. Crane knows how to get him out.'

'Ha!' Crane turned towards Thatcher with a look of relief on his face, and flashed him a smug grin. 'Exactly,' he condescended.

At the other end of the beach hut, Thatcher slowly raised himself up until his head was almost brushing against the sloping roof, then stepped across the scattered junk towards Dorothy. With a groan he crouched in front of the girl, blocking Crane from her sight. Taking her hands in his enormous grip, he smiled at her kindly.

'Dorothy,' he began, quietly, urgently. 'I don't think you understand what you're asking me to do.'

Dorothy scrutinised her friend. He was being unusually evasive that morning, and she wondered whether she was missing something. It seemed unfair to make her deal with layers of subtext so early in the day, especially when she was feeling more befuddled than normal. But Crane was definitely right on this one – yesterday's debacle had shown them that they weren't going anywhere without money, and the pills they stole from West did seem to be their most valuable asset. There was no way she was just going to give up and go home. Thankfully, she had the casting vote.

'You swore to God,' she reminded him.

'Leave God out of this,' Thatcher snarled back at her, unbalancing himself enough that he had to stand up again to avoid toppling over. Towering over the girl, he lowered his head, closed his eyes and drew in a deep breath, before muttering something to himself. When he opened his eyes again, he gazed down at Dorothy and continued in more measured tones. 'What I meant to say was the promise I made was to *you*. Dorothy? Please?'

'Then keep it,' she replied without emotion, certain that she was making the right decision. 'Keep your promise. We're not going back.'

Above her, Thatcher pressed his hands onto his face, roughly massaging his cheeks and eyes. Crane broke the silence. 'Ah, you are no fun when you're like this,' he said playfully to the other man, a broad smile stretched almost all the way across his narrow face. 'No fun at all.'

Thatcher lowered his arms and scowled at Crane, his expression somewhere between humiliation and contempt. He stretched out a reluctant hand and gestured with his fingers; the younger man promptly pulled four ziplock bags of pills from his jacket and dropped them into Thatcher's sizeable palm. The tall man held up the contents for closer inspection, before carefully sliding them into one of the many pockets in his long coat.

With a final futile glance at Dorothy, Thatcher turned and shuffled through the mess towards the exit, shoulders slumped and head lowered. He slid a plastic cricket stump out from where it had been wedged between the handles on the doors the night before, cracked one of them ajar, and peered through the gap into the brightness beyond. Satisfied that the coast was clear, he pushed the door fully open and took an uncertain step into the world outside. Crane called after him, 'Hey! How hard can it be, eh?'

Thatcher turned and glared at the other man, who countered with a conspiratorial wink and his obnoxious grin. 'Five hours,' Thatcher growled quietly. 'Be at the train station in five hours.' He turned to the young girl. 'Dorothy?'

Outside, the Sunday sky was grey and overcast. They were in one of a short row of beach huts, each painted a different colour and in various states of repair. Further down the beach, similar clusters of wooden huts sat between the grassy sand dunes and the promenade, along which older couples and women with strollers ambled. In the distance, the rusting metal remains of a burned-down pier jutted out of the sea, its gnarled fingers corroding slowly in the salt breeze.

Crane had been careful in selecting their temporary lodging – as far away from the centre of activity as they could find in the darkness. Shielded from the rest of the town by crumbling red cliffs, their hut was located at the point where the promenade narrowed slightly as it led uphill to a car park. If they had chosen a hut any closer to the remains of the pier, amongst the ice-cream vans and the shops selling beach supplies, they would now be stuck in the midst of families who were busy unpacking sun-loungers and towels, setting themselves up for a relaxing day by the sea while their kids frolicked on the chilly dunes. So far, however, no one had come to claim any of the huts in their cluster. Although people were already meandering along the walkway behind them, it didn't look like anyone had spotted the splintered wood around the clamps that had once held a padlock in place.

Thatcher squinted into the leaden daylight as Dorothy arrived behind him at the beach hut's doors. She peered expectantly up at the older man, who turned to face her with a strained smile. Reaching behind his head, he unclasped his rosary-bead necklace. 'They'll never believe this,' he muttered, and leant over to hang it around Dorothy's neck, threading the catches through her tangled blonde mane as she gazed up at him. Taking a final glance at Crane, then at the silver crucifix that rested on Dorothy's T-shirt, he whispered, 'Protection. Till I get back.'

And with that, he marched away without looking around, down towards the town and whatever circumstance might have planned for him there.

∽

NOT LONG AFTERWARDS, Crane and Dorothy also left the hut and shuffled off down the hill. Dorothy's head had yet to clear itself of the vagueness that had arrived in the night, and this had been further confounded by a bout of jitters that had set in as she watched Thatcher skulk away. She couldn't decide whether it was a reaction to her friend's unusually dramatic exit, or if it was just that she was now entirely at Crane's disposal, but either way she wished that Parsley was still there with her. Even though his behaviour had been erratic over the last few days, she knew he'd have kept anything bad from happening to her. That said, there was no chance that he and Thatcher would have both fitted into the cramped hut at the same time.

Somehow it had been easy enough to find their way to the beach the night before, even after dark, and Dorothy expected the rest of the town to reveal itself to her with the same casual ease. They walked along the promenade towards the centre of activity, then turned away from the shore and headed inland. The day had started off murky, and a stiff breeze blew in from the sea, seeming to freeze the fractious seagulls stationary in the air above them. Watersports enthusiasts in wetsuits prepared their boards and kites on the beach, while most people contented themselves with just a taste of the sea air.

Crane and Dorothy's aimless stroll took them uphill, towards the centre of the town, past a museum of regional history and a gallery selling landscapes painted by local artists. Faint echoes of a faded elegance leaked through the rotting Victorian architecture, from an age before television and cheap flights to places with nicer beaches. The continual buffeting from salty sea winds had maintained a corrosive barrage long after the income from the middle classes had dried up, slowly peeling away paint and rusting metal to reveal the functional skeleton beneath the façade. The town had been built to exploit sand and shoreline, and now it was struggling to endure without a reason to exist.

Unsurprisingly, Crane took the responsibility for navigating through the narrow streets and lanes, as well as doing most of the talking. He bobbed and weaved in front of Dorothy, walking backwards when he could, snatching brief moments of eye contact. Dorothy was already finding it hard enough to concentrate without having this elaborate dance as an additional distraction, and she drifted along behind him.

'I'm just saying that we need to be realistic,' Crane insisted, before breaking off to cavort around a lamppost. 'Know when to cut our losses. Move on.'

'We're not leaving him here. Not in this horrible town,' Dorothy reiterated. For some reason, this was proving to be a really complicated day. She accepted that sometimes she didn't pick up on everything people said in a conversation, particularly if it was one of those conversations where people don't say what they actually mean, but she was normally spared this much second-guessing when talking to her friends. Today it would have to be her job to keep everyone on mission, and she restated the goal: 'We need to get Parsley out of prison.'

'Yeah, yeah. I know,' Crane replied. 'Absolutely. In a perfect world the police would just give him back, and we could all go find your aunt together.' He stopped in front of Dorothy and caught her by the arms as she walked into him. Fixing her with a deliberate stare, he continued, 'But we've got to be super careful, yeah? If they know who he is, you can bet they're going to be looking for us too. What if the cops are using him as bait so they can catch us as well?'

'Why are you just telling me this now?' Dorothy snapped back at him, pushing free of his grasp, unable to keep her frustration out of her voice. All this backsliding, all these efforts to forestall her, were becoming as wearing as they were perplexing. If Crane refused to cooperate, she'd have to figure out a plan for springing her friend on her own, and she could already feel the threads of anxiety creeping into her thoughts. Whatever the flaws in the other man's plan, it was bound to be better than hers. Anyway,' she reminded him, eager to coax him back to the fold, 'Parsley wouldn't tell them anything.'

They marched along in silence as Dorothy's trepidation grew, desperate for her friend to put her out of her misery. But then the embryonic twitches of a grin crept onto Crane's face, and he glanced over his shoulder towards the young girl. 'You sure he wouldn't talk?' he asked. 'Bet you he's singing like a canary right now.'

Dorothy stared at the side of Crane's head as he allowed a smile to form, releasing her from her torment. It was a joke. It was, actually, quite a good joke, and she started to giggle in relief. Crane joined in with his raspy chuckle. Ahead, the road opened out onto the town's high street. Cars and pedestrians passed in front of them, welcoming them to the next phase of their search. If Parsley was in a cell in a police station, it was bound to be around here somewhere.

As they approached the junction, the amusement on Crane's face dropped away as quickly as it had arrived. He turned to Dorothy. 'Hey, wait a minute,' he enquired, suddenly all business again. 'Do you know what Parsley's real name is?'

∼

THEY HAD ONLY TRAVELLED about two hundred yards up the high street before Crane spotted the police station. It was some way off, but as soon as he laid eyes on it, he pulled Dorothy into an alley, out of sight.

'I can see it,' he declared urgently. 'Up the road. With a blue door.'

Dorothy peeked out from their hiding place, glancing in the direction that Crane had indicated. She could see more shops, and a petrol station, but nothing that said 'Police'. She turned back to Crane for more details, but before she had a chance to ask anything, he was already answering her question. 'Yeah. That's what police stations look like in small shithole towns like this. They just buy an old house or a shop and build the cells for prisoners and the rooms where they interrogate you afterwards. But they always have a blue door so you can tell. Normal people aren't allowed to buy that kind of blue paint, so you know it's definitely the police.'

'Does it say "Police" on it as well?' asked Dorothy, suspiciously. 'I can't see anywhere that says "Police".'

'It will. But you probably can't see it till you get closer,' answered Crane. He pressed Dorothy lightly against the wall and manoeuvred himself into her eyeline. 'Doz, listen to me. I need you to go back to the café that we just walked past, and wait.'

Dorothy's agitation came flooding back. This didn't sound right. This didn't sound right at all. 'But it's just there. The police are just there,' she ventured carefully.

'I'm going to go and get Parsley out,' Crane announced

confidently. 'And you are going to get some food. Yeah? Breakfast? Aren't you hungry?'

Dorothy's brow furrowed as she tried to make sense of what her friend was suggesting. 'But it's just there,' she repeated. 'Why can't I come too?'

'I bet you the police are going to be looking for us as well,' Crane explained in a hushed tone, fixing Dorothy with a knowing stare. 'If they've figured out who Parsley is, they'll be looking for three other people. But if I go in on my own, they may not realise that I'm with you lot.'

'There are two of us,' Dorothy argued. 'Not three.'

Crane pushed her harder against the wall, moving his face closer to Dorothy's, dropping his voice to an even more furtive level. 'And if I get caught, you'll still be free to finish the mission. You need to finish the mission, remember? It's the only way. You got the rest of the cash?'

Dorothy rummaged in the pocket of her puffer jacket and pulled out a handful of coins. She offered the shrapnel to Crane, who glanced down at it in surprise.

'No, no,' he said. 'You take it. Go buy some breakfast. Wait for me in the café. I'll be back soon with Parsley, hopefully. We'll come and find you.' He started to nod again. 'Do you understand?'

Dorothy stared back into her friend's expectant gaze. Very little that Crane had just said stood up to closer analysis. He didn't even like Parsley, and if he did manage to talk the police into letting their companion go, chances are that Parsley wouldn't want to leave with him anyway. And the whole blue paint thing sounded highly dubious as well. But he had got one thing right: she was hungry. Dorothy cursed her meandering concentration, not least because she was giving Crane all the opportunity he needed to treat her like an idiot. Fine. If he wanted to waste his time, she wasn't going to get in the way. At that moment Dorothy didn't have the acumen to argue with her companion, but maybe getting some food in her would help ease her confusion. Then when Crane came to join her in the café, no doubt empty-handed, she would force him to explain his failure in detail, and make him come up with a better plan. They still had most of the five hours left, after all.

'OK. I'll go and wait in the breakfast place,' Dorothy concurred reluctantly. 'If it doesn't work, you can think a bit harder.'

'Good girl!' Crane enthused. He pulled her into an unexpected hug, before angling her in the direction of the café and giving her a light shove to start her on her way. Dorothy staggered forward a couple of steps. When she glanced back at her friend, he was combing his fingers through his disordered hair in a vain attempt to make himself appear less dishevelled. He flashed her a thumbs-up then shooed her away with both hands. With a last purposeful tug on his jacket to straighten his clothes, he stepped out from the safety of their hiding place and strode fearlessly away towards the police station.

Seeing her friend march off up the street triggered the itch on her forearm, and Dorothy pecked at it through her puffer jacket while she watched him depart. After another twenty or so paces, Crane turned and gave her a more forceful burst of double-handed shooing. Without the sound of shiftiness and half-truths to distract her, Dorothy had become aware of a noisy rumbling from her stomach. Even though she was going to have to tolerate her own company for a while, she felt herself start to relax. Now was a good time to regroup and hopefully deal with the strange disorientation that had dogged her all morning. She pulled herself away from the sight of her companion on his way to inevitable defeat, and wandered back down the road.

∽

The café was busy, but Dorothy still managed to find a free table by the window, far enough away from the beguiling chatter of other diners. More fascinating, however, was the crazy hodgepodge of curios that populated the room. A row of shiny white elephants of decreasing size stretched along a high shelf, while on the counter a golden cat waved one of his arms towards her. And all the ketchup bottles were shaped like big tomatoes. But the most bizarre thing was the picture of a waterfall on the wall. When she first glanced at it, it had looked like any normal painting, but the more she stared, the more the water appeared to be actually flowing. The whole point of securing a spot by the window was so she could keep an eye out for Crane and Parsley, but since she had spotted the animated picture she was having trouble concentrating on anything else.

Breakfast, however, was very welcome, and the more she ate the more she came to appreciate the sense in Crane's plan. She eagerly worked her way through a stack of hot buttered toast, ripping each slice with her hands before devouring it. The orange juice, though, tasted a bit strange, and was full of little bits that she had to spit out after each sip. It tasted like they hadn't put enough water in it, and she opted instead for a cup of tea. Tea with as many sugars as she wanted.

After shifting seats so that her back was turned towards the waterfall, Dorothy could now begin her uninterrupted vigil of the street outside. Of the slow-moving older people wheeling bags in front of them, and the sullen teenagers who never looked up from their phones. On the other side of the road, a side street stretched uphill, flanked by a row of cottages and leading up to a small green. In the distance a big granite-grey car was struggling to park, shuffling forward and backward as it inched towards the kerb. It was too far away to see many details except for the imposing black grille on the front. To Dorothy, this had always looked like an enormous moustache, of a type seen only in movies about cowboys or old-timey detectives; since the headlights also resembled scrunched-up eyes, she could never shake the impression that this car was about to tell her off for something.

A cold finger of terror tapped on the back of her neck. Was that West's car?

Although it was too far away to be sure, it certainly looked like West's car. It hadn't taken her long to catch up with them, after all. Before Dorothy had a chance to properly consider what this meant, she had already scraped her chair backwards and thrown herself to the floor, ducking her head below the window and out of sight. Around her, the clanking of cutlery and the hum of chatter abruptly stopped, leaving her aware of the sound of her own shallow breathing. She glanced across at the other customers, who were all now quietly focused on her.

Cowering beneath her table, Dorothy struggled to fathom out what to do next. The first thought that entered her head was that Thatcher had given them up – he had, after all, been the one to suggest that they go back. As unlikely as that sounded, it was even more far-fetched to believe that West could have found her way to this ridiculous little town by complete chance. Whatever the explanation, they definitely should have hidden the car somewhere better. A concerned voice broke through Dorothy's nervous speculation.

'Are you alright, young lady?'

Dorothy glanced over her shoulder at the café owner, who was leaning in with a troubled look on her face.

'Is everything OK under there?'

Dorothy opened her mouth, expecting to find something to say to reassure the owner, but the words never came. Too much information was competing to make itself heard. Her mouth flapped like a fish out of water while her mind wrestled with an unreasonable number of possibilities.

'Young lady?' the worried owner continued. 'Are you hiding from someone? Do you need me to call the police?'

The question forced Dorothy to confront an even more appalling notion: that West had somehow found out about Parsley's arrest from someone *inside* the police. Faced with this prospect, Dorothy started to imagine all the extra opportunities there now were for getting caught, and her brain threatened to spiral off into some useless space. Without realising it, she had launched into one of her breathing exercises; when she found herself methodically trying to empty her head of cares and worries, she hastily pulled herself back into a more productive frame of mind. This did seem like a pretty good excuse for feeling stressed.

Acting in their favour was that West didn't really know what Crane looked like. Her friend might have been right all along in insisting she stay behind. Whatever had brought West there, it was clear that she and Crane needed to be somewhere else, and quickly. Staying out of sight, she crawled towards the front door, knocking against table legs and scattering crockery and cutlery around her.

'Hey!' the owner called after her. 'You sure you're alright?'

When she reached the exit, Dorothy stood up and glanced back at her trail of destruction. Although all eyes were still on her, the other customers had started whispering amongst themselves, and a formless murmuring percolated throughout the room.

'Police,' she muttered to no one in particular. 'Going to find the police.' She opened the door, took one last inquisitive stare at the magic waterfall painting, and escaped onto the high street.

Outside, a row of parked cars separated Dorothy from West's side road, but trying to make progress while staying crouched beneath the level of the car windows proved to be harder than she had imagined. She was also drawing strange stares from her fellow pedestrians. After a while Dorothy gave up in favour of dashing along the high street as fast as she could manage, even though she was having some difficulty spotting the house with the blue door.

'Doz?' Crane called out. 'Oi, Doz! Where you going?'

Dorothy staggered to a disoriented halt and twisted around towards the direction of the voice. Sitting on a low wall up a narrow alleyway, Crane stared back at the girl, a half-eaten doughnut poised at his mouth. Jumping to his feet, he jettisoned the food behind the wall and hastened over to join his friend. 'Hey didn't I say—' he began, through lips white with sugar.

'West,' interrupted Dorothy, panting. 'Back there. It's West.'

Crane's face scrunched up in disbelief. 'Bullshit. How can she be here? She doesn't know where we are.'

'West is down there!' insisted Dorothy, gesticulating along the high street. 'I saw her car!'

Crane exhaled emphatically though his nose. When he addressed her, his words were delivered slowly and precisely, as if he was talking to a young child who had just hurt herself on something he'd already warned her about. 'Dozza, you know that lots of people have that car, don't you?' he explained carefully. 'It's a Lexus. It's very popular. Even that same colour. If you watch...'

The unfinished sentence hung in the air as his gaze drifted off to the side in contemplation. After a moment in thought, his sceptical expression contorted into one of dismay, and he seized Dorothy by her shoulders. 'West is here? Shit! I knew she'd catch up with us! We've stayed in one place too long. We need to go.'

But Dorothy wasn't ready. She shimmied free of Crane's grip and took a decisive step backwards. 'Parsley?' she demanded. 'Where's Parsley?'

'I tried,' Crane muttered, his gaze darting in all directions, on the lookout for danger. 'They didn't let me see him.'

When Dorothy didn't move, he turned to face the girl to deliver a longer version of events. 'I tried to see him,' he explained earnestly, 'but he's in prison. They're not letting him out. I told them everything that happened, and how it wasn't his fault, but they still wanted to keep him locked up. And the police are definitely looking for us as well.' Crane scanned from side to side before confiding quietly, 'In fact, I may have got recognised.'

As Dorothy tried to reconcile herself to the idea that her friend may now be lost forever, something about Crane's story nagged at her. It would take a longer moment and a calmer disposition to properly unpick, but it was time that Crane wasn't prepared to let her have. 'Remember why we're here, Dozza,' he persisted. 'We need to get a move on. Now!'

Even before Dorothy had assembled the group of travellers to join her on her quest, there had been the plan. Sure, the plan had changed pretty dramatically since those days – it had mutated, evolved and adjusted to events, as any good plan should – but at no point had it lost sight of their objective. If Dorothy didn't find her father, there was a good chance she'd wind up dead. Whatever crises they encountered along the way, nothing was more important than the endgame. Ultimately, there was only one question that needed to be answered.

'Are they going to catch us?'

Crane relaxed his shoulders and flashed a sympathetic

smile towards his friend. 'Not if we run,' he answered calmly. 'Let's go.'

∼

IT WAS GOING to take every iota of Crane's guile and cunning to keep them under the radar until they could regroup with Thatcher. But it didn't start promisingly. Caught in a pincer manoeuvre between West and the police, Crane instead chose to carry on down the narrow alleyway in which he had been hiding. When this opened up into a small quadrant littered with cigarette butts but with no way through, he changed his mind and decided that the safest escape route was to head back towards the café. Because speed was of the essence, at every junction they chose the path that led downhill, and before too long Crane and Dorothy found themselves jogging back towards the sea.

Their dash to the beach gave Dorothy her first chance to reflect on what the rest of the journey would be like without Parsley in the party, and it made her feel even more flustered. Up to then, she'd assumed they'd be able to march into the police station and just ask for Parsley back, claiming him like a piece of lost property. She hadn't prepared herself for this eventuality. It wasn't only that Parsley was fiercely loyal and great at keeping secrets, it was that Dorothy relied on him to get in the way of bad things before they happened to her. She felt less safe with every stride that took her further from the police station, even though she knew she was meant to be running away from danger.

By now, the unbroken canopy of clouds was thinning, revealing odd patches of blue sky that crept imperceptibly across the heavens, bathing Crane and Dorothy in bursts of sunshine. Already the beach was much busier than it had been at first light, with the cries of excitable children masking the sounds of the waves and gulls. As the crowds on the promenade swelled, Dorothy relaxed slightly, safely anonymous amongst the growing swarm. She convinced herself that, with a bit of practice, she could probably navigate her way along the shoreline by just following the smells, as they hurried from burnt sugar and vinegar, through dog shit, to finally arrive in sun cream and brine.

It was Dorothy's idea to head back to the beach hut and hide there for a few hours, but as they approached it became evident that some of their neighbours had already arrived. They were still some way off when a shirtless man emerged from their hut, his taut belly suspended over blue cargo shorts and stick-thin legs. Behind him, a policewoman appeared and examined the jemmied lock. Without sharing a single word or look, Dorothy and Crane spun around and hurried away as quickly as they could without arousing suspicion, back into the comforting embrace of the throng.

It was the start of Crane's masterclass in how not to be seen. They spent a while sequestered in the public toilets on the promenade – until Crane was driven out of the sole stall in the men's block by a persistent child, and then had to sneak himself into the women's side to rescue Dorothy. In the beach shop they tried on disguises of straw hats and brightly coloured sunglasses, but the shopkeeper didn't relax his gaze long enough to give them a suitable opportunity for theft. Walking along the base of the cliffs rather than following the promenade offered some respite from prying eyes, even though they never managed to get past the last of the visitors and onto a section of beach to themselves. And it was really annoying having to stop every hundred yards or so to empty the sand from their shoes. The first time Dorothy bent over to deal with the debris in her bloodied trainer, she felt a surge of sadness that caught her completely off-guard. Up to that moment, allowing herself time to wallow in her own personal heartache had seemed unnecessarily indulgent when compared with her concerns for Parsley's wellbeing, and it wasn't until she tugged on a blood-encrusted lace that she realised just how successfully she'd been able to partition Henry out of her thoughts. She resolved to conduct every subsequent purge of sand with her head pointed upwards, staring away from all the activity, purposefully thinking about anything else. Thankfully, it wasn't too long before Crane announced that he was fed up with hiding on the beach, and wondered aloud what else there was to do to in a pointless coastal resort.

On the flattest rock they could find, Dorothy fished the remains of their funds from her pocket, and they carefully separated the coins into piles to count them. After arriving at wildly differing totals, and after a couple of recounts, they settled on £3.36, along with an American quarter which Crane threw into the sea, claiming it was bad luck. It didn't sound like much.

Disheartened, the two reluctant sightseers retraced their steps back to solid ground and sat quietly amongst the sun-baked guano on a dead woman's bench. A day spent by the seaside, and all that bracing sea air, had done nothing to curb the apprehension Dorothy still felt after seeing West's car earlier in the day. However, she was also starting to wonder whether her travelling companion cared as much about getting caught as she did. Crane had become listless and crotchety, and his ill-humour was beginning to rub off on her. He was getting careless just because he was too bored to stay alert. As if to reinforce her misgivings, two police officers appeared a few hundred yards along the promenade and began to drift in their direction. Crane's strategy had run its course. This was the time to assert herself. Hanging out by the sea made

Dorothy feel far too conspicuous, and she demanded that they spend the rest of the day hiding in the train station. And then, whenever five hours was up, Thatcher would come and find them. In any case, he was the only one of them that owned a watch.

~

BY THE TIME they found their way back to the station, the sun had burned away the last remaining clouds, leaving behind only a few wispy stragglers to mar an otherwise perfect sky. Following Dorothy through the town had done nothing to improve Crane's mood, and she was eager for the time to be up so that her companion would have somewhere else to direct his venom. As the sliding doors parted to welcome them onto the concourse, Crane barged in front of Dorothy and strode off past the ticket machines and the coffee shop. He slumped down onto an empty row of seats, making no attempt to stay out of sight.

There were plenty of times that Dorothy really didn't like being around Crane. Times when he was petulant and grumpy and unable to assert his authority. Normally she would just go and find something else to do while he bullied someone until he was happy again, but right now he was a liability. He was doing as little as possible to avoid getting spotted by West, and he was doing it on purpose. Without glancing at her friend, Dorothy ambled past the chairs to feign an interest in the timetable on the wall behind him.

'Look!' she declared in a stage whisper out of the side of her mouth as she stared at the rows of incomprehensible numbers. 'By the coffee place. On the ceiling. It's a camera. It's looking at us. Looking at you.'

'So?' Crane replied, turning towards Dorothy and ruining

her ruse. 'What do you want me to do? Pull it down or something?'

'Hide!' Dorothy urged quietly, motioning with twitches of her head. 'Behind the sign over there.'

Crane turned to examine the hoarding, which warned the travelling public that railway operators didn't tolerate physical or verbal abuse aimed at their staff. He blew a dismissive raspberry. 'Well, they shouldn't be such extraordinary wankers then,' he called out to no one in particular, before swinging back to Dorothy. 'Bollocks to that. My knees hurt. And Snatcher's late. Probably.'

This felt like one of those moments when everything could so easily fall apart, and Dorothy wished that she could get past whatever it was that had messed with her ability to focus since she woke up. Without Parsley there to protect her she was a sitting duck, and now they might have lost Bill as well. Bill looked out for her, in his own manner. He cared about what happened to her – too much sometimes – and he'd certainly have thrown himself in the way of Crane's hostility before it could spill over onto her. The plan would no doubt have to change, again, and since she was unable to concentrate on anything, she was powerless to help. Dorothy's anxieties started to stir. She needed to get out of range of Crane's rancour before it infected her too.

A train rattled into the station and pulled up to the platform, forcing a cold draught through the ticket gates. Dorothy shivered. The doors opened and a mass of people disembarked, strolling towards the barriers and filing through one by one. Sensing an opportunity, Dorothy drifted across the concourse until she was enveloped by the horde. Some travellers moved straight through the station and out of the glass doors without looking back; some stopped in smaller groups to finish their conversations; others just milled about aimlessly for a while.

Relaxing once more into anonymity, Dorothy allowed herself to be slowly jockeyed through the hall, invisible and unattended.

So passed the rest of the day, while outside the sun withdrew towards the horizon and the sky darkened. Whenever Dorothy checked in on her angst, she found that new concerns were adding themselves to the list. No longer worried only about Parsley's absence and Crane's obstinate apathy, Dorothy now found herself imagining Thatcher in a police cell, making a deal to give up his former companions if the police let him off his drug-peddling charge. She worried that no one seemed to care whether she found her father or not, and how little saving her life meant to her supposed friends. She worried that they were wasting time that she didn't have. And then another train would pull in to the station, and Dorothy could lose sight of herself within the crowd. For a short while she managed to calm her unease – just enough to stop it from flaring up into something insurmountable.

The evening wore on, and the trains became less frequent, less busy. For the second time that day, Dorothy found herself thinking of Henry, although now he had become the target for her frustration and anger. It was his fault, after all, that she was stranded in this miserable little town, so far from anyone that cared for her. It was his stupidity and selfishness that had put her life in danger. Dorothy was getting close to the point when she'd have to go and take her resentment out on Crane, regardless of the very public row that was sure to ensue, when Thatcher finally sauntered onto the concourse.

The wave of relief that passed through Dorothy didn't last long. Her friend was traipsing through the station in a very un-Thatcher-like manner. As soon as he spied her, Dorothy expected him to hurry over, full of apologies and excuses. Instead he took a moment to shake his head patronisingly before swaggering towards her, with a bounce in his step that Dorothy had never witnessed before.

Crane leapt out of his seat and darted across to intercept the other man. 'Where the fuck have you been?' he demanded.

'Where the fuck have you been?' Thatcher mimicked Crane's nasal drone, scrunching up his nose and exposing his top row of teeth. His expression morphed into a languid grin and he playfully ruffled Crane's hair. 'Looking good today, gorgeous,' he responded, glancing around the concourse. 'No Arseley?'

'We thought you'd been caught,' Dorothy declared, unsure how the conversation was going to unfold.

Thatcher turned and winked conspiratorially at the young girl, further adding to her disquiet. 'Catch the Thatch?' he drawled. 'Not in this life, baby.'

'Did you get the money?' Crane asked.

A look of mild unease replaced the sprightly smirk on Thatcher's face, and his head flicked from side to side as if he was trying to pinpoint the location of a buzzing fly. 'Did you hear that?' he enquired of Dorothy. 'That tweet … tweet … tweet? The song of a little lost blackbird, chirping in my ear.'

The delivery was half musical, half menacing. The irritation on Dorothy's forearm flared up for the first time since that morning, and she pinched at it through her coat. 'Bill? What's the matter?' she asked, confused and flustered. 'What's the matter with you?'

Thatcher turned his attention back to the girl, an unhurried smile again settling on his face. 'Oh, nothing matters to me, my little honey bee,' he reassured her, looking like he was savouring the taste of each word as it bubbled up and escaped from his mouth.

Crane's shoulders slumped and he tilted his head back to gaze at the ceiling, forcing out a long, disappointed groan.

'What the fuck, Bill?' he demanded with exaggerated exasperation. 'Really? You couldn't just leave it alone, could you?'

Without letting his genial façade slip, Thatcher leant forward until he loomed over the smaller man, rocking his head from side to side. 'What the fuck, Crane the Brain?' he mocked, his voice a poor imitation of Crane's whine.

Unbowed by Thatcher's intimidation, Crane pushed himself onto his tiptoes until the two men were close enough to kiss. 'You need to get your shit together, you junkie twat.'

'And still the sonorous blackbird!' sang Thatcher through his fading grin. 'Always – fucking – tweeting. Why don't I make you shut up?'

'Well, it's nice to know I didn't underestimate you,' Crane spat as he squared up to the bigger man.

The men stared into each other's eyes, neither backing away, neither bothering to mask their mutual disdain. Their hostility made Dorothy feel nauseous. She would have gladly forced herself between them to vent some of the building pressure – if she could only figure out whose side she should be on. There was always some tension when the two men spent too much time in each other's company, but today's discord was too brusque, too random.

It was Thatcher who broke the impasse. He rocked back onto his heels and the cordial smile returned to his face. With a mischievous glance at Dorothy, he reached into the pocket of his long coat and pulled out an impressive wad of banknotes. Thatcher gawked at the money as if seeing it for the first time, his face contorting into a comical expression of awe and surprise. He lifted it to his nose and inhaled, closing his eyes, luxuriating in its perfume, before contemptuously flinging the bundle at Crane's face with a deft flick of his wrist.

The notes burst around Crane's narrow head like a wave breaking around a rock, then began their slow flit to the ground. Crane eyeballed his antagonist for a second longer, before dropping to his knees to scrabble around on the floor after the scattered money. Thatcher beamed serenely, detached from all the hectic activities below. 'You have absolutely no comprehension of what I can achieve, Mr Crane,' he called good-naturedly to the younger man. When Crane looked up, his face was etched with a grudging respect that apparently left him unable to form a coherent riposte. Thatcher, however, had no such problem. 'Tickets? Go on, off you fuck.'

Having stuffed the last of the fallen money into his jacket pocket, Crane had no choice but to comply. He loitered beneath Thatcher's aggressive smirk for another moment before shuffling off in the direction of the ticket office. After watching his companion disappear, Thatcher turned his grin on Dorothy. She countered with an unconvincing smile of her own. He gestured towards the exit. 'Why don't you and I venture outside, Miss Gale?' he suggested agreeably. 'I have a feeling you're going to enjoy this rather wonderful summer evening.'

Without waiting for an answer, Thatcher offered her his arm. The last thing Dorothy wanted was to have to endure any more of that town, and she was surprised that her friend seemed to have enjoyed himself there as much as he had. It was impossible to make much sense of what was going on, but then again everything about the day had been perplexing in some way or another. Thank God they would be on their way soon. Dorothy looked up at Thatcher, hoping for some clue as to what was going on, and after an awkward pause he gently took her hand and tucked it into his arm. With a curt nod, and his relentless smile, he led the girl into the night.

The cloudless evening had darkened into a perfectly clear night, allowing an unobstructed view into space and the innumerable spots of light that peppered the heavens. Tonight the sky was especially full, and especially impressive. Her friend had been right. Dorothy so rarely got the chance to wander about outside in the night-time, and it would have been unforgiveable to miss this opportunity. As Thatcher steered the young girl away from the single lamppost that illuminated the car park, more and more of the extraordinary celestial spectacle was revealed. Dorothy found that, if she stared at a star for long enough, a hundred other dimmer lights slowly appeared all around it. When they eventually came across a suitable bench, it was so dark that Dorothy worried she might trip over something.

They sat a while in silence as Dorothy stared upwards, transfixed, her eyes slowly adjusting to the darkness. Thatcher spoke first. 'A glorious vista to stir feelings into even the coldest of hearts! An old man could lose his way on such a night were he not to tread carefully.'

Dorothy liked it when Thatcher lapsed into poetic language – when he 'talked like a twat', as Crane referred to it. She didn't always understand everything he said, but that didn't really matter because somehow she could always follow what he was trying to say. For the first time since his arrival at the station, Dorothy allowed herself to relax in his company. She glanced across to watch her travelling companion as he marvelled at the heavens, and it came as a shock when she instead found herself staring directly into his eyes.

In the subdued light, Thatcher's smile took on a more sinister aspect. Without breaking eye contact, he gave her a playful nudge. 'Don't look so worried,' he urged. 'This is an auspicious occasion!'

Dorothy's first reaction was to wonder how she looked when she was worried; however, this train of thought was quickly derailed when Thatcher put his hand on her leg and started gently stroking her thigh, inching slowly upwards and inwards with every caress. The unwelcome intimacy of his touch caused Dorothy to tense where she sat, frozen from bewilderment more than fear, struggling to conjure up an innocent narrative that explained his actions. In all the time she had known Thatcher, she had not once even considered that they might be anything other than friends. It wasn't that he was so much older than her, or that even when he looked happy it was always undercut by a deeper sadness; it was just that their relationship was already perfect as it was. Every unwanted caress put their friendship in further jeopardy, and it wouldn't be long before this bond would be broken forever. Perhaps they had even passed that point already.

As she tried to think of the best way to escape the situation with the minimum of fallout, Thatcher leant across to try and kiss her. Dorothy's primal mind took over. She leapt up from the bench and took a step backwards into the darkness. 'Bill? What are you doing?' she demanded. 'What are you doing with me?'

But Thatcher was already standing and bearing down on the girl, a monstrous silhouette with a gleaming white smile and dark voids where his eyes should be. He shot out an arm and caught the front of Dorothy's coat, screwing his colossal hand around the zipper so it acted like a straightjacket. A rush of panic cut through her, and for the first time that day she felt as if her whole brain was thinking in the same direction. She tried to struggle, but Thatcher was holding her so tightly that she could only thrash her arms in ineffectual circles. He pulled her towards him, lifting her up so she couldn't dig her heels into the ground, and grabbed the front of her waistband with his other hand. He curled his fingers over the elastic, seizing hold of Dorothy's leggings and pubic hair, raising her further into the air until the tips of her bloodied shoes barely touched the path beneath her.

Dorothy leant backwards as far as her jacket allowed, recoiling from the terror that reared above her. She tried to scream, but her breath caught in her throat, leaving behind only the sound of quiet retching. Thatcher pulled her closer, looming over her as she writhed and contorted. In the gloom, his dogged grin looked ever more deranged, and spittle had collected at the corners of his mouth.

'Surrender, Dorothy!' he hissed through clenched teeth.

Dorothy turned her head to one side and screwed her eyes closed, determined not to have to witness the coming assault. She felt the warmth of Thatcher's shallow breaths on her cheeks, and listened to his muffled growls and the wet rattle that never stopped even when he inhaled. And then she felt a jarring crash that knocked her free of Thatcher's grip and flung her to the ground.

Crane had arrived at speed, emerging without warning from the darkness and slamming into the side of the bigger man. Dorothy looked up to see Crane manoeuvre himself between her and Thatcher, shoving her assailant backwards, preventing him from regaining his balance.

'What the fuck?' an astonished Crane demanded, sounding like he was actually expecting an answer. 'What are you doing?'

Thatcher stood up to his full height and turned his attention to the other man, with his relentless smile still fixed in place. 'You know, I'd be obliged if you wouldn't mind waiting inside, Hunk,' he called down amiably. 'Can't you see that the grown-ups are busy?'

Standing over the fallen girl, Crane held his ground. 'Why are you—'

His question was cut short when Thatcher reached over and drove his knuckles hard into the younger man's face. In the same movement, Thatcher hooked his immense hand below Crane's chin and lifted him backwards, hoisting his opponent into the darkness. Crane's feet danced over the tarmac as he struggled to stay upright, until four steps later the back of his head smashed into the brick wall that marked the end of the car park. Thatcher tightened his hand around Crane's throat, pinning him against the wall.

'I get you, Mr Crane,' Thatcher confided to his travelling companion, leaning in until their faces were almost pressed together. 'Moping about. Always bitter that it was only Henry who got a little grease from the oil can.'

Behind the men, Dorothy clambered to her feet, dazed and disoriented. From where she stood, it looked like Thatcher was now trying to kiss Crane instead of her. Her saviour's face was turning red as he clutched onto Thatcher's wrist, frantically kicking towards the ground in an attempt to stay on his feet. Crane was staring at her with a desperate glare, and as Dorothy approached he became more animated, letting go of Thatcher's wrist and furiously shooing the girl away with one hand. Thatcher, meanwhile, was not done talking.

'Come on! You know she's got to be worth a gallop around the paddock,' he continued in a whisper, his grin widening. Thatcher winked at the suffocating man imprisoned on the end of his arm before squeezing his spare hand into a fist and plunging it into Crane's stomach. 'Yeah?' he enquired pleasantly as he released his grip and let his companion collapse to the ground in a winded jumble. 'You get what I'm saying, don't you?'

Dorothy's hesitation vanished when she saw her friend tumble to the ground, struggling to breathe. 'Stop hurting him!' she howled, edging past Thatcher to tend to Crane. But before she could help, Thatcher caught her wrist and lifted her away, back to upright again, then higher still. With a shriek, Dorothy reached up with her free hand and attempted to peel Thatcher's fingers back from their steely grip around her arm.

Below her, Crane was already lifting himself onto his hands and knees, desperately sucking air into his lungs. Grabbing onto Thatcher's long coat, he attempted to clamber hand over hand up the front aspect of the tall man, wheezing and whistling in pain with every fresh hold he made. Thatcher turned to focus on the figure beneath him, pausing as Crane continued his halting ascent. When the breathless man finally glanced up, Thatcher unleashed a vicious downwards haymaker with his spare fist that connected with the side of Crane's upturned face and smashed the smaller man back into the tarmac.

'No!' screamed Dorothy, suspended uselessly above her crumpled friend. Below her, the noises from Crane's breathing had stopped, and he wasn't moving. Dorothy redoubled her efforts to free herself from Thatcher's grip, but her assailant's attention had already turned back to her. The persistent smile was gone. He grabbed the zip on Dorothy's jacket and jerked it down, exposing her dirty beige T-shirt. His eyes had lost their sparkle and humanity; whatever was about to happen, Thatcher looked as if he would derive no pleasure from it. He lifted Dorothy away from Crane's carcass, moving further along the wall into the murky blackness beyond.

As Thatcher dragged Dorothy across the rough brickwork, her thoughts were still on Crane. 'Bill! Please! He's really hurt. You've really hurt him.'

Finally letting go of her wrist, Thatcher pinned the girl against the wall with his elbows, freeing up both his hands. The sudden pressure of his weight on her torso knocked the wind out of Dorothy, and her pleading turned into a surprised gasp. With practised expertise, Thatcher's huge hands grabbed the neck of her T-shirt and ripped it down the middle.

Defenceless in the half-light under the spectacular canopy of stars, Dorothy felt a flutter of cool night air against her pale flesh, like a breath from Thatcher's cold heart. A strange acceptance descended on her as she realised there was now nothing else she could do. She knew that Crane's intervention had bought her the opportunity to get away, and she had squandered his sacrifice. Given the mess Parsley had made in the pub the night before, Dorothy wondered what kind of punishment he would have meted out to Thatcher to rescue her from this situation. Her tall companion had certainly picked his moment. What was about to happen was going to hurt, and it would leave scars that would be painful long after the hurt had healed. But it wouldn't last forever. Whatever horrors were about to be unleashed, she would endure them and she would survive them. Dorothy closed her eyes and emptied her thoughts, braced for the violation to come.

The dark brought with it a stillness and an unexpected calm: a reassurance that the rest of the world was going about its business regardless. Air-brakes hissed as a train prepared to depart from the station; a distant car door slammed shut and the engine revved into life; and further away she could hear the sea pounding the shoreline with wave after wave. Her chest felt chilly and her wrist bruised, and from every angle a menacing presence enveloped her. Poised. Waiting. Trembling.

The train picked up speed, the rhythmic clank of its wheels becoming faster and fainter until they were swallowed up by the night. Still the uninvited presence waited. Even with her eyes closed, Dorothy could sense that something in Thatcher's demeanour had changed. She dared herself to take a quick peek.

Her assailant stood in front of her, staring down at her chest through the rip in her T-shirt. Silent tears drained from both eyes, running down his craggy cheeks and dripping from his jaw. Dorothy followed his gaze. She could see all the way down to her navel, with only a dirty white bra crossing her unprotected torso and guarding the last of her modesty. Between her breasts, a silver crucifix hung from a string of rosary beads. She glanced back at Thatcher, who was now fixated on the metal cross.

Another moment passed in silence. Having prepared herself for the worst, Dorothy actually felt her anguish rising again with this unexpected pause, into which she had no insight. Thatcher gently lifted the crucifix away from her sternum, his fingers brushing against her flesh. His giant hand quivered as he rested the silver cross on his fingers, rotating a rosary bead with his thumb. Thatcher examined the necklace for a moment longer before looking up to meet Dorothy's frightened stare. He drew in a faltering breath to speak. 'Doro—'

And then with a sharp tug on her neck Thatcher was gone, blindsided for a second time. Rosary beads scattered across the ground with fragile pings as Crane bulldozed Thatcher away from Dorothy with a robust shoulder-barge. This time, however, Thatcher made no effort to maintain his balance, allowing himself to tumble to the ground. Above him, Crane reeled drunkenly, pressing one hand against his ribs. Without even glancing towards Dorothy, he staggered forward and fell on top of Thatcher's prone body, kneeling on his chest, wildly slapping Thatcher's face with open palms, spurred on by a careless rage.

'You ... stupid ... fucking ... junkie!' he screamed, punctuating each blow. 'Die, you fucking junkie fuck!'

Thatcher raised his arms on either side of his face, pressing his wrists against his ears to block the onslaught, but after a few of Crane's blows landed ineffectually on his forearms he dropped his guard and permitted the smaller man's clumsy aggression to connect.

Above them, Dorothy's heart was hammering so hard in

her chest that it made her teeth chatter. 'Stop it! Stop hurting each other!' she shouted. She reached down to try and trap one of Crane's erratic swings, narrowly missing his arm and coming dangerously close to catching the back of his hand across her forehead. Before she had the opportunity to try again, however, Thatcher had pushed Crane off, dropping him into an untidy pile on the nearby tarmac.

Thatcher stood up slowly, giving Crane time to stumble to his feet and position himself again in front of Dorothy. She felt her panic surge again as her aggressor raised himself up to his full height, imposing and intimidating, but something had changed. For the first time that evening, Dorothy recognised the man who stood before her. Even in the grip of fear and confusion, part of her wanted to go and give him a hug and tell him that everything would be OK. Thatcher stared at the ground next to the girl, one fist clenched around what was left of his crucifix, broken twine trailing through his fingers. 'I'm...' he mumbled. 'It's not...'

His words fell away into the darkness. There was nothing he could say or do to make things OK again. There was no way back from this. Despite the horror and distress, Dorothy felt a twinge of grief at this unexpected bereavement. She knew that she would never see her friend again, and that it must be breaking his heart. Taking one final look at Dorothy and the indifferent universe behind her, Thatcher turned and scurried into the shadows, claimed by the night.

His departing footsteps were the last thing she heard before the world was completely silent again. Dorothy stared into the void after her assailant, while Crane leant forward, greedily gasping for air.

'Doz?' he stammered between gulps. 'Did he get you? Did he do anything?'

As her saviour clutched at his aching ribs, Dorothy's

consternation slowly dissipated, leaving a sense of foreboding that warned her that she was actually in more danger now than she had been before Thatcher's departure. She called into the darkness after the fleeing man, 'Bill! Where are you going to go, Bill?'

When the darkness failed to answer back, Dorothy moved to follow Thatcher into the gloom, but Crane caught her arm. With a shriek Dorothy jumped away, startled by the uninvited contact.

'Hey! Whoa! Easy!' Crane exclaimed, trying to pacify her as she launched into a frantic scratching session on her forearm. 'Where are you going? He's gone. He's lost.'

Dorothy stared into the unlit beyond, trying to catch a glimpse of anything that could help her make sense of what had just happened. But there were no answers to be found. She zipped her jacket up as far as it would go, shielding her torn T-shirt and uncovered flesh. 'We need to get out of this town,' Crane declared, bruised and winded. 'We need to leave. Right now.'

Although there were only two of them left, they still had custody of the plan. And they still had a job to do. Dorothy nodded carefully to Crane, who gestured towards the train station before setting off at a fast hobble. After the briefest moment of contemplation, Dorothy fell into step beside him, heading back towards the light and out from beneath the treacherous night sky.

SATURDAY, 21ST AUGUST

The Cowardly Lion

*C*urled up beneath starched sheets on a single bed, in the smallest guest room in the Gatekeeper Hotel, Dorothy's eyes flicked open.

Dorothy hated the first few moments after waking up somewhere unfamiliar. It hadn't happened for a while, thankfully, but not so long ago, it used to happen all the time. It was so annoyingly inefficient: just when she really should be devoting her attention to preparing herself for the challenges of the day ahead, instead she had to waste all that energy trying to remember how the previous one had ended. Rebuilding yesterday's narrative forced her to audit her memories, to put everything into some kind of order, to sort out what was real and what only seemed real because it had happened in a particularly lucid dream. And usually with everything blurred by the fuzzy afterglow from whatever drugs she had taken the night before.

It used to happen so often that Dorothy had developed a system. Step one was to close her eyes and pretend to still be asleep as she assimilated whatever data she could from her surroundings. Her bed was soft – softer than she was used to, anyway – and she could feel a thin covering of linen wrapped around her body. It left her legs feeling a little too cold, and a little too sore from all the walking and climbing she'd done the day before. The smell from her pillow was unusually musty, and she took a moment to savour its surprisingly intoxicating scent. She could hear the music of the rain as it flung itself onto a window pane; she recognised the same staccato rhythms as those that had played throughout her dreams the night before. And the throaty rumble of snoring, which sounded like someone on the verge of suffocation, gasping for each breath just as they were about to expire.

So, Parsley was there. That was a good start. Nothing bad would ever happen to her as long as Parsley was there.

For the second time that morning, Dorothy opened her eyes. Despite the strange surroundings, she felt remarkably perky. Her brain was already sparking with new ideas, and all the colours around her seemed brighter and more vivid than she remembered from the previous evening. They were in the buggery and blow-job place, and she was there with her friends on an adventure of sorts. She needed to take a moment to remind herself that actually everything was not OK. Dorothy knew that she should really be feeling despondent but, other than the dull ache in her legs, she felt great.

In front of her, crammed into the narrow gap between her bed and the wall, Crane was stretched out beneath a blanket. Her blanket, in all likelihood, as she seemed to be wrapped in only a sheet. His eyes were shut, but he was clearly already awake as well – masked by the noises of rain and snoring, Dorothy could hear him squirming inside his covers. Without warning, Crane's hand snuck out from under his blanket and dropped something into his mouth before retreating again. Dorothy might have suspected that he was popping one of his pills, had he not expressly promised not to bring any drugs on the trip. That said, it could equally well have been an errant crisp or a piece of doughnut from their meal the night before.

Thatcher and Parsley were asleep on the floor on the other side of her bed. Even if he had been staying there on his own, Thatcher would have been too long for the mattress, but from where she lay it looked like he was too long even for the room. Sheltered under his ridiculous black coat, her friend's feet were propped up against the door, while his head nestled underneath the basin. Between them, his extended frame bent to follow the contours of the room, settling along the recessed bay underneath the rain-rattled window.

Splayed out on his back, occupying the lion's share of the floor, was Parsley. Although not quite as tall as Thatcher, Parsley was an absolute behemoth, wide in every direction. It wasn't possible to discern how much raw muscle lurked beneath the many layers of fat, but everybody knew how freakishly strong he was. His age, like so many other things about him, was a closely guarded secret, and informal estimates put him anywhere between twenty and forty. It didn't help that he had chosen such an unorthodox look: his hair and beard had been ineptly clippered to the same short length, while his clothes looked like they had been selected simply because they might fit. Parsley's overall appearance was less about personal vanity than it was about seized opportunities for warmth and modesty. Although nobody really understood what motivated him to do the things he did (and Parsley himself was tight-lipped on the subject), no one ever doubted the courage of his convictions.

And Dorothy had got the bed. While Crane had managed to claim a snug nook to sleep in, Parsley had to make do with whatever was left. Without blankets or pillows, he was laid out on a mattress of empty crisp packets and a box of sugary cardboard that used to contain a dozen doughnuts. His head rested in the centre of a red stain on the carpet, next to a discarded wine bottle and a small but untidy pile of vomit.

Dorothy sat up in bed, eager to share the day. 'It's the morning! Up time!'

Crane was quickest out of the blocks, springing bolt upright and holding an anxious finger to his lips. 'Hey! Keep it down, Doz!' he whispered. 'No one knows we're here, remember?'

On the other side of the room, Parsley was already on his feet, transitioning instantly from his desperate raspy sleep into a state of readiness, and scattering flakes of dry sick onto the floor. Beside him, Thatcher slept on.

'Jesus fuck – how'd you do that so fast?' Crane demanded quietly of the behemoth, before shaking his head. 'You freak the shit out of me sometimes, caveman.'

When Parsley didn't answer, Dorothy stood on the bed and began to brush crumbs of food from his clothes. 'We need to go and get on a train,' she confided to her friend. 'Find the station. We should probably get out of here before someone catches us.'

The sensation of the weave in Parsley's jumper beneath her fingers felt uncommonly textured that morning, and her cleaning movements soon turned into long strokes that lingered on her friend's substantial chest. Dorothy quickly realised what she was doing and stopped herself; if Parsley had noticed, he kept it to himself. Behind them, Crane offered some clarification. 'Yeah – we've got to go. Don't want to stay in one place too long,' he muttered. 'Yo, Arseley? Want to give Big Bad Bill a kick in the bollocks to wake him up?'

∼

As Dorothy watched from the top of the staircase, Thatcher gingerly descended to the ground floor of the small hotel, tiptoeing from one creaking step to the next. The threadbare carpet underfoot did little to dampen the noise as he negotiated his way across its faded patterns, sometimes skipping like an oversized ninja, sometimes plodding like an old man with aching testes. At the bottom, he craned his head around the bannister to peek down the hall. So far, it didn't look like he'd been spotted.

With a thumbs-up to his travelling companions, Thatcher cautiously opened the front door. After taking a final glance back down the hall, he beckoned to the others. Dorothy was next to steal down the stairs, closely followed by Parsley, who shoved Crane aside and stamped a disorderly path in Dorothy's wake that made Thatcher wince with every noisy step. Crane loitered on the landing for as long as he dared before chasing after the others. He had only just made it outside when Dorothy heard a door squeaking from deep within the hotel. She grabbed Parsley's sleeve and dragged him into the morning rain and out of sight while Thatcher blocked the view. Safely crouched in the front garden, she watched her tall friend nervously spin a couple of rosary beads on his necklace before he snapped on his most charming smile and turned to address whoever was approaching from the other end of the corridor.

'Ah! And the very finest of mornings to you, Mrs Jackson,' Thatcher effervesced. 'You have just waylaid me en route to a cigarette.'

'Good morning, Mr Snatcher,' the landlady replied suspiciously. 'A horrible day for such a nasty habit. Did you manage to sleep alright after that fall you took?'

'Like a kitten!' Thatcher gushed. 'You have such a wonderful hotel.'

The compliment must have caught the woman off-guard.

'Oh. Thank you, that's very kind,' she replied, sounding genuinely surprised. 'Are you ready for some breakfast? What would you like?'

'Toast, Mrs Jackson. Toast, if you'd be so very kind,' replied Thatcher as he pushed the front door shut behind him. 'And plenty of it.'

∽

It was another half an hour before Thatcher finally emerged from the hotel. Although the rain had eased slightly from the window-rattling intensity of the night before, a persistent drizzle fell from the overcast sky, and the other three had withdrawn some way down the road into a bus shelter. There they waited in respectful silence, unwilling to risk discussing any details of the plan lest they be overheard. After a couple of buses had come and gone, Dorothy noticed that Parsley had been standing in a spot where only half of his body was covered by the roof. Through his efforts to lurk as close to her as possible, he was now soaking wet on one side, and he didn't even have a coat. As Dorothy dragged him into the shelter, he began to hum an unrecognisable melody. A sense of unease threatened to spoil her unshakeable good humour – she didn't remember her friend being quite this clingy before. But it was only a fleeting concern, and she quickly returned to studying the complicated patterns made by the raindrops as they landed in a puddle.

Thankfully Thatcher came bearing gifts. With the excited grin of a schoolboy who'd just got away with doing something naughty, he offered the others a peek into the substantial pockets in his coat, revealing them to be crammed full of slices of hot buttered toast. His companions gratefully took it in turns to reach inside and share in the spoils, before setting off towards the station (directions to which Thatcher had also beguiled out of Mrs Jackson). For Dorothy and Crane, breakfasting in the rain involved picking as much lint and fluff off the bread as they could before it became too soggy to eat, and by the time they hopped over a fence and crossed into the station car park, Crane had become too annoyed to be bothered. 'When we get on a train,' he grumbled, 'Dorothy and I are going to blow whatever dosh we've got left on proper sandwiches. Dry sandwiches.'

'But what about Parsley?' Dorothy demanded. 'He might be hungry too.'

'Sod him,' Crane replied. 'He was happy enough to eat all Snatcher's pocket shit.'

Parsley stared impassively at his cantankerous friend. If he had taken offence, he didn't let it show, although to be fair he had indeed eaten the bulk of Thatcher's stolen breakfast, lint and all. Dorothy reached up and stroked the side of his face, smoothing his uneven beard with her buttery fingers. He responded with a muted purr, contentedly humming a tune to himself.

The party crossed the car park and shuffled into the concourse. Without the distraction of the rain, Dorothy felt cold for the first time that morning, her damp puffer jacket clinging to her bare arms. She looked at Crane expectantly, water dripping from the ends of her long blonde hair, impatient to hear about the next phase of the plan. Crane addressed his fellow travellers. 'OK. Right. Tickets.' He turned to Thatcher and continued, 'Off you go, Twatcher.'

Thatcher peered down at him, a curious look on his face. This part of the plan was evidently news to him as well. 'I'm sorry,' he said. 'To where, Mr Crane?'

'Get some tickets so we can get on the train,' Crane replied. 'Get a move on – I'm starving.'

Thatcher shifted his weight uneasily. 'Mr Crane, I don't believe that we have sufficient funds in our reserves.'

Dorothy gazed up at Thatcher, bemused by his explanation, and he smiled back at the girl. 'Not enough money,' he clarified.

A flicker of annoyance sparked inside Dorothy's head. She could normally rely on Bill not to treat her like an idiot, even if Crane never seemed to get the message. Of course she understood what he meant; she was only trying to figure out why he had shot the plan down so quickly. Dorothy stamped on the spark before it could flare up, determined not to let it sour her mood. She reached into her jacket pocket to pull out a fistful of coins, bundled loosely around a couple of damp banknotes, but Crane stepped in to stop her. 'No, no. You're alright, Doz. Give Thatch the credit card we got from West. The plastic card.'

Thatcher's face fell. 'Oh, come on!' he chided Crane. 'We can't use that.'

'We can't, no,' Crane acknowledged with a shrug. 'But you can.'

'Really? Then please enlighten us why it is that *you* don't go and purchase the tickets with West's credit card?'

'Because *you* know how to do this,' Crane rebutted. 'What do you think you're here for? Go work the hustle, bitch!'

Dorothy fished a credit card from out of a deeper, dryer pocket, and held it up to the bickering men, waiting for one of them to claim it. Thatcher raised both his hands and backed away from the offering, declaring apprehensively, 'Actually, no. No. I really don't want to do this.'

'So what?' Crane retorted. 'Who cares what you want?'

Thatcher turned to Dorothy and smiled wistfully. 'I imagine that Dorothy cares.'

Dorothy shook her head. Already the two men were locked

into yet another of their verbal rallies, just like all the other arguments she had been forced to witness. It didn't really matter what the subject was – dinosaurs, movies, Jesus – Crane would typically start things off by serving an opinion at Thatcher, intended mainly to make him feel sad. Thatcher's role was to address the flaws in Crane's point of view, and then the squabble was under way. Sometimes Crane delivered an ace that was impossible to return ('If God really loves you, why did he make you such a massive wanker?'), but sometimes the to and fro could last for hours ('What kind of drugs work best to get rid of the taste of a stranger's dick?'). On occasion, Dorothy would be encouraged to contribute a theory of her own, but she was never normally asked to adjudicate.

However, this time she did have the answer, and Thatcher hadn't done himself any favours by asking her to settle the disagreement. She did care what Thatcher wanted – they were friends after all, but all bets were off when the plan was in danger. And he knew that. This is why she had made him promise to do what he was told, before they'd even started the trip. Without a moment of hesitation, Dorothy twisted around to offer him the credit card.

'There you go,' added Crane smugly. 'Perform your magic, you fucking criminal.'

The three of them faced each other in an expectant stand-off, and an uncanny silence descended over the concourse. For an instant the constant percussion from the rain slipped away into the background; no passengers shuffled across the concrete floor; no distant trains signalled their approach. All that remained was Parsley's mumbled song, quietly composing itself in his throat like the buzz of a trapped insect.

And then that was gone as well. Dorothy glanced up at the colossus, who glided past her with his arms outstretched and gave Thatcher an enormous shove. Having evidently taken it on himself to resolve the impasse, Parsley moved in for a second attempt to bulldoze Thatcher into submission, but Dorothy threw her arms around one of the behemoth's substantial elbows and pulled him to a halt. Stopped in his tracks, Parsley bared his teeth and growled at his tall companion without taking his eyes off him.

Thatcher turned to Dorothy with an anxious pout. Even Crane's self-satisfied grimace had slipped off his face. Dorothy slid an arm away from restraining her friend and offered the credit card to Thatcher again. This time he plucked it out of her hand without any protestation.

With a last nervous peek towards Parsley, Thatcher turned the card over to examine the signature on the reverse. Using the index finger on his other hand he traced the pen strokes into the air with tiny twitches, first slowly and deliberately, then getting faster and faster. With a final flourish he pocketed the card, took a deep breath, and abruptly disappeared towards the ticket booth at the far side of the concourse.

Screened by the now uninterested Parsley, Dorothy tried to make it look as if she wasn't watching the exchange with the teller in the ticket office. Although she was too far away to hear what was being said, she could tell that Thatcher had opened with a lame joke, which raised a polite smile from the station operative. The conversation continued, and before too long the teller was pushing buttons on a machine and running his finger down a list on a clipboard. Thatcher nodded respectfully and made a play of patting down his pockets, adopting a distracted air as he searched his clothing before triumphantly diving into a pocket and returning with the credit card. He attempted to pass the card to the man behind the glass. The teller shook his head and gestured towards the chip and PIN machine on the counter. Thatcher's counterfeit expression of accomplishment gave way to a more genuine look of confusion;

again he tried to hand the teller the card, and again he was directed to the chip and PIN machine. Dorothy could hear his voice getting louder and more insistent, but still the teller shook his head. Thatcher threw up his arms in exasperation, and finally a coherent sentence found its way across the concourse: 'I ask you, sir, how is this any way to run a rail network?'

Thatcher turned back towards his gawping companions, a contrite expression on his face. It didn't look like they were going anywhere just yet.

∽

'ONE LITTLE TASK,' muttered Crane, as the four travellers ambled through the incessant rain in no particular direction and towards no particular destination.

The group had left the station without exchanging anything more than a series of stares — looks of confusion and withering disappointment. Although Dorothy didn't completely understand what had just happened, it was clear they needed to figure out a new plan. She fell into lock-step behind the two sulking men while Parsley brought up the rear.

Despite all their efforts yesterday to get to this town, and away from the perils of the countryside, Dorothy didn't want to stay there any longer than was absolutely necessary. She needed Crane to step up and find a way past this setback. Her friend, however, seemed to be more interested in scolding Thatcher for his many inadequacies, enjoying the opportunity to vent some of his indignation.

'I'm completely soaked,' he complained. 'And Dorothy's probably going to get even more sick from the cold, just because you couldn't use a credit card. I mean, how hard is it? I've seen children with credit cards.'

Pretty soon it was clear that Thatcher had had enough, and he sloped off to the back of the procession. But if he thought that Crane would let him reflect on his failure in silence, he was wrong.

'Oi! Where are you going, shit-lips?' the younger man called out before trudging after him. 'Think you can just walk away from this? No fucking chance.'

The one-sided exchange between the two grown-ups left Dorothy at the head of the party. Around her the day still bristled with fascination and sparkle: the elegant watery curves thrown up whenever a car tyre passed through a puddle; the extraordinary textures of paving slabs; the electrifying taste of the charged air. She certainly wasn't upset about being wet, although she was getting increasingly perturbed by Parsley's behaviour. Rather than joining her for a chat, he had taken to lurking in the space immediately behind her, stalking her with his hulking presence. Whenever they encountered other people stomping through the rain on missions of their own, Parsley would veer off to position himself between them and Dorothy. It was a bizarre manoeuvre to witness, and one that invariably forced the startled pedestrians to divert into the street, or cross the road completely. Although Dorothy welcomed having her gigantic friend there to look after her, she was finding it hard to relax when he insisted on skulking in her blind spot. She took a moment to marvel at the droplets of water that had somehow got caught up in her guardian's hair without bursting.

But it was Parsley's unexpected brusqueness with Thatcher at the station that troubled her the most, especially since Thatcher actually seemed to like Parsley. As far as Dorothy was aware, Thatcher had never been rude to the colossus, and she had no idea what vibe Parsley was picking up that had caused him to behave like that. She turned onto a side street to avoid having to frighten their way through a group of smartly dressed men leaving a community centre, while the behemoth lumbered closely on her heels.

'And another thing...' announced Crane, as the censure continued behind her.

Their path took them up a steep hill past areas of overgrown grassland, and across a brand-new road bridge that spanned a stream far below. After rounding a bend in the road, Dorothy realised that she was leading her friends into a labyrinthine housing estate, the normal patchy white paintwork and pebble-dashed façades of the buildings replaced by a pervasive bland yellow brick. The rain had tailed off to a persistent mizzle, bringing with it a damp that felt like it was being held in the air rather than dropped from above. It wasn't long before Crane also noticed the change in scenery. 'Yo! Dozza! Hold on, girl. Where we going?' he called.

Dorothy turned to her companions, who were trailing some way behind. Crane skipped up to talk to her, leaving a thankful Thatcher to dawdle after him in peace.

'You've gone wrong, Dozza,' he declared. 'This isn't the way.'

'Where did you want to go instead?' Dorothy asked, nonplussed. As far as she was aware, they were just heading away from the station. 'What's back there that isn't down here?'

Crane rolled his eyes and opened his mouth to speak, but he caught himself before any sound came out. 'OK. Fair enough,' he finally conceded. 'But if we get lost, it's your fault, right?'

'We're not lost,' Dorothy reassured him. 'We just don't know where we're going yet.'

'Yeah, we do,' Crane retorted, gesturing towards a small

parade of shops in the distance, deep within the maze of identical houses. 'We're going to find something dry to eat.'

∽

It was, predictably, just another opportunity for Crane to punish Thatcher for his incompetence. As they approached the newsagent, Crane demanded that Dorothy hand over the remains of the group's funds, before venturing inside while the others sheltered under an awning. He soon reappeared with three long sandwiches, passing one to Dorothy and another to Parsley. Crane started unwrapping the third baguette while staring at Thatcher, daring him to complain. But even if Thatcher would rather stay hungry than risk a conversation with his travelling companion, Dorothy wasn't going to let this pass unchallenged. 'What about Bill?' she demanded. 'Where's his food?'

'Oh, haven't you heard? He's got a credit card,' Crane explained. 'He can go buy whatever he wants.'

Dorothy shook her head in dismay, even though there was something perversely impressive in just how long Crane could bear a grudge. She tore her sandwich in half and offered a piece to Thatcher. But before he could accept the gift, Parsley shifted over to block the exchange, glaring at the tall man and baring his yellowed teeth. Thatcher dutifully held up a hand. 'Thank you, Dorothy, but I'm not hungry. You eat.' Dorothy resolved to have a long talk with Parsley when they were on the move again, but when she bit into the sandwich, she was grateful for his intervention. A thick layer of butter scraped across her teeth and onto the roof of her mouth like a cooling balm, bringing with it a taste of ham so unctuous that it sent her tongue into spasms of pleasure. She closed her eyes and luxuriated in every chew.

THE ZOO

After they had eaten, they set off again in silence, following the same route through the estate. Even without a specific destination in mind, something nagged at Dorothy: an impression that they *were* actually moving forwards rather than just rambling randomly through this odd little town. The answer revealed itself slowly, unwrapping itself in her subconscious while her brain fizzed with all the extra sensory data. To her right, a range of gentle hills stretched into the far distance; to her left, terrace after terrace spread out down side streets and around small parks. But ahead of her, in the gaps between buildings, there was nothing. They were walking towards the end of things to see.

When they finally arrived at the last row of houses, they had no choice but to turn left and follow the road back through the estate. But Dorothy instead continued straight onwards, guiding her friends through a wide opening between two houses that looked like it might actually have been part of someone's land. She took them across a perfectly manicured garden, through a flowerbed, and around a split in a wooden fence that opened onto a sodden field. On the far side lay only sky and clouds. A brisk wind had picked up, billowing Dorothy's hair out behind her and poking fingers of cold through her soggy jacket and thin leggings. Dorothy leant into the wind and pushed forward, determined to uncover whatever it was that the forces of nature were trying to stop her from seeing.

The revelation that awaited her on the other side of the field was so obvious that it left her questioning her sanity. They had spent a night and a day in this unremarkable little town, yet until that moment she hadn't realised that they were by the sea. The party had arrived at the summit of a cliff, with a shingle beach some fifty feet below them, and only a thicket laden with ripe blackberries provided a barrier between them and a sheer drop onto the rocks. Ahead, the sea churned with a sandy brown hue. Looking down along the shoreline offered a picture-postcard perspective of the town: a panorama made up from millions of tiny, beautiful details, almost too much information to have to take in. Although it was still overcast, the rain had stopped, and even through her amazement Dorothy felt an involuntary pang of hope. Somehow it seemed that their mission might finally be back on track.

As she collected her breath after the struggle across the wet field, Dorothy found herself wondering how Henry would have dealt with their situation, and with it came the realisation that this was the first time that day that he'd entered into her thoughts. All the stimulation and the intoxication from everything she'd seen since waking up that morning had left her no room to dwell on him. She knew she should be feeling mortified by the disrespect she was showing to his memory, but today even Henry couldn't undermine her equanimity. Dorothy stared down at her bloodstained trainer for inspiration.

Along the cliff, an informal footpath had been beaten into the ground, following the course of the thicket downhill and back towards the town – evidence of sightseers trekking up from the beach to enjoy the same view. 'So, that's where we were going,' Crane remarked. 'Nice one, Dozza. Take a minute, everyone, but then we've got to go. If we approach along the sea line, we should avoid running into West.'

This was the first time anyone had mentioned West, and the possibility that she might be nearby cut through Dorothy's positivism like an icy blast. 'Where's West?' She shivered anxiously. 'Do you think she might be here? In this town?'

'Almost certainly not,' reassured Thatcher, before turning to the other man. 'Mr Crane, can you please refrain from troubling Dorothy without good reason?'

'Yeah? And that's why I'm in charge, dick-house,' Crane

replied dismissively. 'Course West's going to be looking for us. Once she finds her car, this'll be the first place she comes.'

Getting caught by West would scupper everything. Dorothy tended to a nagging itch on her forearm while she considered what she'd do if they were spotted. Crane's expression softened when he saw the nervous look on her face. 'Hey, don't get too worried, Dozza,' he said in more encouraging tones. 'Chances are we'll be fine. Just need to keep an eye out. Not do anything stupid.'

This did little to calm Dorothy's jitters, but before she could dwell on it any longer the air was suddenly filled with the noise of humming, so loud that it almost drowned out the sound of the crashing waves below. Standing dangerously close to the edge of the cliff, Parsley was pawing great clumps of blackberries into his mouth directly off the thicket, along with any leaves and barbs that happened to get in the way. Sparks of delight flashed in his eyes as the sweet juices popped on his tongue and dribbled down his chin. For a moment the others watched in disbelief as the colossus molested the briar, before bursting into fits of laughter. Above them, the first rays of sunlight broke through between the clouds. If their freedom relied on them not doing anything stupid, they were in deep trouble, but for a glorious shared instant that didn't seem to matter.

∽

THE WALK back into town along the coastal path was an exercise in staying upright, scrabbling for traction on the wet, slippery grass. Before long, Dorothy was forced to focus only on each next step, and quickly lapsed into silent meditation; by the time they finally stepped over a low metal railing and into an empty car park, she had fallen so deeply into her daydream that she had absolutely no idea how much time it had taken to get there.

A promenade now followed the course of the clifftop all the way down to sea level, its rough concrete providing welcome purchase underfoot. Following Crane's lead, they continued their march downhill to where the clifftop met the beach, past sullen joggers, past rows of untended beach huts in various colours and states of disrepair, all the way down to a shop whose front was draped with inflatable animals and plastic beach tools. It was there that Crane finally stopped to address the party.

'So far, so good,' he explained. 'Now all we need to do is go find somewhere warm. Dry off a bit and figure out what to do next.' He turned towards Thatcher, a mischievous smile forming below his mirthless eyes. 'Anyone fancy a drink?'

∼

THE HORSE & Colours pub was old, certainly as old as the town's heyday, and was the only detached building amongst a row of terraced houses. Inside, smoke-stained burgundy wallpaper covered every wall and sucked all the light out of the room, welcoming the fugitives into its dark folds. The intricate flock pattern was interrupted by the occasional missing strip, and punctuated by brasses and paintings of fox hunts. Hanging over the front of the bar, a black-and-white photograph showed the pier in all its splendour before it had burned down, while below it a line of accomplished drinkers perched in silent solidarity.

The four travellers converged around a wooden table, far enough away from the entrance for Dorothy to feel comfortably hidden, but still allowing an unobstructed view of the front door lest West or one of her minions come in to search for them. The table was littered with empty glasses and an untidy pile of pistachio shells. Dorothy peeled off her damp puffer jacket, eager to get settled so that she could run her fingers across the furry patterns on the wallpaper. She set about tracing the tactile motifs on the wall behind, her soggy beige T-shirt clutching the contours of her bra. The fuzzy shapes dazzled the tips of her fingers as she stroked them, but left an oily film on her hands that smelled disgusting. She soon gave up and turned back to join the others at the table, only to find Thatcher peering at her with a strange intensity. Her companion quickly snapped out of his trance with a sharp intake of breath, and shifted his attention towards the mess on the table.

A relaxed interpretation of the legal drinking age ensured that the pub was already busy, even though Saturday evening was barely under way, and it was clear that most of the clientele had been there for a while. A hum of friendly background chatter permeated throughout the room, interspersed with bursts of raucous laughter. From an unseen lounge the sounds of reckless karaoke filtered into the mix, the music leaking into the public bar in bursts whenever the connecting door was opened. And still Dorothy couldn't stifle the exhilaration that had clung to her all day, even as she sat in a darkened room in damp clothes. They were probably less than a mile from the train station, and had spent the intervening time achieving absolutely nothing other than getting wet, yet her shimmering mood appeared to be unbreakable. In fact, it was only Thatcher who seemed in any way troubled by events. Since arriving in the pub, he had developed a fractious energy, continually fidgeting in his chair and scanning the room with uneasy glances. Even Crane seemed in uncharacteristically high spirits. 'Alrighty! Gonna grab us some drinks,' he advised the others. 'Dozza, want to give me the dosh?'

As Dorothy riffled through her coat pockets, Thatcher pulled out the useless credit card and offered it across. Crane responded with a sarcastic sneer and opted instead to cherry-pick his way through the notes and shrapnel from Dorothy's cupped hands, before disappearing into the gloom. The girl relaxed into her seat and surveyed the room, at all the people too busy with their own stories to care what she was involved in, or question whether she should be there or not. There were definitely worse places to hide while they brought their journey back on track.

Dorothy tugged on one of Parsley's sodden sleeves, guiding him into the chair next to her. Being inside again, in the warmth and the subdued lighting, seemed to have settled her friend back to his normal agreeable disposition, and she started to brush the water out of his beard in long, firm caresses that were more about cleaning the foul-smelling residue from her fingers. He responded by humming a counter-melody to the muffled music coming from the adjoining room, and by the time Crane reappeared with the drinks, Dorothy had become completely lost in the sounds of Radio Parsley. When she opened her eyes again, she found that Thatcher had chopped the discarded pistachio shells into three perfectly parallel lines with the credit card. He quickly jumbled the clutter back into its previous state of disarray before snapping the card in two and tossing the pieces into the debris.

Crane offloaded the drinks from a tray and distributed them to the others in the party. He passed three pint glasses filled with tap water to Parsley (who poured them down his throat as quickly as they were handed across), an alcopop bottle crammed with straws to Thatcher, and a small glass of orange juice to Dorothy. She glanced up with a look of confusion until Thatcher reached across to swap their drinks over. He carefully sniffed the juice before pushing it to one side, untouched. Crane sat down at the head of the table, holding a pint of lager. He closed his eyes and took a long pull, before tilting his head back with a sigh of mock ecstasy.

They needed a new plan, and Thatcher was clearly keen that they hatch it quickly and move on. 'Why are we here?' he entreated Crane. 'I'd feel much more comfortable if we could go somewhere else. Please?'

'Where?' Crane demanded. 'Come on, where we gonna go? We can't go anywhere, douche-flaps, and whose fault is that?'

A sinking feeling threatened to spoil Dorothy's impeccable humour. Ever since they had embarked on the adventure, Crane had been responsible for coming up with the plan. They were still a long way from finding her father's farm, she knew that, but the fact they'd made it this far was largely down to Crane's savvy, even after he had insisted on getting rid of the car. If they were going to find a way out of this quandary, it was going to have to come from him.

'How do we get on a train? If we don't have any tickets?' she asked, cajoling her friend into kick-starting the thinking process.

A hush descended while everyone racked their respective brains. Eventually Thatcher spoke. 'Couldn't we conceal ourselves in the lavatories? I'm sure I saw that in a film once.'

'What the fuck are you wittering on about?' Crane snapped. 'We're not worried about places to hide. We need to figure out how to get through the barriers.'

'Do they sell really cheap tickets?' Dorothy offered helpfully. 'For other trains? Could we use those just to get through the barriers?'

'We're in the middle of nowhere, Dozza.' Crane shook his head. 'Ain't no such thing as a cheap ticket. Otherwise everyone would be getting out of this poxy town.'

'Well, I thought it was an interesting idea,' Thatcher declared. 'Thank you, Dorothy.'

'Oh, piss off,' Crane retorted. He took another long draw from his pint, returning from his drink with a thoughtful expression on his face. 'Shame the weather's so shitty. Could maybe have nicked a boat. Taken it in turns to row. Or just let the Neanderthal do it all.'

'No. We'd all have to help,' Dorothy replied, annoyed that Crane could even contemplate something so inequitable.

The sounds of chatter and muffled singing were interrupted by a squeal from the front door, the groan of unoiled hinges drawn out by an especially languid push from the other side. A dishevelled young couple jostled through the opening, eyes pinched and slightly wobbly, and shuffled towards the bar. After gazing over his shoulder to check on the new customers, Crane turned to Thatcher with a grin on his face.

'Two more from the herd,' he declared. 'Go on.'

'No. We're not playing that game,' Thatcher responded. 'We've got other things to worry about.'

Crane, however, was not easily dissuaded. 'Come on, junkie!' he urged through a broad smile. 'You're good at this.'

'Really? I don't know,' Thatcher muttered, before glancing up at the couple for a longer inspection. 'Well, he's been smoking. Definitely. Sativa, I suspect, and he's been at it for a few hours already. She's ... she's more of a lush. Very hungover, in any case. Was there possibly some cocaine in there last night as well? Difficult to tell.' His contemplative stare lingered on the pair as he tracked their meander across the room, before he raised his eyebrows in surprise. 'You know, I do believe she's checking me out.'

'*She* is? Yeah, right. Thought you'd be more up for her pal,' Crane sneered.

Without relaxing his eyebrows, Thatcher's expression

turned to disdain. 'Oh, you know how I delight in confounding your schoolboy prejudices,' he retorted.

'Then it's a shame you're too old and you're too fucking ugly,' Crane spat back, venting whatever wind Thatcher had allowed to build in his sails.

The tall man stared wistfully down at the detritus covering the table. 'Has anybody considered...' he started, before looking up at the others. 'Maybe this is all just a sign? Maybe this is as far as we're supposed to get.'

Crane flicked a shell at Thatcher, while Dorothy shook her head sadly. If her friend didn't want to help with the new plan, that was one thing, but it was quite something else to actively try to stop it from happening. Thatcher knew very well what was at stake if they didn't succeed. They'd all be better off if he just kept quiet.

As the three travellers reflected on their options, Parsley quietly rose from his seat to tower above the conversation, before brushing his chair aside and ambling away from the group. Crane idly tracked his movement, calling after him, 'Oi! Caveman? Parsley? Where are you going?'

If Parsley heard the question, he gave no acknowledgement as he drifted away into the depths of the pub. 'Idiot,' Crane muttered. 'Do you think one of us should run after him? Make sure he pisses outside his trousers?'

Even though Crane hung out with Parsley most days, Dorothy wasn't convinced that he liked him very much. But even so, Crane knew how protective she felt towards the behemoth, and she often wondered what he thought he stood to gain by being rude about Parsley behind his back. It also made her question whether her friend also shared his opinions of her whenever she was out of the room. Her doleful look must have been caught by Thatcher, who reached over and placed an affectionate hand on her arm. He turned to address the younger man. 'You know, you might try being a little less ... pernicious, Mr Crane.'

Crane raised his hands in a crude surrender. 'Sure,' he capitulated. 'When you start being a little less ... fuck off. Why do you even care, anyway?' Taking another conspicuous pull of his drink, he let his gaze drift away before suddenly sitting forward. An alarming smile cracked across his face. 'Actually, big lad like Parsley,' he speculated. 'Reckon there's got to be a butcher in town who'll give us a hundred quid for the meat.'

Thatcher let out a belly laugh and broke into a fit of giggles. Dorothy frowned up at him, disappointed that her friend had decided to participate in Crane's mean-spirited banter. She pulled her arm away. 'That's not funny,' she said to Thatcher. 'You need to be nicer to Parsley. Both of you.'

'You're right,' Crane replied with a grin. 'Sorry, Doz. He's probably way too fatty anyway.'

Thatcher convulsed quietly, struggling to stifle his mirth. His gaze flicked from Crane to Dorothy as his face contorted and reddened, but the sight of her consternation seemed to be making things worse. Before too long, Dorothy also found herself chuckling in sympathy with her friends. There was something in the rarity of the situation, where Thatcher got to share in Crane's wit rather than having to endure it, that had made her buckle. She prayed that they'd all be back to their normal sober selves by the time the subject of the joke returned.

Their irrepressible laughter blended into the babble of the other pub-goers as Saturday evening finally arrived to bring some respectability to the revelry. From deep within the darkness, a woman shrieked her delight at some unheard comment; elsewhere, a call of 'Cheers' was followed by boisterous clinks and the sound of shattering glass; somewhere a door opened and an earnest rendition of 'Over the Rainbow' wafted across from the karaoke machine. The verse ended in a percussive snap, with the female singer calling out, 'Oi! Hey! What are you—' after the retreating microphone. Her objections were swallowed in a whine of feedback before another voice emerged from the distortion, picking up seamlessly from where she had left off.

Across the pub, the hum of conversations gradually quietened, distracted by the unfamiliar sounds coming from the karaoke in the adjoining room, until the place was almost completely silent. It wasn't the technical perfection of the singing that was capturing everyone's attention – in places it was barely even proficient – but there was something intangible in the delivery, something extraordinary. The singer's voice had a coarseness that was almost too painful to listen to: sometimes jagged and confrontational, sometimes frail, but always raw, always honest. And utterly mesmerising. The singer clearly understood the fragile nature of dreams, knew that chasing fantasies was a futile pursuit, but there was no bitterness or cynicism in his voice. It was as if simply daring to give voice to a vision of a better world might actually be enough. It was a tantalising glimpse of something pure, insistent like an unfed addiction.

Crane dared to break the silence. 'Oh shit,' he muttered anxiously to the others. 'He's at it again.' Pushing his chair back as quietly as he could, he got up and hurried towards the source of the singing, weaving a nervous path through the hypnotised throng.

Dorothy turned to Thatcher, unsure what was going on, to find her friend squeezing the bridge of his nose. He opened an eye. 'You know, I have a sneaking suspicion that those two were only placed on this earth to test me,' he mumbled, more to himself than to the girl across the table. 'Come on.'

Following closely behind Thatcher, Dorothy glided through

the doorway and into the back room of the pub. Perched on a raised dais that was once the extent of the hearth around a fireplace, Parsley was singing into the microphone, his blank expression in stark contrast with the astonishingly soulful melodies that were coming out of his mouth. Crane stood nearby, ready to pounce on his companion once the song was finished, while a handful of bewitched bystanders gaped at the performance. The song's lyrics scrolled by on a small TV screen, behind which a diminutive woman was quietly scolding her partner. 'Thanks for that, limp-dick. You're my fucking hero.'

'Go swap out your jam-rag,' her friend replied above his breath, obviously more interested in listening to Parsley than having this conversation. 'Have you seen the size of this bugger? Have another go when he's done.'

During her brief journey across the bar, Dorothy had also become the focus of someone's interest. As she lurked by the doorway, an unkempt patron sidled up behind her. Dressed in earthy colours and coarse textures, Dorothy's admirer was almost certainly a beneficiary of the pub's tolerant attitude to underage drinking. Although he was still growing out a short back and sides, he was already twisting his hair into proto dreadlocks. In one hand he clutched a half-full pint glass; the other he cupped around his nose and mouth to test his breath. Apparently satisfied, he engaged his most charming grin and shuffled into Dorothy's eyeline.

'What a cock-head, eh?' he volunteered with a smirk, more to the ghostly outline of the bra underneath Dorothy's drying T-shirt than to her face.

Unsure whether she was the intended target for the comment, Dorothy glanced behind her before unintentionally locking eyes with the young man. 'Who is? Is it me?' she queried.

'Eh? No, you're alright, girl.' He gestured towards the stage. 'I mean Judy fucking Garland here.'

'Oh, you mean Parsley? Is Parsley Judy fucking Garland?' Dorothy enquired, trying to appear casual.

'What – is he a mate of yours?' the young man stuttered. Dorothy shrugged and turned back to watch the performance. Whatever Parsley was doing, it was considerably more interesting than this conversation. Unperturbed, her new friend adopted a different tack. 'You here on holiday, then?'

Dorothy took a second to consider the question. The truth was, they were only in town because they couldn't get away to anywhere else, and she wondered whether there was a word that accurately described their situation. 'Holiday', however, definitely wasn't it. In the end, she just shook her head, opting for a simple 'No.'

'But you're from out of town, yeah?' he persisted. 'You're too gorgeous. I would have clocked you already if you'd been here before.'

The longer this unwanted conversation went on, the more annoying it was becoming. A mere six feet from where she stood, her friend was baring his soul into a microphone, and this man seemed to be the only person in the bar who was immune to Parsley's talents.

'Oh,' she stalled, hoping that he'd at least let her listen to the end of the song. 'Clocked…'

Disappointingly, her reply only seemed to encourage the young man. 'Yeah!' he gushed. 'What's your name, gorgeous?'

It was clearly not meant to be. With a sigh, Dorothy turned to face her new friend. 'Dorothy. Dorothy Gale,' she answered without enthusiasm, before clarifying, 'Or Doz. My aunt calls me Dotty, but nobody else does.'

'Yeah? Dorothy? Pleased to meet you, gorgeous. I'm Tarka, and I'm way 'otter than all the other boys.' When his joke rebounded ineffectually, he gave up and went in for the kill. 'So, wanna come join us for a drink? Got some smoke as well, if you fancy it? You into that?'

Without waiting for an answer, Tarka moved his hand towards Dorothy's face, causing her to flinch slightly. However, it turned out that all he wanted to do was to lift a strand of her hair from her forehead and move it over to the side of her face. Dorothy's eyes tracked its transit across her view; from somewhere in the bar Parsley's singing stopped abruptly, mid-chorus. Tarka tipped his head forward and stared up at Dorothy through his eyelashes; a mush of synthesised violins was interrupted by the dull thud of a microphone hitting the floor. Tarka winked at Dorothy and his mouth opened in a friendly smile – then an enormous hand seized hold of his undersized dreadlocks and dragged him away from the conversation.

Without pausing, Parsley raised his other hand and steered the young man's face directly into his stationary palm, a peculiarly inefficient action which nevertheless burst Tarka's nose open by the sheer power of the impact. The respectful hum of the enraptured audience gave way to startled gasps as Parsley tugged back on Tarka's hair and thrust his face once again into his waiting hand.

Dorothy screamed.

Waiting to one side of the stage, Thatcher was the first to react. He pounced on Parsley from behind and tried to wrap his arms around the colossus' shoulders, but even his extended reach was not enough to encircle Parsley's chest. Thatcher's hands flailed ineffectively as they tried to grab for each other, and all the while the assault continued unabated.

'For the love of God, man!' he wailed. 'Stop it! Put him down!'

Emboldened and shamed by Thatcher's apparent heroism,

a handful of regulars bounded over to assist. After a critical mass of reinforcements had arrived, they began to grab onto Parsley's arms and head. At first this only served to slow the beating, but eventually they succeeded in pulling Parsley's arms apart. With an overwhelming force now preventing him from continuing with his aggression, Parsley gave up manhandling the young man, leaving him dangling from one fist. It wasn't clear whether Tarka was still conscious, although he was certainly struggling to breathe, gulping down pockets of air and releasing sprays of bloody spittle as he exhaled. His nose was crushed out of shape and his face so covered in gore that it was impossible to see what other damage might be buried below his red mask. Trickles of crimson ran through Parsley's grip from his victim's ripped scalp. One of the larger drinkers started to prise the behemoth's gargantuan fingers apart, until Parsley released his clutch and allowed Dorothy's suitor to collapse into a pile at his feet.

The whole brutal affair had frozen Dorothy to the spot in shock. In the centre of all the activity, Parsley stood calm and unflappable, no trace of anger or malice on his face. He hummed gently to himself through the last chorus of 'Over the Rainbow', presiding stoically over the fallen man before lifting his head to meet Dorothy's stunned stare. Their eyes locked, but there was nothing there: no acknowledgement of what had just happened, no concern about Dorothy's wellbeing, no pride in his work. She was looking into an empty vessel where her friend used to be. The sight triggered a rush of nausea that left her feeling light-headed. She rocked backwards on her heels, hoping that someone would catch her before she fell over.

Elsewhere in the room, the initial stupefied hush was giving way to noisy dismay and revulsion in equal measure. Now that the beast had been restrained, the usurped karaoke singer squatted and gently cradled Tarka's head, while horrified onlookers fought a path to the exit, colliding into people arriving from the adjacent bar. A growing crowd amassed around a smartphone, calling to each other, 'What just happened? Did you get that on video?' And from all sides a frantic commentary struggled to make sense of what they had just witnessed.

The flustered men that hung from Parsley's limbs joined the discourse. 'What are you doing?' one cried. From the behemoth's right elbow another shouted, 'You're going away when the police get here, you fucking animal!' Yet another called down to Tarka's nurse, 'He gonna be alright, love?' Taking advantage of the calm that followed the assault, Thatcher had finally managed to lock the tips of his fingers together to form a clamp across Parsley's chest, and was trying to crane his head around to check on the status of the victim. 'Oh Parsley,' he muttered into his friend's ear. 'What have you done? What did you do to this poor man?'

With the crisis now under control, one by one the pub regulars loosened their holds on the emotionless man mountain. A flicker sparked in Parsley's eyes, and for a tiny moment Dorothy thought that she saw her friend return. He held her gaze an instant longer, then turned away to focus once again on the man on the floor. The colossus rolled his shoulders and thrust his chest outwards in a manoeuvre that resembled a giant hiccup, shrugging off the men who were still holding on to his torso and arms. He fell to his knees next to where Tarka was being cradled and grabbed the young man's collar, launching into a second barrage of open-palm punches.

This time Dorothy was ready. She lurched forward, reaching out towards Parsley, but before she could disarm him she felt a pair of strong hands catch her around the waist.

'Stay back, love!' a man behind her bellowed in her ear. 'He's gone fucking mad!'

Pinned in place, Dorothy stretched out her fingers to try and touch her friend's face, but she was too far away. She was powerless to do anything but watch, even though she was the only person in the room who might actually have been able to end the punishment. The gory tableau in front of her swelled and contracted as the re-energised men jostled for position, and all the while Parsley's hand moved back and forth like a piston, pressing against the bleeding mass of Tarka's head, squeezing out droplets of blood that swam through the air in slow motion, following their own perfect arcs. Dorothy gawped at the patterns, trying to find order in their trajectories, tracing the dark red lines until they splashed into pools on the floor.

'Break something on his head!' screamed a former captor as he staggered to reclaim his grip on Parsley's flailing elbow. 'Hit him with a bottle!'

Again, the men vigorously dragged the monster's thrashing limbs to a halt, eventually stretching Parsley's arms out to his sides and pinning him into a stress position by leaning on his back. Beneath them, Tarka's nursemaid wrestled to disentangle herself from the unconscious man, starting to freak out at the prospect of a stranger dying in her arms.

Now that Parsley had been subdued for a second time, a fearful silence descended over the witnesses in the room. The only noises came from the replay of the first assault on a smartphone and the sound of Tarka's laboured breathing. The distant howl of a police siren was just becoming audible above the charged stillness, and all around the room people glanced uneasily at each other.

With a screech of tyres and a slamming of car doors, two police officers hurried through the front door and were ushered through to the karaoke bar. At the sight of the pool of blood that surrounded Tarka, the younger police officer stumbled to an unsteady halt and grabbed hold of the back of a chair for support, leaving his partner to deal with the situation alone while he teetered uselessly on the spot. The second officer, an overweight policewoman, gawped for a moment at the grisly scene before regaining her composure and calling on her radio for an ambulance, and the police van, and whatever other back-up they could find.

The policewoman turned her attention to how best to detach the prisoner from the group of agitated men that were still holding him in place, and get access to the casualty below. 'I'm going to need you all to release your grip on this man and let him stand up,' she explained carefully to Parsley's subjugators.

'Not likely,' the man on the left shoulder replied anxiously. 'We tried that and he went mental. Can't you Taser him or something?'

Although she was no longer being held back from leaping into the fray, Dorothy was still rooted in the same spot. Her mouth was pursed in the shape of a silent scream as she gawped at the hideous scene in front of her, transfixed by all the blood. Even though she had failed to keep a memory of Henry in her head all day, now he was the only thing she could think about, and she was trying everything she could to shift her attention to something – anything – else. Ahead, she could see Thatcher poised, ready to throw himself back into the fracas if required, as Crane crept up behind him and tugged on his coat. Thatcher turned to face his companion, who gestured towards the exit, dragging him away before he had a chance to reply. Without making eye contact with her, Crane shuffled past Dorothy and hooked her by the arm, towing her away from the carnage and towards the door.

Leaving behind a crowd of traumatised music lovers, the mood in the other half of the pub was marginally brighter.

Most people sat and debated in earnest whispers, but some continued to order drinks, or wander to the toilets and the smoking area.

'What are we doing?' Dorothy asked in a loud whisper, shaking herself free from her trance. 'What are they going to do with Parsley?'

As he negotiated his way through the bar and back towards their table, Crane adopted a rictus grimace. If he was intending to convey a casual innocence to the other drinkers, it wasn't working. 'Coats!' he sang quietly out of the corner of his counterfeit smile, before shepherding Dorothy and Thatcher outside and into the cool of the evening.

The rain had stopped and a stiff breeze blew in from the sea, bringing with it the metallic taste of salty air and the chatter of seagulls. Bathed in the flashing blue light of the nearby police car, Dorothy turned to Crane to repeat her question. 'What's going to happen to Parsley?'

'It's the fucking police,' Crane retorted. 'If we stay here any longer, they're going to want to talk to us.' He gave Thatcher a hard shove to propel him down the road and into the shadows of an alleyway before calling back to Dorothy, 'Come on, Doz! Can we get out of the limelight, please, before all the other coppers turn up?'

Since he had been dragged away from the violence, Thatcher was behaving in an uncharacteristically pliant manner. However, after being hustled out of sight, he quietly cracked. 'What is the problem with that ungodly freak?' he spat, angry tears welling in his eyes. Anxiously, Dorothy braced herself for whatever was about to follow.

'Did you see that kid?' Thatcher continued. 'That poor kid? What did he do to you, Dorothy?'

There was no good answer. None of it made any sense. The cooling wind buffeted her face, but it couldn't dislodge the image of what she'd just been forced to witness. Dorothy racked her brains to imagine what kind of danger Parsley must have seen in the actions of that irritating boy. 'Parsley was looking after me,' she mumbled unconvincingly. 'That's all he ever does.'

'Oh, the great and powerful Parsley has obviously got matters well in hand,' Thatcher declared through his muffled fury. 'Rescuing Dorothy from a perilous chat-up. Excellent work.'

'He was trying to look after me!' Dorothy insisted, desperately searching Thatcher's face for some shred of understanding. Instead, her tall friend started to pace up and down.

'Well, that's that,' he muttered. 'That's it, right there. The adventure is over, people.'

It was Crane's turn to front up to Thatcher. 'What?' he demanded. 'You want to go back to the Zoo?'

Thatcher threw his arms open. 'Oh, I'm sorry,' he gushed sarcastically. 'I presume you have a better plan? God knows, you normally do.'

Crane took a combative step forward. 'What the fuck does that mean?'

Thatcher deflected the challenge with a shake of his head. 'Oh please, Mr Crane,' he implored with contempt in his voice. 'We await to be enveloped by your fabled insight. It's worked so damn well up to now.'

'Are you trying to ride me, junkie?' retorted Crane, getting closer to the bigger man's face. 'Who put you in charge?'

'In charge of what? This whole enterprise has just advanced from ill-conceived to unmitigated disaster.'

'Fuck you!' Crane growled. 'We still have a mission. Nothing's changed. Get over yourself, dog-fucker!'

In the cramped alleyway, the two men leant in towards each other, glowering, threatening. Framed between them like a child watching a parental dispute, Dorothy waited for a gap in the abuse before muttering 'No'. Distracted from their confrontation, her friends turned to look at her. She continued, 'We're not going anywhere. Not till we get Parsley back.'

'Dorothy, we're not getting Parsley back,' Thatcher explained. 'That's not what we're talking about.'

'Yes, we are,' Dorothy insisted, exuding a calm authority. This was not open to debate. It was not up to Thatcher or Crane, or anyone else, to just decide to abandon one of their companions. She was sure that, if the roles were reversed, Parsley would be doing everything he could to convince the others to come and look for her.

Thatcher threw up his arms in frustration. 'I'm sorry,' he said to no one in particular. 'Was I the only one who saw what just happened in there? Why are we having this conversation?'

'He's our friend. We don't leave our friends behind,' Dorothy countered again with the confidence of someone stating a moral certainty. Thatcher exhaled dramatically and turned towards Crane, lifting his hands to invite the other man into the argument.

Although they were sheltered from the sea breeze by the high fences on either side of the alleyway, the wind tripped noisily across the exposed parapets and spun off in chaotic eddies, ruffling hair and rustling clothing. From the pub, wafts of incoherent speech broke through the turbulent rumble; sounds of slamming car doors, a gurney being snapped open, squeaky wheels rattling over uneven paving, the familiar protest from the hinges on the pub's front door. When Crane broke the uneasy silence, it was in an unusually placatory tone.

'OK. I have a plan, if everyone else can just calm down for a moment,' he began. 'What if we go to the police station tomorrow? If they let Parsley out, great. We take him with us.

But if they don't, we leave him behind and go anyway. The mission comes first.'

Thatcher clasped his head in his hands and gave an exasperated groan, but the more Dorothy considered Crane's idea, the more it felt like the right thing to do. Her tall companion seemed to be actively trying to ditch their friend in this godforsaken seaside town, and it was making her question what he stood to gain by Parsley's absence. Maybe this antipathy was what the colossus had been picking up on all day.

'But ... he's ... why are we...?' Thatcher stuttered, struggling to form a coherent counter-argument. Crane glared at him with an insistent expression on his face, until finally Thatcher relented. 'What? Fine. OK. Whatever.'

This was why Crane was the one with the plan. Now that the heat had dissipated from the exchange, Dorothy felt herself shiver in the unruly draughts. Her puffer jacket was still damp, and the cold was starting to seep into her arms again. Everything that had once appeared bright and alluring now felt flat; it seemed that her sunny disposition was breakable after all. They also had a new problem to deal with: they had to find somewhere to stay for the night, and it was highly unlikely that they had enough cash left for another hotel. She cast her mind back to everything they had seen on their epic walk earlier in the day, doubtful that there was much more of the town to explore. There *had* been something, she thought. Something that had reminded her of the den at the end of her aunt's garden.

'I wonder what they keep inside all those sheds,' she speculated. 'The ones by the beach.'

FRIDAY, 20TH AUGUST

The Yellow Brick Road

*P*ropped up in the passenger seat of a granite-grey Lexus, the left side of her face smeared against the front window, Dorothy's eyes flicked open.

She had no idea how long she'd been asleep. When they got into the car last night it had been dark outside, and they'd been in a city. Now it was daylight, and they were gliding along a narrow country road framed by tall trees. On her right, an old brick wall stretched as far down the road as she could see, the boundary of some ancient estate; on her left was a towering embankment that appeared to be made of earth and ivy. As the car bumped over a cattle grid, a metal gate revealed a forgotten field on the other side of the mud wall, then sea for the rest of the way to the horizon.

This morning (if indeed it was still morning), something felt unusually mushy in her head. Normally, she could transition almost instantaneously out of a deep sleep to wide awake, like being brought out of a hypnotic fugue by the snap of a finger. But today something in her brain felt different, blending sleep and consciousness into something woollier and less binary. It felt like the kind of anesthetised hangover she would get after taking certain kinds of drugs, even though she'd allowed nothing more dramatic than a cup of tea into her system yesterday. That said, a lot had happened over the last couple of days, and that was probably messing with her normal sleep patterns, exacting a toll. She had expected to wake up feeling sad, still grieving, and while she didn't want to burst into tears again or do anything as histrionic as that, Henry was already on her mind. Him, and an unpleasant sensation of nausea.

Dorothy closed her eyes again to allow herself to process all this conflicting information before she'd be obliged to deal with other people. The frequent gaps in the roadside bank flashed bursts of light through her eyelids, while the vibrations from the side window gently massaged her brain. She welcomed the coolness of the glass against her cheek, the tranquil purr of the tyres on the tarmac, the sounds of Parsley's peaceful humming directly behind her. On her right, Crane was still driving the car, and he and Thatcher were already engaged in one of their debates. Although he was sat in the back, Thatcher was leaning so far forward that his head had popped through the gap between the front seats. Even at these close quarters, the discussion was being conducted in an unnecessarily loud whisper.

'Although I'm still struggling to comprehend why that has anything to do with it,' countered Thatcher, evidently annoyed by some earlier insult.

'Really?' Crane replied. 'So, you're not allowed to get wasted. You're too old to get paid to suck a dick. Ain't nothing left but a dose of the Lord Jesus once all the fun is gone.'

'There is absolutely no correlation!' Thatcher now sounded exasperated. 'What in God's name are you talking about?'

'Just admit it – you'd take your old life back in a heartbeat.'

'What? No! You don't ... I'm not...' Thatcher stuttered. 'Absolutely not! No!' It appeared that he had already arrived at his highest level of vexation, a state that Crane liked to refer to as 'peak pique'. Although Dorothy kept her eyes shut and her face firmly pressed against the window, she couldn't prevent a small smile from curling around the edges of her lips. They must be playing a game that Crane had invented a while back, but which didn't get an outing very often now that Thatcher was wise to its rules. With the tall man already inflamed to the point of stammering, Crane was clearly winning this bout.

'Shame,' Crane prompted. 'Bet old Snatcher was way more fun to be around than the boring twat he is now.'

'I have ... you really, really don't...' Thatcher sputtered, before catching his breath and exhaling slowly through his pursed mouth. When he continued, he had regained some small measure of composure, although he couldn't hide the frustration in his voice. 'From which dark recess in your brain does all this vitriol stem?'

'Hey, don't go confusing my curiosity with your character flaws!' Crane replied.

Thatcher slumped back into his seat in acknowledgement of Crane's victory. 'You have no idea how often I pray for your soul, Mr Crane,' he muttered.

'Yeah? Well, don't. Trust me on this one. I'm smarter than you.'

And with Crane's inevitable last word, the game was over. Dorothy smiled again, but she knew that this was the point at which she had to insert herself into the conversation. Left to his own devices, Thatcher could stay upset for hours, days sometimes, while Crane had probably already moved on. Parsley's humming was now papering over an uncomfortable silence; while Dorothy always found it soothing to have his music playing, she was also aware that not everybody shared her point of view. In fact, sometimes it could even make things worse. With some effort she peeled her face away from the glass and turned to address Crane and Thatcher.

'Where are we?' she asked. 'How long—'

'Whoa!' whooped Crane. 'About time! The sensible chat just woke up! Look! We're by the sea. On our way!' He flashed a welcoming smile towards the young girl that looked like it might actually be genuine.

From the back seat, Thatcher reached a paternal hand across and placed it on Dorothy's shoulder, shifting effortlessly out of his moping into an affectionate concern. 'You've been out for hours, sweetheart,' he said sympathetically. 'How are you feeling? Are you doing OK?'

Dorothy placed her hand on his and patted it encouragingly, indulging Thatcher's protective instincts. If she didn't let him think he was helping, his low-key interest in her wellbeing could easily develop into a state of anxious supervision, and then no amount of reassurance could rescue her. She turned and gave him a friendly nod, intended to be just enough to calm his misgivings. Thatcher, however, persisted. 'We were worried about you. You've been asleep for a really long time. Do you realise that while you were out, we actually parked the car so the rest of us could get some shut-eye? And we were convinced you would be the one to wake up first. But we've been back on the road for over an hour. Are you sure you're feeling OK?'

It was a simple question, but one to which there was no easy answer. Dorothy contemplated her unusually clouded brain. While it certainly didn't feel normal, it didn't feel particularly unpleasant either. Even with everything she'd put it through over the last couple of days, she wondered whether she was actually going through a peculiarly benign form of detox. Regardless, there didn't seem to be much to gain from talking about it. It was all just a pointless distraction until they had finished their mission and found her father. She needed to change the subject. 'Yeah, I'm not ... I'm really not,' she mumbled thoughtfully, before attempting to distract Thatcher with her broadest smile. 'What were you speaking about? You and Crane?'

'Oh, please,' Thatcher replied dismissively. 'You really wouldn't want—'

'No, no! Let Doz have her say!' Crane interjected. 'Come on! Help us out here, would you, Dozza? God or no God?'

Thatcher lifted his hand off Dorothy's shoulder and shaped it into a stranglehold, which he shook towards the other man's neck. 'Mr Crane – enough, if you please. There is no need to entangle Dorothy in your tawdry crisis of faith.'

'Crisis of faith? Ain't no crisis here,' Crane retorted. 'Can't you just shut up and let her answer?'

With all eyes on her, Dorothy's plan had officially backfired. She had hoped to just relight the touch paper and then sit back quietly to enjoy the bout as the two men sparred with each other, giving her a bit more time for her mental fog to clear. And to make things worse, this was one of those annoying questions that didn't even have a right answer. Whatever she said next was going to upset one of them. 'Well,' she started. 'Isn't he...'

She tailed off, allowing Crane to come to the rescue. 'It's no,' he assisted. 'Course it's no. You believe in dinosaurs, don't you?'

While this was not where Dorothy had expected the discussion to lead, at least she felt more comfortable with the question. 'Um, yeah?' she ventured nervously, before suffering a moment of doubt that she had got dinosaurs and dragons mixed up. 'But they're real, aren't they? I mean, they were real once?'

'Not according to Snatcher.' Crane beamed.

Thatcher leant forward again and crammed his head through the gap between the front seats. 'Mr Crane, you know very well that's not what I believe!' he exclaimed, finally provoked into continuing a debate that he had already lost.

'Oh, so the world didn't start with two people, then?' Crane enquired.

'You're simply not listening to what I'm saying! I've never advocated that the Bible should be interpreted literally. It's ... *allegorical*.'

Crane blew a dismissive raspberry. 'Allegorical? Is that another word for bullshit?' He cackled at his joke before doubling down. 'I mean, it's all bullshit. It's totally ridiculous. What's so great about faith, anyway? Why is just believing in something a good idea? Seriously?'

Thatcher twisted one of the rosary beads in his necklace and cast a hesitant glance towards Dorothy. A moment passed before he answered, and his words were delivered in so quiet and respectful a manner that they almost slipped unnoticed beneath the noise of the car. 'Dorothy believed in the Programme.'

'Ha! And that's totally my point!' Crane declared. 'What do you think we're doing now? We have to figure out whether that was all bullshit too.'

'No, I understand that.' Thatcher's tone was measured, hiding his earlier irritation, and he targeted his comments towards Dorothy. 'But I suppose my point is: wasn't life ... wasn't everything ... better when it *was* still possible to just believe in things?'

Whether it had been his intention or not, Thatcher's question triggered a fresh surge of nostalgia in Dorothy, dragging her back to a time before she lost her innocence. At some point, her memories might bring her a measure of comfort and solace, but right now they were just making her sad, and her friends obviously weren't going to give her the space to grieve in her own way. So much of her life had been insurmountably complicated, even before she'd been sent to live with Aunt Ruby, but with Henry things had been different. When she was around him, seeing the world through his eyes in all its absurdity and silliness, everything had been simple, effortless. What things needed to be taken seriously and what she could laugh off; the reasons why people did the things they did and the reasons they gave to everyone else; cause and effect. When her life calmed down again, when the mission was over, it was this clarity she would miss the most. It wasn't even that long ago – she could still remember how it tasted to be happy. Dorothy looked down and studied her hands. 'Things were better,' she conceded. 'Everything was better.'

Thatcher placed his hand back on her shoulder and gazed at her with a warm-hearted smile.

'Bloody hell! Not you too?' Crane railed at Dorothy. 'Moment you start acting the twat like Thatch, I'm gonna have to—'

Crane's punchline was cut short by an enormous hand that suddenly appeared from the back seat of the car and pressed against his head, squashing him against the side window with a surprised yelp. The car lurched to the right until it straddled the unbroken white lines in the centre of the road, then veered into the empty carriageway opposite. Dorothy's heart skipped a beat, pulling her out of her wistfulness, as the car swung further over into the path of any oncoming traffic. Behind Dorothy, Parsley had shifted his substantial mass into the centre of the vehicle, compressing Thatcher into a cramped nook that was already too small to hold his angular frame. The behemoth was leaning through the gap and shoving his sizeable weight onto Crane's face, forcing the driver to twist his body sideways, blocking his view of the road ahead. Crane stamped his foot wildly on the floor, searching for the brake, but with the strange angle his body now occupied, this served only to wedge his leg into the gap between his seat and the door until it was pinned in place.

'Hey! Parsley!' Thatcher complained. The headrest of the seat in front blocked him from seeing the terrifying view through the windscreen. 'What on earth are you doing?'

Even through her fear, Dorothy was surprised by his surliness. If he had a better understanding of their situation, he'd probably be losing it as well. In front, Crane was desperately entreating Parsley to stop, although the words whistled out in a meaningless mush through his immobilised jaw. The car continued to drift onto the wrong side of the road until the passenger-side tyres bounced noisily over the line of cat's eyes.

As Crane blindly jerked the car left then right, attempting to guess a safe line along the country road, Dorothy leant across and cupped her hands around Parsley's wrist, gently stroking his splayed fingers, willing herself to appear more composed than she felt. 'It's OK. It's all OK, Parsley,' she reassured her friend, fighting to stay calm. 'Crane was just trying to be funny. You know how he likes to be funny sometimes.' Across from her, Crane's mewling protestations paused as he struggled to nod in agreement; Parsley's crushing, however, didn't let up. Dorothy continued, unable to keep the shakiness out of her voice. 'Crane is just about to apologise. To me. If you let him go, he can say sorry. But he can only say it if you let him go. You can let him go, Parsley.'

The tyres bumped again over the raised rubber markers in the middle of the road as Dorothy continued to caress Parsley's hand. If she had to ask him again, it was probably going to come out in a hysterical scream, even though that was sure to make things worse. But then her friend released the pressure on Crane's face, shuffled back into his seat and started to hum quietly to himself, as if the previous minute had never happened. Crane snatched at the steering wheel to drag the car back into the correct lane. After a couple of twitchy corrections, he managed to regain control over the speeding vehicle.

An incongruous melody percolated forward from the back seat, cutting through the tension that clogged up the rest of the car. Another moment passed before Dorothy sucked in a noisy gasp of air, unsure whether this was the first time she'd remembered to breathe since the start of Parsley's outburst. Her heart was racing, and her early morning haze had completely evaporated.

It was a visibly shaken Crane who spoke first. 'Jesus. Fuck. *Fuck*,' he muttered slowly, staying focused on the road ahead. 'You fucking ... ugly ... primate ... motherfucking ... troglodyte! What the fuck? What the actual fucking fuck?' He delivered the tirade through a clenched jaw, forcing pauses between words, barely maintaining a check on his muzzled rage. 'You want to get us all killed? Really? You have got to be the most stupid of all the stupid fucking twats. And I've spent my entire life surrounded by stupid fucking twats. Congratulations. You're the fucking stupidest and twattiest of them fucking all.' With an obligation still to fulfil, Crane finally allowed himself a quick glance away from the precious road ahead towards Dorothy. 'Doz, I'm sorry. I'm sorry about what I said. But Parsley, you're the ultimate fucker.'

Behind the driver, Thatcher's face trembled momentarily as he desperately fought to disguise a smile. Catching him squirm in the rear-view mirror, Crane's fragile patience instantly vaporised to reveal the boiling animosity beneath. 'Really, shit-sniffer?' he exploded. 'Who the fuck invited you anyway?'

Slumping back into the driver's seat, Crane drove on in a

sulky silence as the nonchalant humming continued from the back seat, harmonising with a beeping noise that seemed to be coming from the dashboard, where a light was flashing. Even though the danger had passed, Dorothy was having trouble shaking her apprehension, and she was wondering whether she should have brought Parsley along after all. She could think of plenty of times in the past when she'd had to put up with Crane being much ruder than that, and Parsley had always let these go without incident. She just had to hope he'd got whatever it was out of his system. Dorothy peeked over towards Crane to see how well he was doing at regaining his composure, and was gobsmacked to find him staring at the dashboard light instead of the road ahead, despite their recent brush with disaster.

After another couple of minutes of strained calm, Dorothy realised that it was up to her to defuse the stifling tension. 'Hey,' she chirped. 'The purse we got from West. Where's the purse?'

Crane reached inside his jacket pocket, pulled out a slim brown leather wallet and flung it casually towards his passenger. Thrown with a little too much force, it hit Dorothy on the side of her head before tumbling into the footwell. With a muffled shriek, Crane yanked himself forward in his seat until his chest was pressed against the steering wheel. He stared into the rear-view mirror at Parsley. Only when it became clear that his misjudgement had gone unnoticed did he settle back to brooding in his seat.

Unruffled, Dorothy rummaged through the purse, emptying out all the cash before jettisoning the leather shell back into the footwell. She counted out the banknotes onto her lap before proudly announcing, 'Forty-five! Forty-five pounds. *And* a credit card!' Dorothy gawped at the stolen booty. 'That is so much money! That's more money than—'

She let the sentence hang in the air as she struggled to think of a suitable comparison.

Thatcher smiled wisely. 'Keep it safe, Dorothy. I suspect it won't last too long.'

'But we can stay in the car? All the way?'

'I don't see why not,' Thatcher replied. 'We've made it this far, after all.'

In the silence that followed, it was almost possible to hear the cogs turning in Crane's brain. Eventually, he turned to address the others, his bad mood seemingly forgotten. 'Actually, Doz might be on to something there,' he declared. 'Bet you West will have reported it stolen by now.'

'Reported it to the *police?*' Dorothy asked incredulously. 'Do you really think West has gone to the police?'

'Well, either way, nobody can find us if we don't have the car,' Crane explained. 'We need to get rid of it. Dump it where no one can see it. We should do this here. Really soon, before we get spotted.'

'But then we'll need to find another car,' Dorothy insisted. 'We're not there yet.'

'I reckon a train is our best bet. Incognito. Seriously, we've got money, we've got a credit card. The pigs will be chasing after the car – no one's gonna be looking for us on a train.'

'That's all well and good, Mr Crane, but we're deep in the countryside,' Thatcher interjected. 'I suspect there will be more convenient opportunities to abandon our only form of transport.'

'No, this is much better. This is totally the right place to do it.' The car stuttered forward with a misfired cough. 'There!' Crane cried enthusiastically, gesturing towards a break in the earth bank a few hundred yards ahead under a canopy of overhanging branches. 'We'll dump it here. Take 'em days, maybe even weeks, to find it here. By then we'll be home and dry.'

The car coughed for a second time. Crane shifted it out of gear, coasting towards the gap. 'Gonna stealth it in, just in case there's someone watching from a field,' he explained to Dorothy without missing a beat, as the car gradually decelerated towards its destination. With a final sharp jerk on the steering wheel and a heavy stamp on the brake, the car sputtered into the covered parking space, leaving the back end hanging out into the road.

Crane snatched at the handbrake, shut off the engine, and nodded to himself in apparent acknowledgement of a difficult manoeuvre executed efficiently and with no small amount of driving talent. 'Right,' he announced to the other passengers. 'Job done. Let's go find a train.'

On the back seat, however, Thatcher remained unconvinced. 'You know, I'm really not sure this constitutes the best location for—'

'Hold on just one second,' Crane interrupted with a raised finger. He opened the car door, scrambled out onto the country lane, and hurled the key fob across the endless brick wall on the far side of the road. He climbed back into the driver's seat and pulled the door shut, before turning to the man behind him. 'Sorry, Snatch. What did you need?'

∼

For all of Crane's earlier eagerness to get far away from the stolen vehicle, it took the party an inordinate length of time to sort themselves out before setting off. It was Dorothy who suggested that there might be stuff in the boot of the car that could assist them on their journey; it was Crane who experimented with a number of branches in an attempt to jemmy the back door open; and it was Thatcher who eventually spotted the catch in the driver's footwell that opened it automatically.

Throughout, Parsley stood dutifully next to his door, patiently waiting for the others to get their act together.

Dorothy was delighted to see that her instincts were right. The luggage space was loaded with a number of cardboard boxes, and Crane set about rummaging through each in turn with growing disappointment. After passing up on a laptop, a collection of brand-new umbrellas and a stockpile of clean shirts, he chanced upon a box filled with medical paraphernalia. From amongst the hermetically sealed packs of syringes and the vials of clear liquids, he pulled out a smaller box that contained unopened bags of pills in thick plastic wrapping. They looked like they had started off life in a pharmaceutical lab somewhere: each had a sticker on the side describing the contents, helpfully listing all the side effects next to a yellow triangle and skull and crossbones. Further notes were scrawled on the bags in black magic marker in an undecipherable code. Crane grabbed a couple of samples and turned around eagerly to present them to the others. 'Jackpot!'

'Ah – no!' responded Thatcher when he caught sight of the contraband. 'No, I strongly recommend you put those back, Mr Crane.' He reached up to his necklace, anxiously spinning one of the rosary beads between finger and thumb.

'What? You shitting me?' Crane enquired, stuffing the bags into his jacket pocket.

'Are those drugs?' Dorothy demanded as Crane pulled more packets from the stash. 'Did West leave some drugs in the back of her car?'

'Not for us, Doz. Rules, remember?' Crane answered. 'But you never know when these'll come in handy.'

'Handy where?' challenged Thatcher. 'If you're looking for something to sell, take the laptop.'

'Sell 'em?' asked Crane. 'Good shout, Snatch. I hadn't even thought of that.'

Dorothy was happy to let the two men argue this one out between them. She had already moved on the box of umbrellas. Reaching in, she retrieved one of the samples and picked away at the plastic sheath. 'Can we take an umbrella? Can we have this?' she pleaded with Crane.

Having stuffed the last of the pill packets into his jacket, Crane plucked the brolly from Dorothy's clutches and ripped off the remainder of the factory wrapping. He motioned for the others to take a step backwards before opening the umbrella up behind the car. Its matt-black canopy was punctuated on three sides by a corporate logo – a stylised lower-case 'a' formed from two entwined snakes, set above the word 'Almiratech'. Crane tapped a disapproving finger on the emblem. Shaking his head, he collapsed the umbrella, tossed it carelessly into the boot of the car, and slammed the door shut.

The four travellers stood for a moment in silence. Without warning, Dorothy felt a sudden chill pass through her, and was reminded just how little she enjoyed being in the countryside. There was never anyone around to hide amongst in the great outdoors, and the only people you ever ran into always insisted on talking to you, asking how you were doing and wishing you a good day. Even when she had lived on the farm with her father, she had found it hard to relax, and now she was fenced in by nature in every direction. The rest of their adventure looked very different from outside the car. But before she had a chance to dwell on the issue, Crane invited the others to join him with a simple, 'Shall we?' He set off without waiting for an answer.

∽

FACED with no choice but to follow the road, the party formed into single file, with Crane setting the pace a full thirty feet ahead of the others. Although Dorothy had no idea what the time was, she guessed it was still fairly early in the morning; the sky was concealed by an unbroken covering of low cloud, and it took a concerted effort to figure out which bit of grey masked the sun from view.

They had only been walking for ten minutes or so before Crane's assertion that no one would discover the car for weeks was called into question. The first motorist to pass them slowed to a walking pace alongside Thatcher, and the driver leant across to ask whether they had broken down and needed any assistance. Crane was forced to hurry back to join the conversation in time to deny that the Lexus was theirs, or that they'd even seen an abandoned car on the roadside. The driver clearly didn't buy Crane's explanation that they were just out enjoying a ramble through the beautiful countryside, and eventually drove off with an exasperated, 'Sod you, then.'

But before too long, the brick wall on the opposite side of the road abruptly turned through ninety degrees and disappeared up a hill in an almost perfectly straight line, marking the limits of the estate and exposing a vast swathe of gorseland adjacent to the private grounds. Crane stopped at the end of the boundary wall and turned to address the others. 'See?' he demanded, gesturing up the slope. 'We need to get to the top. We'll be able to see everywhere, figure out where the trains are, everything. All part of the plan.'

'Of course it is,' Thatcher replied dismissively.

'What? Your knees too old for a little climb?' Crane asked. 'You're welcome to go back and wait in the car, Granddad.'

'Come on, Bill.' Dorothy smiled at her tall friend. 'This looks a good way not to get caught.'

And so the trudge continued upwards, over a barren landscape of weeds and hardy grasses, and away from the exposed road. Below Dorothy's feet the morning dew had yet to be burned away, and every step churned the ground into an earthy mulch that made for slow progress. The unruly grasses gave up balls of moisture whenever they brushed across her leggings, until she was sodden from the knees down.

The higher they climbed, the stronger the breeze from the sea became, snatching at Dorothy's hair and clothes and howling in her ears. Whenever she lifted her gaze from the obstacles immediately in front of her to look up the hill, it always seemed as if the crest of the ridge was just a short walk away. However, as she approached these supposed peaks, each time they proved only to be local plateaus, revealing other false summits ahead. Behind her, the horizon beyond the sea expanded with every step, until the only evidence she could see of human civilisation were the far-off ships navigating along the Channel.

Were it not for Crane's dogged progress and his insistence on staying just out of earshot at the head of the group, Dorothy would have probed him further about the details of his plan. Despite Crane's insistence that he had everything in hand, this was the first she had heard about trains and hills, and she felt uneasy about being kept out of the loop. She understood that all good plans needed to be flexible, to adapt to new circumstances, but it'd be very different if it turned out that Crane was just making it up as he went along. The higher they climbed, the more her anxiety grew, yet she could never quite catch enough breath to muster the bellow needed to compete with the clamouring wind, or find the strength in her aching calves to break into a jog and close the gap on their guide. She had no choice but to grimly march onwards, in the hope that Crane might actually know where he was going.

Eventually, the relentless uphill march ended in a summit of sorts. To their right another, higher peak presented a familiar hurdle, obscuring the view in that direction, but for the first time the terrain ahead sloped downwards on the far side of a patch of level ground. A vista of gently undulating hills and fields flushed in shades of green spread out under the leaden sky. A tiny copse of trees stood on top of the crest, their jet-black fruit shuffling and rippling amongst the leaves. As Crane approached, the air suddenly exploded into life as a murder of crows leapt from their branches as one, circling overhead in a cacophonous frenzy. He spun around with open arms to welcome the other travellers to his summit, his face split in half by a crooked smile while the skies behind him broiled in chaotic black.

It was impossible to estimate how far into the distance they could see from the crest, but the surrounding countryside revealed no evidence of trains, or even an indication of a community that might need a train. Other than a single faraway farm, there were no signs of human habitation at all, and certainly nothing that looked like it could help them get on with their journey.

The vast rustic panorama added to Dorothy's jitters. 'Where's the station?' she demanded, anxiously scanning the scenery, reconciling herself to another long walk whatever the answer. In every direction, all she could see was an expanse of more pointless countryside that would now need to be endured and conquered. 'I can't even see any train tracks.'

Standing next to her, Thatcher appeared to be thoroughly underwhelmed. 'I don't suppose you have any comprehension of where we are, Mr Crane?' he enquired. 'It could be that the decision to abandon the car was premature after all.'

'No, we're still going in the right direction,' Crane countered. 'There.' He pointed into the valley below. 'Field, field, big green hedge, road. Head down there, follow the road, find a town. Bingo. How hard can it be?' He grinned up at Thatcher, seeming to draw energy from the despondent look on his companion's face. 'You didn't have to come, Snatcher.'

And with that Crane was off again, focused on the most direct path to the distant road, his feet juddering and sliding down the hill. Dorothy sighed – it didn't look like she was going to get the opportunity to catch her breath after all. It was almost as if her friend was trying to put as much distance between himself and the others before he had to deal with their next round of suggestions.

∽

THE RELUCTANT EXPEDITION skidded and slipped their way down from the crest, with Parsley finding it especially challenging to maintain his balance on the steep wet grassland. Whenever he took a fall, and he took plenty of these before the ground levelled off again, he would kick his feet into the air and land hard on his back. The first couple of tumbles made Dorothy feel nauseous with empathy; however, each time the colossus simply climbed back to his feet without acknowledging any pain or humiliation. By the time they had completed their descent the sound of heavy falls from the rear of the party had become part of their routine. It took such a level of concentration to navigate a safe pathway off the slippery hill that when they reached the big green hedge, Dorothy realised that no one had uttered a single word since the summit.

The hike continued onto the road. Even though walking again on flat gravel was considerably less taxing than shuffling down the hillside, Thatcher had already settled into an impenetrable sulk. It seemed that the only member of the group still sporting even a semblance of good humour was Crane, who rejoined the others to kick off a new game of winding Thatcher up. The other contestant, however, didn't look like he was interested in playing, and brushed his companion off with a heartfelt growl.

'Are we going to find something to eat?' Dorothy asked Crane before he could disappear again. 'Or drink. I could really do with a drink of something.'

'Better ask Twatcher how he manages,' Crane replied cryptically, prompting the other man to fire him another look of disdain. He turned his attention back to Dorothy. 'Yeah. We definitely should have grabbed some water first. I was actually counting on there being some in the back of West's motor. Anyway, keep an ear open – maybe we can hear a river, or a stream, or something.'

Dorothy stared at her friend, aghast. 'A river? I'm not drinking out of a river. We need to find a tap, or a place that sells it in bottles.'

'Suit yourself,' Crane responded with a shrug. 'We're not far from civilisation anyway.'

They plodded in silence along the service road away from the farm, then followed a country lane that was only wide enough for one car. They walked beneath tree branches that had reached across the road and knitted together to form a tunnel of leaves, or in whatever dimming light had managed to force its way through the dense clouds above. Dorothy had hoped that her distrust of the countryside would eventually burn itself out, but it lingered on stubbornly, refusing to let her go. Regardless of how Crane wanted to spin it, they had brought an urban arrogance with them into the wilds, and because of it they were lost.

In an attempt to take her mind off their circumstances, Dorothy tried to imagine what Henry would be doing if he were there with her. Even after all their exertions, she could picture him dancing along the road with his enthusiasm intact.

Actually, by now he would have probably skipped off into the undergrowth and returned with a massive bunch of wild flowers. A fleeting irritation forced her out of her daydream. So, even if Henry was there, they'd still be lost and wandering about aimlessly, only now she'd also have an unwieldy bouquet that she'd be obliged to lug around.

Just as the daylight was fading, and the first rumblings of panic were starting to bubble up inside Dorothy, a village appeared on the other end of a bend in the road. The sight was so unexpected that the companions stopped dead in the middle of the lane to stare at the settlement, nervous it might vanish like a mirage if they dared to approach any closer. 'Ta-da,' Crane sang weakly, sounding more relieved than pleased with himself.

The final few hundred yards into the village were the most painful of the long walk, but for the first time since they had abandoned the car, Dorothy had an inkling of where they should be going. It didn't take them long to find the centre of the community – a small parade of shops and takeaway restaurants, an oversized church and a traffic camera. A welcoming light beckoned them towards a small supermarket, and with it their first sight of another human being since leaving the car all those hours earlier.

Inside the shop, Dorothy and Thatcher were given the task of sorting out snacks, while Crane went to ask for directions. Parsley had been instructed to wait outside and try not to look like an enormous bearded baby, but he followed his friends into the shop anyway. Dorothy watched as Crane strode up to the closed Post Office at the rear of the supermarket and leant on the bell until someone came out and opened it again. After what seemed like a fairly terse exchange, the four travellers reconvened outside to compare notes.

'No train. No station. Just a bunch of fucking bumpkins,' summarised Crane between mouthfuls of crisps.

'But how does the plan work if we can't find a train?' demanded Dorothy, chugging on an enormous bottle of fizzy pop.

'Well, yeah. Exactly,' Crane mused. 'And the nearest one is seven miles in that direction, apparently.'

Without really knowing how far seven miles was, Dorothy couldn't gauge whether this was meant to be reassuring news or a complete disaster. They might already have walked that distance today, or maybe even further. Equally, they could still be hiking when the sun came up tomorrow even if they set off now. Thankfully, the off-duty Post Office worker had offered a possible solution. 'The grumpy bitch did say there was sometimes a bus,' Crane continued. 'Although it doesn't come every day. And it might have already been.' He helped himself to another handful of crisps as the others stared at him expectantly. 'Tell you what, we've got to get away from these yokels, but I'm buggered if I'm walking any more today. Come on.'

With that, he marched off, taking four purposeful strides towards the church before slowing to a hobble. Behind him, Dorothy turned to Thatcher for guidance, but he could only produce a noncommittal shrug. 'It's this way, I guess,' he speculated, and limped after Crane, away from the comforting glow of the supermarket and into the twilight.

∽

IN THE SHADOW of a giant wooden thermometer that had sprouted up amongst the graves outside the church, the four of them dutifully lined up in single file at the bus stop. When their transport out of the backwoods didn't immediately arrive, Dorothy found herself squirming from side to side in discomfort, and decided to risk her place in the queue to find somewhere to sit and rest her legs. Moving towards the graveyard, she gently lowered herself onto the pavement and leant back against a stone wall, legs outstretched.

Crane watched his friend get comfortable before rebuking her. 'Oh, Dozza. Really? You know that's where the dogs piss? Right where you're sitting?' But it wasn't too long before he also persuaded Parsley to keep his place in line and flopped down alongside her. Thatcher was next, although he was tall enough to perch on the top of the wall and still have his feet touch the ground. Only Parsley seemed content, somehow managing to stand completely still at the front of the bus queue, humming an ever-evolving melody to himself.

When the bus finally appeared, the clouds that continued to obscure the sky were almost black, and they were still the only four people at the stop. At the first sight of their ride back to civilisation, Dorothy leapt to her feet and danced about excitedly, having already secretly prepared herself for an overnight trek through the wilderness. While he must have been just as relieved as she was, Crane couldn't stop himself from answering the bus driver's welcoming smile with a curt, 'Where the fuck have you been?' The four of them gratefully shuffled inside to sink onto more comfortable seats, away from the unpredictable perils of the countryside.

For a service that didn't even run every day, the bus was surprisingly full of other refugees. By far the largest contingent was a noisy squad of ruddy-faced young farmers that occupied the rear section: all male, and all dressed in immaculate quilted jackets and flat caps. Although they were clearly underage, their boisterous chat consisted entirely of anecdotes from recent drunken evenings, and bold predictions for how drunk they were going to get that night. All the other double seats were occupied by less demonstrative travellers, mostly women riding solo next to bags of shopping, older couples, and random unshaven men in knitted beanies. The party stumbled towards the first four available spaces amongst the sullen passengers. While Thatcher politely gestured his intentions to his prospective neighbour, Crane flopped down unannounced next to an older woman, who had to scramble to pull her groceries onto her lap before they were squashed. Dorothy aimed for an empty seat adjacent to a rosy-cheeked middle-aged woman whose hair was covered in a patterned scarf; directly behind her, Parsley squeezed in beside a dishevelled man in a donkey jacket, who was either too polite or too nervous to complain about being crushed against the window.

For the first time since abandoning the car, Dorothy allowed herself to believe that their mission might be back on track. Even though she trusted in Crane's planning, she recognised that everything that had happened between stealthing the car into the parking space and the bus finally arriving had relied on forces outside their control. Today's experiences served mainly to fuel her distrust of the capricious countryside. Sure, she understood why it was needed – all the cities and towns would just crash into each other otherwise – but it definitely looked more appealing when viewed through a window.

Behind her, Parsley's music had started again. Dorothy relaxed her head against the back of her seat to savour the soothing melodies. As the throbbing in her legs slowly dulled, she noticed an itchy tingle on her left forearm. When a cursory scratching session through her puffer jacket didn't deal with the irritation, she struggled out of her coat to examine its source. Amongst the many puncture scars, a small plastic cannula was taped down against her arm, just below the crook of her elbow. The edge of the adhesive pad that held it in place was lifting away from her skin, where it had trapped orange fibres and flakes of black lint.

Jostled by Dorothy's flailing arms, the middle-aged woman next to her chanced a glance towards the medical implant. Dorothy prodded around the point at which the plastic tube entered her vein, searching for the source of the itchiness. She finally identified a tender patch underneath the adhesive pad, and carefully peeled it back to expose the skin below. When a focused scratching session failed to deal with the tingle, she opted to pick at the rest of the sticking plaster, delicately lifting it away to keep the stinging to a minimum. Dorothy's neighbour continued to stare at the process, the colour slowly draining from her face, no longer able to disguise her interest. She let out a low moan that droned harmoniously under Parsley's hum. After Dorothy had completely removed the adhesive pad and let it fall to the floor, she returned to jiggle with the cannula itself; beside her, the woman's moaning became louder, before her chin dropped to her chest and her eyes rolled in their sockets. Having failed to address the discomfort, Dorothy pinched her thumb and forefinger around the implant and cautiously withdrew the thin plastic tube from her vein. In the next seat, her neighbour ogled every gory second of the extraction. When the tapered end popped free with a small spurt of blood, the older woman finally fainted, and her catatonic head flopped gently against the window pane.

The bus rumbled along the tight country lanes, sedating Dorothy with the soporific vibrations from its diesel engine and an unhurried rocking from side to side as the driver steered along uneven cambers and around potholes. Even after her supposedly epic sleep the night before, she felt herself again being lulled by the sway of the journey and the tranquillity of Parsley's music. She closed her eyes and allowed herself to drift, until her reasoning became jumbled with half-dreamed images and illusions. She was aware that the bus stopped a few more times, releasing passengers into the Badlands. She was aware of the unruly excitement from the rear of the bus quietening into a more clandestine conversation, unintelligible murmurings without words or articulation. In her thoughts she saw fleeting visions of people she used to know – just enough of a glimpse each time to grasp the sense of someone, just enough to know who they were meant to be.

By the time the bus reached its terminus, it had already passed through the centre of the town and deposited its payload of provincial thrill-seekers. When Thatcher gently shook Dorothy's shoulder to rouse her from her nap, they were the only four people left, apart from Dorothy's sleeping neighbour. As the drowsiness lifted, Dorothy suddenly felt cold and intensely hungry. 'Is this the place?' she whispered to Thatcher as she climbed carefully out of her seat, not wanting to wake the woman next to her. 'The place with the train station?'

'So I'm assured,' replied Thatcher, steering her towards the night-time on the other side of the door. 'I wonder whether we've left it a bit late for today, though.'

Out on the tarmac, Crane was busy thinking similar thoughts. 'I'm starving,' he announced. 'We need to go find some proper food. Not sure we're gonna get a train tonight, either.'

'Are you advocating that we find somewhere in this town to spend the night?' questioned Thatcher.

'I'm not avocado anything till I've eaten something,' Crane grumbled. 'Get a shift on.'

∽

AT LEAST TOWNS and cities behave like normal places, Dorothy mused as they attempted to navigate their way back to the town centre. She soon found herself quietly celebrating the little improvements: the pavements that kept them out of the way of cars; the streetlights and the noises and the promise of crowds. Being away from the countryside had also breathed new life into Crane's leadership, and he bounded away with a spring in his march, declaring confidently that everything they needed could most likely be found within two hundred yards of where they had started.

And his assumption was almost right. Turning into a street about five minutes' walk from the bus terminus, Crane led the party down a wide, leafy avenue on which every property appeared to be a purpose-built hotel or a townhouse that had been converted into a Bed and Breakfast. Although some places had already closed up for the season, others still competed for the last dregs of the summer trade, announcing their rates and availability on wooden signs that sprouted from every front garden. It was an unexpected moment of serendipity at the end of a painful day, and one that Dorothy took to be a premonition of easier times to come. That was, until Crane reappeared from his first meeting with a prospective hotelier, slamming the front door shut behind him and stamping back along the garden path.

'Total bitch!' he spat when he'd re-joined the others on the pavement. 'Unbelievable. Un-fucking-believable! Do you know how much money that fucker wanted? Must have figured out I was from the city. Thought I had an ATM for an arsehole.'

'But we have plenty of money,' insisted Dorothy. 'Did you tell them we only wanted to stay for one night?'

Crane thumbed towards Parsley. 'Seems they took one look at Cro-Magnon and doubled their rates.'

Dorothy twisted around to check on her enormous friend, who lurked attentively behind her like her shadow made monstrous. But if Parsley had been offended by Crane's childish jibe, he wasn't letting it show. With a sympathetic smile, she reached up and stroked the uneven stubble on his chin, switching on the music.

'Oh, magic,' Crane muttered. 'That'll help.' He was just about to resume his stomp down the road when Thatcher caught him by the arm.

'That hotel over there appears to have the lowest rates,' Thatcher indicated dolefully. 'We may need to rethink our options, Mr Crane.'

Across the road, hidden in the shade of a larger hotel, a townhouse skulked in the darkness. A faint glow from deep within the building barely lit the frosted glass in the front door; otherwise, there was no indication of life. Illuminated by a street light, a sign proudly advertised that the Gatekeeper Hotel was open for business: *B&B £25 per night. VACANCY.* The sliding panel that once covered the word *NO* above *VACANCY* had been replaced with masking tape, declaring a perpetual state of insufficient occupancy.

The others turned to follow Thatcher's gaze. 'What's a B&B?' asked Dorothy.

'Buggery and Blow jobs,' Crane responded. 'Probably more up Thatch's alley.'

Thatcher closed his eyes and shook his head slowly. 'It's actually Bed and Breakfast, Dorothy. It's ... well, it's just like a small hotel. And we're short by quite a bit if it's twenty-five pounds each.'

'Too much dosh if we all want a room,' Crane agreed, letting a snarl settle on his lips. 'I've got an idea – let's draw straws.'

'I'm sorry,' Thatcher said. 'I'm not quite sure how that's going to work.'

'Well, at least you, me or Doz will get a kip in,' Crane

explained, before clarifying the rules. 'Actually, if *you* win we'll pick again.'

Dorothy's heart sank. For a moment she had let herself believe that Crane had come up with a solution, but it turned out just to be another attempt to rile Thatcher. Besides, Parsley would need to be part of the draw too. 'We could just get one room,' she suggested. 'And then all sleep in it. Would they let us do that?'

Crane pounced on the idea. 'Sneak everyone in! Nice! Like it, Doz!' He fidgeted with his fingers, animated again. 'OK. So, one of us gets the room. The others can't be anywhere near here. Can't get spotted. And later, they open the door, everyone slips upstairs. But we've got to be super quiet. Especially Parsley. And we need some food.' He rubbed his hands together triumphantly, firing a grin towards Dorothy and Thatcher. 'Right. Why don't I go and book us a room? Give me the cash, Doz.'

While not exactly the concept that Dorothy had in her head, she was delighted to witness one of her ideas blossoming into an actual plan. She pulled West's banknotes from the pocket of her jacket and offered them to Crane, but he gestured instead towards Thatcher. 'Actually, give it to the Snatcher. They may offer him a discount if he volunteers to suck their cocks.'

It was shaping up to be one of those evenings. Dorothy never completely understood what Crane stood to gain by goading Thatcher, although she sometimes marvelled at the ease with which he was able to conjure a continual barrage of abuse. It was alpha male behaviour, but regurgitated by a beta-minus personality. When they all had nothing better to do, Dorothy liked to consider that the two men were playing a friendly game of attrition, where Crane could pit his wearisome wit against Thatcher's legendary patience. Normally, her tall friend had the option of walking away (and more often than not, this was the only way to know whether Crane had won or not), but today he had nowhere to go.

'My God! Could you be a little more unhelpful, Mr Crane?' Thatcher barked, the first cracks appearing in his composure. Even with his familiarity with the game, it clearly didn't stop it from being incredibly annoying.

Crane awarded himself a smirk for drawing blood. Thatcher didn't usually allow himself to be dragged into Crane's World, and it made Dorothy wonder whether the stress of being lost all day was getting to him. 'Please?' she asked quietly, eager to put some distance between her two companions before someone got hurt. 'Can you go and ask, Bill? You look the nicest of all of us.'

Thatcher screwed his eyes tight and pinched the bridge of his nose. 'I'm sorry,' he confided to his young friend. 'Of course I can.' It looked as if someone had opened a valve and was slowly letting his air out; sure enough, as he reached across to pull a couple of notes from Dorothy's hand, he had to stagger slightly to rebalance his deflating frame. 'Look, might I suggest that the three of you take the rest of the money and go to purchase some food?' he implored. 'We can rendezvous back here later, once the coast is clear.'

Dorothy looked towards Crane for a ruling, who responded with a shrug. 'Alright,' he conceded, addressing Thatcher. 'Keep your ears open. I'll make a noise like a bird when we get back, let you know it's us. And whatever you do, don't give them your real name. Capiche?'

Thatcher nodded wearily. Evidently satisfied with his new plan, Crane signalled their onward direction, but after a couple of brisk steps he stopped and turned his attention back to his sparring partner. Without any explanation, he broke into a wild mime of someone performing fellatio, and after a rapid but dramatic climax he winked at his companion. 'Just don't go filling up before dinner, eh?'

~

RETRACING their route into town took Dorothy, Crane and Parsley onto a wider boulevard, past large, walled residences that must have once housed the town's rich, then along the edge of a small park with trampled flowerbeds. Some way ahead, shops clustered around a set of traffic lights at a T-junction, and as the party approached, a brightly lit street revealed itself on the other side, throbbing with movement and activity.

'Look! Over there!' Dorothy gushed, her head darting from side to side as she tried to pick out details in the distant bustle. 'So many people!'

'So few bullets,' muttered Crane.

'No – we need more people,' Dorothy assured him. 'You can't get comfortable when there's no one around. See you in there.'

And with that, she bounded away towards the crowds, leaving Crane and Parsley to shuffle along at their own pace. 'They're just cattle,' Crane called after her. 'Don't get lost in the herd, Dozza.'

But the herd was exactly where Dorothy needed to be. Of all the things that made the countryside so hard to endure, it was the isolation that got to her the most. The relief she had felt after spotting all those other people going about their business made her realise that she must have been on edge all day, but had just stopped noticing it after a while. Nothing good ever came from spending that much time inside her own head. Already she could make out a strange mix of Friday-night visitors: the excitable young farmers in their flat caps and shiny coats; a shuffling tribe of stoners who were laughing contemptuously at the drunken hicks; gangs of very young children; and retirees who were just passing through, spectators to the start of the weekend's revelries. As Dorothy emerged into the throng, she finally relaxed.

Approaching quickly from her left, a squat middle-aged man stomped along the pavement. His colourfully tattooed arms stuck out of a shapeless black T-shirt, which was liberally spattered with flecks of paint and clumps of dried plaster. A pair of similarly decorated headphones were clamped around his head. Dorothy stepped into his path and waited with a placid smile for him to stop and engage her in conversation. She could actually smell the layers of sweat that oozed from his unwashed work clothes by the time he caught sight of her feet and pulled up with a gasp. It was an understandable reaction, Dorothy reminded herself, given all the blood on her trainer, and she hoped she wouldn't be asked to fill in any of the details.

'Good evening,' she began as her startled confidant caught his breath. 'Please can you tell me where I can find some food?'

Regaining his composure, the man lifted the headphones off his head. 'Christ on a bike, love!' he scolded her amiably over a bed of tinny dance music. 'You scared the living shit out of me. What you saying, my dear?'

'Food?' Dorothy replied, unsure whether he needed a full recap of her original request or just a reminder.

'Oh.' The decorator seemed disappointed. 'Better you just fuck off then, gyppo.' He replaced his cans and set off again on his journey, leaving Dorothy in a state of confusion. She replayed the exchange in her head, before running after the man and tugging on his T-shirt. He swung around angrily, snatching the headphones off his head in the same movement. 'What?' he demanded. 'I don't give money to beggars.'

'No, I don't need your money. Look!' Dorothy dug deep

into her jacket pocket and returned with the remains of the kitty, thrusting it towards the decorator. There had clearly been a misunderstanding, and it was up to her to sort it out. 'See? I just want to find a shop that sells food. And then buy it with *my* money.'

'Eh? You want to know where the nearest restaurant is? Or a supermarket?'

'Yes please,' Dorothy replied unhelpfully.

'Oh, OK,' the man ventured slowly, evidently still perplexed by the conversation. 'Sorry about that whole gyppo thing. We get a fair few round these parts. Bloody nuisance. Anyway...' He pointed up the street in the direction from which he had just come. 'A couple hundred yards or so. See that building with a big clock on it? If you turn right there, you'll see—'

'Mooooooooo! Mooooooooooo!' Without any warning, Crane's howling face had materialised over Dorothy's shoulder, leaning in towards the astonished decorator, shocking the man onto his back foot for the second time. 'Moo for me, cattle!' Crane roared, his eyes blazing with reckless contempt, keeping Dorothy firmly wedged between himself and his prospective antagonist. 'Where is your herd, cow? Moo for your herd!'

Dorothy spun round to confront her friend. 'Stop it! Stop it, please!' she implored, pushing Crane away. 'He was trying to help!'

Without breaking eye contact, Crane continued to moo aggressively as Dorothy barged him out of the way.

The outburst left the decorator looking more bewildered than offended. 'What the fuck are you on, mate?' he called out after the retreating Crane.

As soon as the words had left his mouth, Dorothy stopped manhandling her friend and switched her attention back to the tattooed man, advancing on him with an accusing look on her face. 'Why did you ask that?' she enquired curtly. 'He's not on anything. Why do you want to know what he's on?'

Scuttling back into the fray, Crane quickly renewed his onslaught, his tongue flicking back and forth like a snake. 'Moo for your herd, cattle-boy!' he commanded, before tilting his head back and baying into the night sky.

Shaken out of his confusion, the decorator propelled himself towards Crane with violent intent. 'Yeah?' he yelled. 'Come on, then, what's-yer-twat! Over here!'

Dorothy faced up to Crane to try to quieten him down, but he continued to moo over her shoulder, bobbing from side to side to ensure that she always blocked the way, feeding on his opponent's fury and rising frustration.

'Oi!' the decorator shouted. 'Stop hiding behind your bitch! You still as smart without your girlfriend to wipe your arse? Come on!'

It was less the insult than the intimation that she and Crane were romantically involved, but this was one misunderstanding too far. Dorothy rounded on the enraged decorator and stuck her index finger firmly in his chest. 'I'm not his girlfriend,' she clarified indignantly, prodding him into retreating. 'He's not on anything, and I'm *not* his girlfriend.'

Tailing her at a safe distance, Crane continued to bellow farmyard noises. Behind him, Parsley stepped out of the shadows, pulling noisy gasps of air into his lungs as he struggled to catch his breath. He lurched over towards the confrontation without breaking stride. The sight of the approaching behemoth was enough to suck all the wind from the decorator's sails. 'Who the fuck are *you* meant to be?' he whimpered, allowing himself to be jostled backwards slightly faster. Taking one last glance at the expressions on the faces of the three friends, he declared, 'You're all fucking ... mad!' before turning and hurrying off down the street.

'No,' Dorothy called after the departing man. 'No, we're not.'

∽

WHEN ALL WAS SAID and done, the exchange hadn't proved to be entirely fruitless. From the vantage point by the building with the big clock, it was possible to see the welcoming lights of a supermarket in the distance, and before too long the travellers found themselves retracing their steps with a bag full of food.

Getting out of the front garden and into the darkened B&B, however, proved to be more challenging. After tiptoeing to the front door, Crane warbled his imitation of a dove's coo in a hushed voice and stepped back to wait for the sound of a latch. Behind him, Parsley took this as a cue to join in, and added his own mellifluous birdsong to the mix, but at such a volume that Crane and Dorothy had to drag him back down the road before he woke everyone up. When it proved impossible to switch the birdsong off again, Crane left Parsley in Dorothy's care to chirp out of earshot, while he sneaked back to the hotel to try his luck with a different breed. Next on his repertoire was an impression of a chicken, for which he simultaneously flapped his elbows and bobbed his head back and forth. After an especially raspy 'ba-kaw', Dorothy was confronted by the possibility that Thatcher might have been stood behind the entrance all this time, laughing at his companion's expense as he made a fool of himself outside.

The only other impression in the Crane aviary appeared to be some kind of parrot, but a succession of loudening calls also failed to attract Thatcher's attention, even when Crane started dropping words between screeches in his parrot voice: 'Door *squawk* open the *squawk* fucking door.'

But eventually the message got through. The front door creaked open and Thatcher's face poked around the crack. Crane welcomed him with a caustic sneer, and his companion smiled back enigmatically, a moist sheen in his eyes. At a safe distance, Dorothy had finally managed to stifle Parsley's warbling into a much less intrusive hum, sufficiently quiet at least to be able to sneak him into the hotel. Thatcher took lookout duties as she and Crane whisked the bag of food up the stairs and into their room. Parsley stomped after them at his own pace and volume. But with the bedroom door shut behind them, and the television turned on to mask their whispered speech, all the painful memories of steep climbs and the monotony of country lanes were forgotten. For the first time since escaping from the Zoo, it felt to Dorothy like the kind of adventure that befitted so important a mission.

The centrepiece of their evening meal consisted of three enormous boxes of doughnuts, which had been marked down in the supermarket to an inexplicably cheap price. So cheap, in fact, that Crane had decreed that they could also afford to splash out on a bottle of wine as an accompaniment. When the contents of the bag were tipped onto the bed, Thatcher shook his head dejectedly. Crane leered at him, carefully watching for a reaction. The tall man, however, appeared to have no issues with the doughnuts on offer, wolfing them down hungrily, savouring each bite with indecent relish.

Perched on the single bed, Dorothy excitedly filled her friend in on the events in the town centre. Even though it was technically his room, Thatcher had already been consigned to sleeping on the floor, and had gathered a collection of cushions and towels into the bay under the window, one of the few places wide enough to accommodate his prone form. Behind him, Crane hammered the cork into the wine bottle using an old biro he'd found in a drawer of the bedside table. The stopper capitulated with a gentle pop. He rewarded himself with a long chug before offering the bottle to Thatcher, who silently declined by shooing it away with his hand.

'Come on!' Crane dared him. 'It's bloody lovely.'

'That's enough, Crane,' Thatcher muttered, turning away to nibble the glaze off a cinnamon roll.

'Really? One drink?' Crane persisted through a venomous grin. 'How bad can it be?'

But Thatcher could not be persuaded. Crane instead extended the bottle to Parsley, who sat peacefully on the floor by Dorothy's feet. The behemoth accepted it without a word, placed the opening to his lips and turned it upside down, draining the contents without seemingly needing to swallow.

'What the hell, Parsley?' exclaimed Crane as he watched his precious nectar rapidly disappearing down the gullet of a philistine. 'Not all of it! Give it back!' He grabbed the upturned bottle by the base and tried to level it out, but Parsley's grip was too strong. This unwelcome interference did, however, provoke Parsley to lean over and growl at Crane, baring his yellow teeth and sloshing the remainder of the wine into a puddle on the carpet.

'Oh, that's just marvellous,' Crane declared, as the final drops of ambrosia splashed to the floor. 'Thanks for sharing, Arseley.'

Parsley switched his attention back to the empty bottle, and a strange tumult unfolded across his normally expressionless face. He opened his mouth, as if about to break into more birdsong, but instead vomited down the front of his jumper in a series of wet heaves without making any effort to direct the mess somewhere less problematic. The sight made Dorothy retch in sympathy, although she found it impossible to stop herself from watching. Thankfully it wasn't long before her friend was done disgorging. Parsley dropped the bottle to the floor and attempted to push himself to his feet; he got as far as his hands and knees, took a moment to consider his options, then collapsed forward onto his face with an almighty crash. Within seconds he was fast asleep. The others stared nervously at each other.

From somewhere at the top of the house came the sound of a door opening and the steady thud of someone walking down a flight of stairs. There was a brief moment of silence, then an anxious knock on the door.

'Hello? Mr Snatcher?' a woman's voice called out from the corridor. 'Is everything alright in there?'

Thatcher scrambled towards Dorothy as quietly as he could. 'Sorry. Hi. Yes, it's fine. Everything's fine,' he babbled, trying to sound like he was addressing the landlady from the bed. 'Er ... sorry about the bang. Just very clumsy. Ever since I was a child, if truth be told. I maybe should have mentioned it?' His voice petered out and he bit his lower lip. It didn't look like he believed his explanation either.

'Oh. OK.' The landlady sounded unconvinced. Dorothy held her breath, expecting the game to be up, until the woman finally capitulated. 'Well, then. Goodnight, Mr Snatcher.'

'Good night, Mrs Jackson,' Thatcher replied gratefully. 'Again, my apologies.'

The three companions stayed frozen as they concentrated on the departing footsteps, while a studio audience whooped hysterically at the humiliation of some minor celebrity on the television. From her roost, sitting cross-legged on the bed, Dorothy had watched as Thatcher's silent scuttle across the room brought his head indecently close to her lap, with his hand now resting in the puddle of wine that Parsley had spilled. As the last sounds of the landlady's movements faded, Thatcher turned to Dorothy with a relieved smile, only to be confronted by a close-up of her crotch. Instead of immediately backing away, full of whispered apologies, his expression turned to confusion, and he lingered there for a moment longer than Dorothy was comfortable with. Only when he glanced down and realised that he was leaning in Parsley's slops did he finally spring backwards. Thatcher stared blankly at his damp hand for the longest time, before lifting it to his nose and taking a couple of careful sniffs. The smell seemed to snap him out of his daydream, and he quickly rubbed his palm dry against his trousers.

It was a predictably chaotic end to a long day. Dorothy wondered whether they were really any closer to finding her father than they had been when she woke up that morning. A nagging instinct warned her that their journey wasn't going to get any easier over the coming days, and Thatcher was already showing signs of wear and tear. Maybe the undertaking was too much for an old boy, after all.

THURSDAY, 19TH AUGUST
Emerald City

*H*uddled in the foetal position underneath a metal-framed bed, and swaddled tightly in a lattice-weave blanket, Dorothy's eyes flicked open.

Even in the shadows under the mattress, the diffuse daylight stung. Her head felt peculiarly leaden, as if someone had closed a door between her senses and the place in her brain where all the actual thinking happened. She could still make out everything, still feel the coolness of the ceramic tile against her cheek and the dull ache of her limbs, but the way the information tasted wasn't quite right. It was heavier, slower, missing detail and nuance. It had to yell to be heard.

All she knew for sure was that she was completely alone in the ward.

Despite all the concern that had been shown to her yesterday, all the screaming and the stamping and the drugs, Dorothy didn't feel any better that morning. She couldn't really describe herself as feeling sad, even though everyone had told her she would be. But Henry was still the first thing that had entered her thoughts when she woke up. Henry could make her properly laugh – laugh till her face was wet with tears and snot, and she worried she wouldn't be able to breathe – and he always said things and did things that made her happy in other ways, and Dorothy knew that she would miss these moments. Maybe that was all that being sad was: just an absence of joyful things.

Trying to make sense of what her room looked like at floor level further fed her disorientation. Dorothy couldn't remember a time when she had even checked under her bed for something, let alone lain down underneath it. It was a world populated by strange objects: discarded underwear and clothing; balls of dust and hair that roamed freely at the merest hint of a breeze; a forest of metal bed legs.

Through the open door on the far side of the ward, Dorothy could hear distant clanking and the indecipherable murmuring of conversation from the canteen. Normally, everyone would have to be cleared out of the bedrooms in time for breakfast, and she didn't understand why she was allowed to still be in there. Was it because she was hidden, or had she been granted a special pass? Whichever, she had woken up with a sticky thirst and a mouth that tasted like she'd been sucking on old coins, and the very best thing for her right now would be a cup of tea. Life always seemed more confounding if she didn't stick to her routines and, as dazed and cheerless as she felt, she didn't want to have to deal with the extra agitation of knowing she hadn't had anything to eat.

Dorothy wriggled free of her cocoon and slid out from under the mattress. Although she didn't recall going to bed the night before, someone had remembered to connect her up to her IV – a half-full drip bag of clear liquid hung from a stand, running down a tube and into the cannula on her left forearm. With a practised twist she unclipped the connector and let it fall to the floor, before stretching out the stiffness and twinges caused by her night on the hard tiles. So, this was what grief felt like. She had expected something more incapacitating, something that would stop her from being able to walk, or talk, or feel hungry. Something that would drown out all the hurt she normally felt.

Being upright again offered her a more familiar view of the room. Poppy ward was well known throughout the rest of the Zoo for being the most untidy, so much so that it had become an in-joke amongst the occupants ('Wow – your hair looks Poppy-pretty this morning!'). Even some of the male patients had taken to using the expression, despite not being allowed to look inside the room to see what they were actually talking about. Today was no exception: a sea of unmade beds, with dirty clothes and crumpled pyjamas scattered over every surface.

Only Glinda's bed in the far corner had been straightened out, with perfect hospital corners holding the sheets and blankets in place, and her stuffed giraffe tucked in securely so that its head rested on freshly plumped pillows. Poor Glinda had begged to be moved to a ward named after any other kind of flower, but the prevailing wisdom amongst the people who made the decisions was that learning to cope with the explosive detritus of eleven other women would be good for her. It was, Dorothy imagined, much like teaching a child to swim by throwing them into the deep end of a pool. That being said, the powers that be had agreed to give Glinda a spot in the corner so she wasn't surrounded on all sides by stressors, although this did mean that she now had the berth next to a habitual bed-wetter. While her dorm-mates started each day by throwing pillows at each other and rummaging through disorderly piles of clothes for something clean-ish to wear, Glinda could normally be found meticulously pushing the edges of her blankets under the mattress as she danced around puddles of urine.

It didn't come as much of a surprise when Dorothy discovered that she was still wearing the same clothes from yesterday: her tight rainbow leggings and a beige T-shirt whose colour she didn't really like but which felt incredibly soft against her skin. These would be fine for breakfast – she didn't want to arrive in the canteen after everyone else had finished and be forced to endure even more of her own company. Somebody had gone to the trouble of removing the shoes from her feet, and when she spied them poking out from under her bedside table she understood why. She had originally chosen her trainers for their commitment to a perfect white design, manufactured from white canvas on white rubber soles, and held in place by fat white laces. But now her left shoe was covered in ruby-red spatters of dried blood – way more blood than you would expect to see from a cut or a minor accident. It was all a bit too much to process, especially before she'd had anything to eat. Dorothy burrowed her feet into the trainers before shuffling sluggishly out of the room.

In the lime-green corridor outside, she was assailed by the smell of bodily fluids and bleach. At one end of the hall, a teenage boy in a hospital gown was being steadied by one of the agency nurses. He was a recent addition to the community, and still under an aggressive chemical restraint. In the other direction, a couple of the younger orderlies were engrossed in a competition of who could administer the best dead arm, dressed in their long-sleeved grey T-shirts with the City Green Hospital Trust emblems printed on their breast pockets. Without these tops, it would be almost impossible to tell patients and staff members apart just by observing their actions.

Dorothy directed herself towards the canteen, but her attention was side-tracked by a dramatic screech of tyres from outside. Pressing her forehead against a nearby window, she gazed down through the wire mesh to investigate the source of the commotion. A granite-grey car with an enormous moustache was ticking itself cool in the disabled parking bays a couple of floors below her, casually abandoned across two adjoining spaces. The driver was already out of the vehicle and rummaging through the boot. Dr West had arrived.

When West slammed the car boot shut, however, she appeared to be behaving in an unusually antsy manner. Up to then, Dorothy had never seen the woman looking anything less than immaculate. Her perfectly tailored skirt suits clung to the smooth curves of her short frame, always in dark grey but never the same outfit twice, and capped off with flawless tights and precarious heels. Dr West's bobbed brown hair was so straight and lustrous that you could sometimes see a reflection of the room's lighting in it, but this morning it looked like she had left home in a hurry. She was still dressed in one of her trademark suits, but her hair flopped about in a hasty ponytail, and she had to tuck her shirt into her skirt as she scuttled towards the front door, clutching a thick stack of files under one arm.

A hush broke across the canteen as Dorothy entered, but it was quickly replaced by a surge of unintelligible whispers, and within a few seconds normal conversation had returned. Accepting the unsure glances from the various cliques of breakfasting friends as she passed them on her way to the counter, Dorothy stacked a plate with cold buttered toast and poured herself a cup of tea from the large metal teapot. From the back of the room, a mournful Thatcher watched her every step through reddened eyes that had clearly shed their quota of tears. When Dorothy turned to face the room, her breakfast in hand, he waved earnestly to beckon her over to join his table. It didn't look like she had much choice, even though all she really wanted was an opportunity to sit somewhere and be despondent; to half-listen to someone else's conversation without feeling obliged to join in. As Dorothy approached, Thatcher stood up to intercept her, pulling her into a warm hug that she wasn't expecting.

'Princess,' he breathed compassionately. 'How are you holding up?'

Dorothy twisted her body to squirm out of his embrace. She stared disconsolately at her blood-soaked trainer.

'Not a princess. No,' she mumbled. 'Not any more.'

Thatcher guided her towards a space at the table, next to where Crane was manually separating meat from fat on a pile of bacon. As Dorothy sat down, Crane focused even more closely on his task, letting someone else start the conversation for a change. Across from him, a bald man with exceptionally crooked teeth also ogled a spot on the table. As Dorothy moved into his line of sight, he abruptly picked up his tray and hurried away.

'I'm sorry.' Thatcher spoke in muted tones as he resumed his seat. 'I didn't intend to upset you.' He reached over and cupped one of Dorothy's hands in his, fixing her in the eye, a sympathetic smile on his face. 'We all missed you this morning.'

'It's too bad,' Crane muttered to his food. 'I'm really sorry as well. I didn't—'

He didn't get the chance to finish. A tray laden with spilled porridge crashed onto the table, dropped from a great height. Standing immediately behind him, Parsley towered over the conversation, his face unruffled, patiently waiting for Crane to move. The noise of the impact had made Crane jump, and he turned to address the behemoth.

'Sweet fucking Jesus, caveman! Can't you see Doz is upset?' he exclaimed. He scraped his chair backwards into the legs of the bigger man and squeezed through the gap to stand up, castigating Parsley throughout. 'Really nice, Parsley! Quality. Doz is all sad, but actually no – it's fine. Because now you're here to make her feel better. Bringing us some of that Neanderthal wisdom. Can't fucking wait.' Crane pushed his plate into the spot recently vacated by the bald diner, littering the table with shards of bacon, and shuffled round to sit down next to Thatcher.

As Parsley lowered himself into Crane's old seat, Thatcher leant across to his new neighbour. 'Please, Mr Crane,' he said softly. 'I think we all feel that it might be more constructive if you didn't do that. Not today, at least.'

'No – actually today,' Crane insisted in a conspiratorial hiss. 'This is important.'

Thatcher turned back to Dorothy. 'Did you manage to get any sleep, sweetheart?'

When strange things happened around the Zoo, this was always the first question that everyone asked, as if things would be any different just because of a good night's sleep. Whatever they had given her to calm her down had made her memory slushy and her dreams that much more vivid, and she had no idea where one had handed over to the other. While Dorothy knew that she should be grateful for all the people who cared about how she felt, it was being overtaken by her resentment at being dragged into the discussion. And it wasn't helping her state of mind that she hated herself for feeling so hostile towards her friends. After taking a draught of lukewarm tea, she ventured an answer, directing her faltering words towards Thatcher's hands. 'I ... I had ... I had an injection. I think Nurse Paul gave me an injection before bed.' She looked up into Thatcher's eyes, as some hazy memories came back to her. 'The room! The room was so big last night,' she declared. 'The ceiling was so far away. I was falling. Falling towards the ceiling. And it kept moving further away...' Dorothy stopped.

Hearing herself describe it out loud, it sounded like it might have been part of one of her dreams after all. 'I had to hold on,' she added anyway.

'Yeah? Well, I know what's happening,' Crane declared, attempting to solicit Dorothy's attention. Thatcher lifted the girl's hand off the table and leant towards her, crowding the other man out.

'You know we're just down the hall,' he continued in his most sensitive voice. 'I can't imagine how horrible it must be for you right now, how bad you must be feeling, and I realise sometimes that people just want to be on their own. But I also know that sometimes it can help—'

'Yeah, yeah,' interrupted Crane. 'Yadda, yadda, yadda. Doz – it's the medicine.'

Thatcher leant in further still, a firmer edge creeping into his delivery. 'Sometimes it can help to have other people around to talk to.'

Snarling with frustration, Crane snatched a triangle of toast from Dorothy's plate and flung it at Thatcher, causing him to jerk backwards in surprise. Crane wagged an accusatory finger at the other man. 'Listen to me, dick-drain!' he snapped. 'It's the Programme! It's the fucking Programme! It's the same shit they're pumping into Doz's veins every night!'

Thatcher flung up his hands in exasperation. 'Did we not discuss this earlier, Mr Crane? This is neither the time nor the venue for your outlandish notions!' He shifted his focus back to the young girl, struggling to collect himself. 'Sweetheart,' he began. 'All I'm trying to say is that—'

'No! Stop!' Dorothy cut him short. This was something that Thatcher had a habit of doing, of trying to shield her from bad news and anything she might find distressing. But now she needed him to shut up. There was too much information in circulation, and she needed just a little more time than usual to properly decipher it all. She was pretty sure she understood Thatcher's message: we're all here to help. Crane, on the other hand, sounded like he might actually have something useful to say.

'Stop talking!' she demanded. 'I want to hear Crane. I want to know what Crane is saying.'

'Oh, but this is—' Thatcher persisted.

'Stop!' Dorothy bellowed. Her shout echoed around the canteen, leaving behind a stunned silence. Across the room a woman burst into tears, her noisy sobs cutting through the dead air, but otherwise not even a whisper broke the stillness. Thatcher and Crane glanced uncertainly at each other; other diners gawped openly in their direction, waiting to see what was about to happen. Dorothy turned towards Crane and nodded expectantly, unaware that she had shut down every other conversation in the room.

After a few more moments of the woman's solitary wailing, a general murmur returned to the canteen. Dorothy bobbed her head again impatiently. 'Well, it's the medicine,' Crane hazarded cautiously. 'I mean, it's got to be, isn't it? Henry wasn't sad, was he? He looked fine in the morning.'

'Henry wasn't sad,' Dorothy agreed.

Crane raised his hands and shrugged. 'Exactly. So, Henry's happy, right? But he's on an experimental drug trial. Which is medicine that no one knows what the side effects are. See what I'm saying?'

'I honestly feel that it would be dangerous to explore this any further, Mr Crane,' Thatcher warned, risking Dorothy's wrath for a second time.

Crane sat back in his chair. 'I'm just saying that Dorothy needs to be careful,' he said. 'She's in the Programme too. Same trial, same drugs. Same poison getting fed into her system.'

Even if she had spent the whole day thinking about what

could have driven Henry to doing what he did, Dorothy would never have guessed that the Programme might be the villain. That didn't make any sense. Henry had been convinced he wasn't being given the same medication anyway. Thatcher, however, didn't seem to be prepared to give her the time to consider this theory properly. 'Really, this is utter nonsense. Please, Dorothy. This is all just rash speculation.' He clapped his hands together and pointed them towards her to hijack her attention. 'You understand that nobody around this table knows anything about the medicine you're taking, don't you?' He jiggled his hands up and down to punctuate his next words. 'But Dr Morgan does. I would suggest that his opinion is the one to which you should give the most consideration.'

If Thatcher meant that to be the end of the discussion, it only served to get Crane more fired up. The younger man sat forward eagerly. 'Well, of course *he's* going to say it's all fine! Of course *he's* gonna want to keep Dorothy in the Programme!' He rubbed the tips of his thumb and forefinger together. 'Cherchez la payola, eh? Don't get me wrong, I like Morgan. He seems like a good bloke. He's just a very bad doctor. How do you know if you can trust him? Wouldn't surprise me if he's getting a massive kickback from that Dr West woman.'

'Good heavens! That's even more ridiculous!'

'Don't be so naïve! You don't think Doz should be getting a second opinion?'

'I'm sorry, but I fail to comprehend what justifies you having an opinion at all.'

By now, the two men appeared to be content just to argue with each other, both gesticulating excitedly, raising their voices. Dorothy was merely a spectator as her friends squabbled about her wellbeing. This was much more like the kind of breakfast she'd been hoping to have.

'Don't be a twat!' Crane retorted. 'A second opinion from a proper doctor.'

'Who?'

'You are!'

'What?' Thatcher did a mental double take before rejoining the debate. 'You know exactly what I mean, Mr Crane. From where are you expecting to find this second opinion?'

'Er ... a building site? A bouncy castle? Fuck me, shit-for-dildos! Where do you normally go to find doctors?'

'OK. So, let me see if I'm understanding you correctly. Your idea is simply to walk into a hospital and petition the first doctor you encounter as to the side effects of Dorothy's experimental medicine?'

As the argument bristled, a middle-aged male orderly with a long grey plait sauntered into the canteen and drifted over towards their table. Without needing to turn around, Dorothy recognised the distinct sucking sounds made by his flip-flops and the nonchalant cadence of his stride. She cocked her head to acknowledge his approach. When he arrived behind her, the orderly placed his hands gently on her shoulders, bent forward and whispered in her ear. She nodded, and rose from her chair. Without a word to her bickering friends, she followed him out of the room.

'Why not?' demanded Crane. 'Someone there will be able to tell you something.'

'You should be aware that's not actually how hospitals work,' Thatcher countered. As she got to the doorway and into the corridor beyond, Dorothy glanced back at the sparring couple, who were now performing solely for Parsley's benefit, and wondered whether either of them had even noticed that she was gone.

~

WHEN SOMEBODY VISITED Dr Morgan's office in the Zoo for the first time, he always opened with the same line, half joke and half apology. It was designed to put the person at their ease and reassure them that he knew what he was doing, despite all evidence to the contrary. 'Come in,' he would say. 'Pay no attention to the curtains. I'm afraid it doesn't look much like the doctors' offices from the movies.'

This, however, dramatically undersold the difference: Dr Morgan's professional space was a cramped mess. At some point in the hospital's history, his office had been partitioned off from a much larger room as part of a tightly budgeted renovation, which also brought the building its first stationery cupboard. It was only when the work had been completed that someone realised that it was possible to hear everything that was said in Dr Morgan's office from the adjoining corridor, and it became necessary for him to swap rooms with the much smaller one originally intended to house the stationery. Above three feet in height, all of the walls in his makeshift office had been constructed of glass; to offer the option of privacy, someone had then hung half-length curtains around the periphery, presumably as a cheaper alternative to Venetian blinds. The stationery had also taken custody of the only external window. Since the curtains always stayed closed, Dr Morgan's office was perpetually bathed in an artificial yellow light.

Inside, one wall was covered in metal shelving, upon which sat an impressive collection of textbooks, conference proceedings, lever-arch files and stacks of paper. These spilled out over the floor, across the top of a couple of filing cabinets, and onto the desk. Every available surface was so cluttered with paperwork that Dr Morgan had recently been forced to decline the offer of a computer, anxious that he would have nowhere to relocate all the documents that would be displaced in the process. Colleagues now had to print off important emails and deliver them by hand, further contributing to the jumble.

But although the room appeared to the untrained eye like a hoarder's paradise, it was only because people didn't appreciate the arcane filing system that Dr Morgan employed. Challenged to find a specific patient file, or asked a question whose answer was on a piece of paper somewhere, he would always move directly to the right place and uncover the relevant document with the minimum of fuss. There was no distinction about what information was kept in the filing cabinets (which were never locked anyway) and what was allowed to roam free elsewhere, but the system guaranteed confidentiality through chaos. It was into this office that Dorothy burst without knocking or waiting for an invitation. She took both Dr Morgan and Dr West by surprise.

Dr Morgan was old – maybe even older than Thatcher. But while Bill continually fought against the behaviour expected from a man of his age, with all the running and the ponytail and the crazy black coat, Dr Morgan appeared to embrace the reality of his advancing years in a more sanguine manner. He didn't seem to mind getting fat, or his hair going grey, or always having two pairs of glasses perched on his forehead or hanging around his neck. And despite what Crane had said at breakfast, Dorothy did instinctively trust him. He didn't have what Aunt Ruby used to call a 'liar's face'. Instead he was earnest and sympathetic and, more importantly, he was always kind to her.

Dorothy marched up to the one available chair and sat down expectantly, as Morgan and West caught their breath. Dr Morgan was hunkered down where he normally sat, partially concealed behind his disordered desk, but Dorothy had never been this close to Dr West before. In her clouded thoughts, it somehow felt inappropriate that the two of them should find themselves in the same room together. It was like coming face to face with someone from television, and she knew that she'd dwell on this moment when her brain felt better again, whether she wanted to or not. The impeccably dressed woman shuffled her seat backwards and out of touching distance, leaving behind a delicate aroma of flowers.

It was Dr Morgan who spoke first. 'Dorothy! There you are! Thanks for ... um, coming so quickly.'

Her arrival seemed to have knocked them both off balance, and Dorothy wondered if she'd just interrupted some of the furtive scheming that Crane had warned her about. Her doctor continued, 'Do you remember Dr West? From Almiratech? She came to talk to us at that big meeting we had just before the Programme started.'

When Dorothy didn't reply, or even sneak a glance in West's direction, Morgan assumed his most consolatory tone. 'Dorothy, you know we're all very, very sad about Henry. Everyone here is. He was a really ... well, you know what he was like, much better than I do. I know that you were very close.'

To hear her doctor talk about Henry suddenly made everything feel more real, and Dorothy felt a deeper sadness struggling to rise above her chemical equilibrium. To her surprise, a trace of real sorrow had also entered her doctor's voice, and he shifted his gaze towards the ceiling. 'It's at times like these that we—'

Dr West leant forward to cut him off. 'Miss Gale? I'm Caroline West from Almiratech. I'm the Senior Trials Manager for Topekazate.'

Dorothy shifted her attention to the woman next to her, who gave her a quick smile before adopting a slower and more deliberate delivery. 'It's a complicated name for a very simple job. It just means I get to make sure you're all doing well with the Programme.'

'Topekazate?' asked Morgan incredulously.

West glanced back towards the other doctor with an excited grin. 'Oh, sorry!' she proclaimed proudly. 'Recent decision. Saatchi's, you know?'

Switching her concentration to the thick file that lay on her lap, West started to riffle through pages of handwritten notes. When it became clear that she wasn't about to say anything else, Morgan stepped in to fill the silence. 'Dorothy, Caroline has come here to make sure that what happened with Henry ... well, we just need to check a few things with you. About your family, mostly.'

Without looking up from her notes, West resumed. 'Miss Gale, Dr Morgan tells me that you've been making excellent progress. Really exceptional progress. And all these reports I'm reading here are very positive. Tell me.' She glanced up at Dorothy. 'Do you feel happy? I mean, not today, of course, but in general?'

Dorothy nodded suspiciously.

'Good. And do you know if anyone in your family has ever ended their own life? Or had suicidal thoughts?'

This was not a question that Dorothy had ever been asked before, and it came as something of a shock. Suicidal thoughts didn't sound like the kind of thing that people would normally bring up in conversation, especially with other members of their own family. Not if all they'd done was just think about it, even if they found themselves thinking about it quite often. She stared blankly at West until Dr Morgan broke in to offer an answer. 'Dorothy came to us directly from a foster family. I believe she was quite a young girl when she was originally taken into care, so she might not be aware of the medical history of her birth parents.'

'But there's no evidence in her patient records that could suggest there had been?' West enquired.

Morgan turned back to Dorothy. 'I'm sorry we have to ask you all these questions, Dorothy. Did Henry ever tell you about his mother?'

Dorothy nodded. 'She's dead. Dead from a long time ago.'

'Did he ever mention to you that she also took her own life? When Henry was only a baby? So did one of his uncles, and a grandparent.'

Again, Dorothy answered with a blank stare, but this time it was West's turn to pick up the baton. 'I think we're just about done here. The important thing is that we don't let one little setback get in the way of all the progress you've been making.' She shut Dorothy's medical records with a flourish and fastened her smile back on. 'I'm delighted to tell you that you're not going to be taken off the trial, Miss Gale. And thank you for doing so well.'

And with that, the meeting was over. Dorothy sat patiently waiting for the next instruction. An awkward silence descended, which Morgan finally cut short with a parting assurance. 'Dorothy, you know that everyone here at City Green, and at Almiratech, we're going to do everything we can to make sure that what happened to Henry doesn't happen to anyone else. Henry was such a lovely man, but he was also very ... *troubled.*'

Dorothy was still finding it hard to think properly through the hazy aftermath of the drugs she had been given the night before, but even so she could tell that something had changed in her head. There was something in there that hadn't been there yesterday; something raw and sensitive; something that seemed to grow every time it was poked and prodded. It felt like a layer of skin had been grazed away, and that someone had covered it up with a sticking plaster when she wasn't looking, hoping she wouldn't notice. But it still hurt. It really hurt. Whether it was having to listen to someone trying to tarnish

Henry's memory, or whether it was because Dr Morgan thought he understood her boyfriend better than she did, or whether she was just waiting for a suitable excuse, his words triggered a monsoon of righteous anger. And this morning Dorothy was happy to let the fiery rain fall. 'Henry wasn't troubled!' she exploded, leaping out of her chair in a fit of fury. 'Henry was happy! He was happy with me! We were going to get married!'

West sprang out of her seat and retreated into the corner of the room, moving so quickly that she must have been preparing herself for such an outburst. She dragged her chair with her to cower behind. Morgan, however, remained unflappable. 'Dorothy! Dorothy!' he urged in an increasingly insistent tone. 'Sit down, Dorothy. You need to calm down. And you need to sit down again.'

But that wasn't going to happen. This was the first time since waking up that morning that Dorothy felt like she might be experiencing a genuine emotion. She pushed aside her sense of relief, determined to lean into her indignation. Up to that moment, she hadn't really bought into Crane's conspiracy theory, but now it was all starting to make sense. She had something to blame for Henry's death, and with it came the opportunity to shed all the torpor that had turned her weak and pathetic. She was taking back her agency, and it made her powerful. And she was certainly not finished with everything she had to say. 'How can you still allow the Programme?' she thundered. 'It was the medicine that hurt Henry!'

'Miss Gale,' West muscled in meekly from behind her barricade. 'I can assure you that—'

Dorothy rounded on the frightened woman. 'It was *your* medicine! It was *your* fault!'

Morgan got to his feet, seizing back the spotlight.

'Dorothy! That's quite enough!' he said in a measured voice. 'Sit down again and we can discuss this like grown-ups.'

Dorothy turned her rancour towards her doctor. 'What do you get?' she demanded. 'What money do you get? From her?' She snorted as the inferno raged in her head, before announcing her judgement: 'I don't trust you any more!'

It took a moment for Morgan to address the allegation, and when he did he sounded genuinely crestfallen. 'Oh, Dorothy,' he started to plead, but the girl was done with the conversation. She screwed up her eyes and opened her mouth as wide as she could, launching into a piercing scream that prompted West and Morgan to cover their ears, wincing in pain. Dorothy continued to fill the room with her deafening shriek until the door to the office slammed open and the grey-haired orderly scurried inside as fast as his flip-flops allowed.

Hearing someone else enter, Dorothy shut off the alarm. She turned to greet the orderly, a confused look on her face, as if she too was busy searching for the source of the clamour. Behind her, West and Morgan stayed recoiled, their hands pressed against their ears. Dorothy cast a final baffled glance around the room, gave a shrug, and breezed past the puzzled orderly out into the empty corridor.

∼

By the time that Dorothy realised where she was heading, she had already got there. Her sudden rage had evaporated as quickly as it had arrived, only to be replaced with a hollow unease that felt much more like real sadness than the nostalgic self-pity that had enveloped her since she woke up. And the sadness had led her to the closed door of Appletree ward.

While it was an inviolable rule of the Zoo that boys were never, ever allowed into any of the female wards, this became more of a rough guideline when applied to girls entering male space. Since the time that Dorothy had first become close to Henry she had effectively been ignoring the decree completely, and because no one else that lived in Appletree seemed to mind her coming and going as she pleased, nobody had seen any reason to enforce it.

Inside, the room bore a striking resemblance to Poppy ward, strewn with clutter and pieces of discarded clothing. It just smelled worse. Much worse. As well as the overall stench that assaulted her every time she opened the door, the walk down the central aisle brought in subtly different notes: here was the fragrance of Mervyn's catheter, here Thatcher's running shoes. In amongst the unmade beds, a stripped plastic-covered mattress was laid out next to a cleared bedside cabinet atop freshly scrubbed floor tiles. As Dorothy approached, the perfume of industrial cleaning fluids started to dominate the smell-scape.

Yesterday this had been Henry's bed, surrounded by his eclectic collection of hanging objects. Today it was just another vacant spot waiting for a new tenant.

Henry had had one simple guideline about what he would allow into his hanging collection: it needed to make him laugh. Over the years the collection had swelled to accommodate a plasticine stick-man that he had found in the day room, fashioned by some unknown visitor, with an unfeasibly large and detailed penis; this had once hung alongside replica military dog-tags for someone called Nigel Beastrider (which Henry had augmented with a surround of pink tinsel) and a ceramic squirrel with a clown's head. And suspended from the ceiling had been his home-made dreamcatcher – a crude ring formed from random pieces of wire and string and feathers from road-kill pigeons. Since he had put it up, Henry maintained that he had never giggled so hard or dreamed so well in his life, with the exception of the night that the cotton thread worked itself free and dropped the whole infested contraption onto his sleeping face.

As she approached the sanitised void where her boyfriend used to live, Dorothy could feel her chest tightening. She had been hoping to unhook something from Henry's collection to take back with her, something to hang from her bed frame to remind her of her anguish. But the hospital staff had already swept through and cleaned everything out. Since arriving at the foot of the bed, her memory had started to bombard her with unwanted images, and she didn't want to imagine how much noisier they'd be if the room hadn't been cleaned up. But the staff could have left something behind. Something to act as a makeshift shrine, so people could come and pay their respects. Something she could steal. Dorothy sat down on the mattress, lifted her legs onto the bed and curled up. Although there was no longer any trace of Henry's musk amongst the stink of ammonia, the cool of the plastic sheeting sucked away some of the fever in her brain. It was enough that her body was now moulded into the indentations that Henry had left. Her breathing slowed and a calmness gradually returned to her thoughts, and before too long she was deep into a dreamless sleep.

~

DOROTHY WAS STILL ALONE in the ward when she stirred, although at some point someone had been in and laid a blanket over her. Waking up for the second time felt much better. Rather than another slow crawl through the haze, she was already feeling more alert, aware of her surroundings, and she drew some fleeting comfort from the fact that normality was finally re-establishing itself. She had also woken up with a need for answers.

Crane was lurking in the first place that Dorothy checked – the day room. This was the hub of all activity in the Zoo, and where everybody tended to congregate when they had nothing better to do. The room was, for one thing, massive. It was always warm and brightly lit, with sunshine that poured in through a triptych of windows. This was where all the games and crafts were kept, and where you had to pass through to get to the smoking room, or if you wanted to go and watch the TV. Part destination, part thoroughfare, the day room always had a lively mix of patients and visitors, nurses and orderlies, all thrown together without clique or hierarchy.

Seated at one of the many tables in the craft area, Parsley was colouring a picture in a thick book of black-and-white drawings, surrounded by a jumble of crayons. Crane stood behind him, leaning over his shoulder and offering advice. 'Oops! There we go again,' he scolded. 'How hard can it be to keep a crayon on one side of a line? Why are you even bothering?'

Dorothy marched over and squeezed between the two men. She began to absent-mindedly stroke the hair on the back of Parsley's neck, triggering her friend into a rendition of some unknown melody while he continued with his task. She turned to address Crane.

'Do you know how to find my Aunt Ruby?' Dorothy demanded. 'Do you know how to find out how to get to her house?'

'Eh?' Crane replied, looking perplexed. 'Didn't you just see her yesterday?'

'I don't want to talk to her. I don't need to see her. I need to find something in her house.'

Crane raised his hands. 'Yeah – still don't get it, Doz. Start from the beginning.'

Dorothy released a huff of impatience before launching into the full story. 'I saw Dr Morgan this morning, and Dr West was there too, and they wanted to know if anyone in my family had killed themselves. I mean, not Aunt Ruby's family, obviously, but my proper family, and this is something only my father would know about. But Aunt Ruby knows where my father lives, and she doesn't want to tell me, but it's on a piece of paper in her house. And I know where to look. If someone did kill themselves, like people did in Henry's family, then I can't have any more of the Programme. Because that means I might kill myself too.'

The confusion remained etched on Crane's face as Dorothy laid out the flawless chain of logic that underpinned her request. 'So, you need to find your dad?' he asked when she was done. 'Or *you* might die as well?'

Crane's version was missing a lot of important detail, but it sounded like an accurate synopsis. 'Yeah. Exactly that,' Dorothy replied.

'OK. Good enough,' he announced. 'You know where your aunt lives?'

Dorothy nodded.

'It's by the sea, right?'

'Well, you can't see the sea. Not from her house,' Dorothy clarified. 'But you *can* walk to the beach. And sometimes you can hear the donkeys that live on the beach. When it's really late and really quiet.'

'Then how hard can it be?' responded Crane, a grin forming on his face. 'We just need to find the coast and follow it round. When do you want to go?'

'Tonight. We need to go tonight.'

Crane cocked an eyebrow and started to fidget with his

fingers. 'Tonight. OK. We might be able to make that work,' he mused uncertainly. 'So, you pick up your happy bag at eight-thirty, and if you're not on the list for a nightcap, then we should be able—'

'No!' Dorothy pointed a stern finger at Crane's face. 'No medicine! Not till we know. No meds for anyone until we know who we can trust.'

A look of realisation dawned on Crane's face. 'Oh yeah. From breakfast! You think I'm right, don't you?' His grin broadened even further and his hand movements became more animated. 'Yeah! OK! Let's do this! No meds, just the mission. They'd only get in the way anyway.'

'Just the mission,' agreed Dorothy solemnly. The objective was established, and now all that was missing was the plan and the players. Crane was obviously in charge of doing the thinking, so while he was working on that she needed to drum up the rest of the party. Dorothy leant forward and whispered into Parsley's ear, turning up the music. The behemoth continued to stare down at his colouring book, an inscrutable expression locked on his face, but when Dorothy was done he dropped his crayon and started to stand up. Dorothy gently pressed him back into his seat and rubbed the top of his head, before spinning around and marching off towards the entrance. She was surprised when she saw Crane hustling after her.

'Where are we off to?' he demanded.

'I need to find Bill,' Dorothy replied. 'To ask him too.'

'Whoa! Easy now!' Crane exclaimed, shuffling in front of Dorothy and stopping her in her tracks. He glanced around the room suspiciously before grabbing the girl by the elbow and leading her over to the window, away from prying ears. 'This is our secret, OK?' he whispered gravely. 'If we get caught before we manage to get away, we are in some serious shit. This is need-to-know only, and Snatcher ain't on the list.' A whine crept into his tone. 'Besides, he's just gonna want to stop us. Get in the way. You know what he's like.' Crane broke into a poor impression of his companion. 'I rather supplicate and enunciate that this activity is contrary to the regulations of the Almighty Lord Jesus. Fuck him.'

'But Bill will want to come,' insisted Dorothy, at a less guarded volume. 'And I want him to come with us.'

'Yeah, but think of all the people who'll want to *stop* us,' Crane explained. 'We don't know which way the Snatch is going to swing, and he's got plenty of opportunity to kill this whole thing dead if he wants to. See what I'm saying? Besides, we've got more important things to do. We don't even know how we're going to get there yet.'

This revelation took Dorothy aback. She had assumed that Crane would have already figured out this fairly important detail. But she had to admit that he was probably right about Bill. This didn't sound like the kind of undertaking that Thatcher would be comfortable with, even though she knew she'd be less likely to run into trouble with him in the party. Dorothy turned away to gaze through the wire squares of the window, searching idly for inspiration in a view that never failed to underwhelm. Even on a bright summer day, it was a challenge to spot anything outside that wasn't coloured some flavour of grey – from the ashen tones of the concrete building opposite, to the darker almost-blacks of the multi-storey car park behind it that blocked out any glimpse of the city beyond. And on a cloudy day like today, all these shades were compressed into one tedious eyesore. Only an additional splash of granite-grey from the disabled parking spaces offered anything unusual against the familiar backdrop of drab. Dorothy found herself staring into the malevolent squinting eyes above the enormous moustache on the front of Dr West's Lexus. Somewhere, a penny dropped. She pirouetted back to

Crane with a quizzical look on her face. 'Can you drive? Drive a car?'

~

WITH THE DECISION TAKEN, Dorothy and Crane went quietly about their separate business, agreeing that it would be better if they weren't seen together. Crane had an assignment that involved a theft from the hospital stores, and it would be best if Dorothy didn't know any of the nasty details. Instead, her job was to act as lookout by the downstairs reception area and the nurses' break room, to keep a keen eye on all the comings and goings. This was going to be their way out of the building, and for the plan to work it was imperative for them to know the exact moment that West left the premises. In any case, Crane didn't want Dorothy wandering around the place, trying to pretend that everything was normal.

Dorothy found herself a seat on a small row of chairs in one of the lime-green corridors that led into the reception area. With the intervening fire door wedged open, she had a pretty clear view of everyone that came and went through the main entrance to the department. Peering over the top of an open magazine, she kept a solitary vigil throughout the afternoon without reading a single sentence. Even though most of the fog had cleared from her head, she was still having some difficulty concentrating on anything, with random memories of Henry flocking to fill the vacuum whenever she allowed her thoughts to drift. At moments when she was in danger of becoming too sentimental, she would remind herself that she had a job to do, and force her focus back to the here and now. And every so often she just burst into tears for a few minutes.

After a couple of hours, Morgan and West finally appeared, strolling through to the reception area. Dorothy clutched her magazine, trying to look as nonchalant as she could, while the two doctors were buzzed through the front entrance. If Henry's death hadn't thrown them off their routine, they would now be on their way to the Hospital Staff Sports and Social Club. The door slammed shut behind them, and Dorothy leapt to her feet. The plan was now in action.

The apparently unlimited size of Dr West's expense account was the subject of much overheard discussion amongst the nurses and orderlies in City Green. If you were lucky enough to bump into Dr West in the Staff Club, so the chitchat went, she would practically insist on buying you drinks, and sometimes dinner too if it was the right time of day. This had developed into such a well-known scam that on the every-other-Tuesdays when West visited the hospital to check on the patients in the Programme, a group of younger nurses and orderlies would purposefully coordinate their shifts to give them a full evening of boozing on Almiratech's dime. And even though he didn't appear to be a particularly talented drinker, the rumoured worst offender was Dr Morgan.

With the two doctors safely out of the Zoo, Dorothy sprinted back to Poppy ward to grab her jacket, then went looking for her friend. Eventually she found Crane keeping a low profile in the TV room, his jacket laid tidily across his lap alongside a stuffed plastic bag that stank of cigarette smoke. Exchanging only covert nods, they moved with resolve towards the reception area and the door to the outside world.

At this stage in the plan, Dorothy's main task was to stand around and look glum, primarily for the benefit of the duty nurse behind the desk. As they approached the reception area, Crane placed a compassionate hand on Dorothy's shoulder and gazed at her forlorn expression. He shook his head wistfully and nudged her towards the entrance, calling over towards the reception, 'Yo, Janice! Door, please?'

Although in theory the front desk could be staffed by any one of the nurses on duty, whenever Janice was working a shift in City Green she usually ended up behind the counter. While not technically obese, Janice was certainly more than big-boned. She had a strangely undeveloped walking style that looked to be as painful as it was inefficient, and so even when she wasn't working on reception she could normally be found sitting down somewhere else anyway. Her round face was always framed by perfect hair, to which she would obsessively attend whenever she had a free moment. Whenever they happened to be passing, Crane would usually take a couple of minutes to engage the nurse in some cheeky but respectful banter; in private, however, he would marvel at why she didn't invest some of the money that she haemorrhaged to her hairdresser on a gym membership.

When the buzzer from the door latch failed to sound as they approached, Dorothy wasn't sure whether Nurse Janice had an actual reason to deny them passage or whether she was just expecting some friendly chat first. Behind the desk, Janice looked up and raised her suspicious, albeit flawlessly threaded, eyebrows at Crane. Leaving Dorothy to concentrate on looking morose by the entrance, he marched across to the duty nurse. 'Jesus, Janice! Come on! I'm not even on a section!'

Without dropping her distrustful expression, Janice nodded towards Dorothy.

'Really?' Crane demanded, sounding like he might actually be offended. 'You heard about what happened, didn't you? I just want to take Dozza outside, help her get her mind off this place for a jiffy. You know – breathe some air that hasn't been farted out of a nutter's arsehole.' He broke out his most charming gurn. 'Twenty fucking minutes? Come on!'

After considering Crane's request for a moment, Janice

capitulated with a gentle shake of her head. 'Twenty fucking minutes, Mr Crane,' she asserted. 'Don't make me regret this.'

Dorothy heard the door latch release. She glanced up from her despondency, but Crane was already bustling her through the exit and out into the freedom of a cloudy afternoon.

As she and Crane hurried away from the Zoo, their escape was interrupted by a loud crash. The front door had been bulldozed open again, slamming into the metal doorstop. Behind it, Parsley thundered out of the building with all the subtlety of a temper tantrum before shuffling over to Dorothy and quietly tagging himself onto the party. She nodded a friendly welcome, although his presence was evidently not part of Crane's plan. He glared at the behemoth in disbelief. 'What the hell are you doing?' he hissed. 'Go on! Fuck off back inside!'

Parsley glowered nonchalantly.

'Look – Dorothy will be five minutes. Just five minutes. Go back inside and she'll come find you later. You can't come with us. You. Can't. Come.' When this also failed to penetrate Parsley's indifference, Crane gave up and turned to Dorothy. 'Doz? Have a word with him, please.'

The girl shrugged, slightly perplexed by Crane's outburst. 'Parsley's going to come with us. I asked him earlier, remember? Why are you saying he can't?' It seemed unfathomable that Crane would even consider embarking on an adventure like this without the security that Parsley offered. And their friend could always be counted on for his discretion, despite Crane's concerns about word leaking out ahead of time. She reached up to stroke Parsley's close-cropped beard. 'He'll be fine,' she reiterated as the music started.

'But ... look at him!' Crane persisted. 'He sticks out like a hard-on in a girls' school!' The whine had found its way back into his voice. Dorothy stared back at him, starting to feel annoyed by his reaction. The mission was already under way, and now they were just wasting time. Parsley's humming filled the gap where a discussion should have been, until Crane finally relented. 'Right. Fine. But he's your responsibility, OK? It's your job to stop him doing anything stupid.' He directed his gaze towards the Staff Club building. 'We need to get a shift on, or we're not going anywhere.'

On the short walk past the research labs and storage facilities, Crane passed Dorothy one of the two long-sleeved grey T-shirts that he had procured from the Zoo's laundry station, and which he'd smuggled out in his plastic bag. Dorothy pulled the uniform on over her T-shirt, enveloping her with the stench of old cigarette smoke and body odour. She wasn't sure why her co-conspirator had stolen their disguises from the pile of dirty clothes by the entrance to the laundry, rather than just grabbing a clean set from the racks on the other side of the room, but by the time they arrived at the City Green Hospital Trust Staff Sports and Social Club building she almost felt like a proper orderly.

At the point where they got inside the Staff Club, the details of Crane's plan became slightly more nebulous. Having no idea what the inside of the building looked like, Crane had limited the scope of their objective to 'Find West, wait till she lets her guard down, then nick her keys'. Dorothy had imagined tiptoeing into a crowded room to surreptitiously snatch West's jacket from the back of her chair while the doctor was preoccupied by showering everyone with cash. Instead, they were immediately greeted by yet another receptionist.

This one was even younger than Dorothy, and she had more important things to attend to on her phone. With a gasp Dorothy froze in her tracks, stalled by a crippling sense of dread. They hadn't even made it two hundred yards from the Zoo, and they'd already hit an obstacle for which they weren't prepared. She braced herself for the possibility that she might be forced to turn and run at any minute. Without a word, Crane broke away from his two companions and cautiously approached the reception counter. Behind Dorothy, the reassuring bulk of Parsley blocked her way back to the Zoo. She clutched his hand while she waited for the receptionist to demand an explanation, but the young woman didn't break eye contact with her screen. Crane shot a glance towards his friends and embarked on his spiel anyway. 'Hi. Er ... good evening? We're just taking Dr ... um ... Parcel down to see the sports?' He left the question hanging in the air, but still the young woman refused to welcome him inside. 'Maybe then get a cup of tea?' he added hesitantly.

After an excruciating pause, the young woman cackled at something on her phone screen, and her thumbs burst into a flurry of activity. Crane took a step backwards and gave a discreet gesture with his fingers for the others to follow him. Dorothy exhaled – it looked like her friend had done enough to be granted permission to enter. Crane signed off with, 'So ... OK then,' and they scuttled inside before the receptionist could change her mind.

From outside, the single-storey Staff Club building didn't look like it would be large enough to hide anyone for too long. However, what wasn't apparent were the multiple underground levels that made up the Sports element of the Sports and Social Club. The ground floor comprised a lively coffee shop and bar area, a formal dining room and an open-air courtyard full of smokers in between. When it became clear that Morgan and West were neither drinking nor dining, the party were forced back into the reception area to deal with the square stairwell that burrowed down into the bunker.

Together they descended into the buried labyrinth, leaving the boisterous chatter and the rattle of crockery behind, creeping into a sterile world lit only by fluorescent tubes. A cloying odour hung in the air from over-stimulated bodies and muscle relaxant. From the first landing, Dorothy could see that the sports facilities stretched out way beyond the footprint of the building above in at least two directions. There were plenty of places to hide down here, and she wasn't even sure how many other floors they had to check. She fought back a twinge of discouragement at the size of the task ahead. In a very real sense, her life depended on the outcome of their quest, but they weren't going anywhere if they couldn't find West. For the second time in as many minutes, she had been reminded about the fragile foundations upon which their plans had been built. She fell into step behind Crane as he crept along the main corridor, the sound of their footsteps concealed beneath the distant metallic clang of weights colliding and the splatter of squash balls.

As it turned out, Drs Morgan and West proved easier to find than she had feared. Sticking her head into a room marked *Male Sauna,* Dorothy's attention was immediately drawn to a branded Almiratech sports bag on the slatted wooden bench. While West wasn't exactly shy about handing out company freebies, the collection of bras and hair straighteners that poked out of the open compartment warranted further investigation.

After Crane assigned Parsley to lookout duty in the corridor, he and Dorothy tiptoed into the cramped changing area. The behemoth stomped in behind them anyway. West's skirt suit hung from a hook above the bag, and Crane immediately started to riffle through the pockets. Dorothy, however, found herself distracted by a circular window offering a view through a wooden door on the far side of the room. Although she couldn't see what was going on, it looked like it might actually be raining on the other side, as drops of water tracked each other across the glass. She inched over to steal a glimpse through the window at the weather beyond.

The wooden room on the other side was inadequately lit by a series of dull orange bulbs cast into a two-tiered bench, and a red glow from coals on a fireplace. On one side, West sat naked on a towel, waving her hands about in animated explanation as part of some unheard conversation. Opposite her, Dr Morgan was listening intently, leaning forward uncomfortably with his chin resting in the palm of his hand, a towel tightly wrapped around his waist. Dorothy stared, bemused, at the couple for as long as she dared, struggling to fathom out what on earth was going on, before finally muttering, 'They're ... melting.'

Her trance was broken by Crane. 'Doz!' he called across the changing room in a loud whisper. 'Dozza! I got 'em. Let's go!'

Snapping back to the mission at hand, she spun around to see her friend waving a set of car keys and a purse at her, and gesturing frantically towards the exit. Their job here was done, and so far everything was going like clockwork.

∼

THE PLAN, however, met another unexpected interruption as they walked along the road back towards the Zoo. Emerging from the evening shadows, Thatcher was practically invisible in his long black coat until he was so close that Dorothy could make out the look of relief on his face. With a wave he bounded up to join the other three, calling out, 'Where have you all been hiding? Nurse Banks asked me to come and find you before she gets into trouble.' His cheer lasted until he spied the crumpled orderlies' uniforms in Crane's and Dorothy's hands. 'Wait a minute,' he demanded, suddenly a different kind of concerned. 'What are you doing?'

Crane pulled the grey T-shirt from Dorothy's grip and

dumped all the stolen clothing into Thatcher's arms. 'Be a good boy,' he implored. 'Take these back, would you? And maybe mind your own fucking business while you go about it?'

He brushed past Thatcher with a look of contempt, who instead turned to Dorothy for answers. 'Dorothy? Can you please tell me what's going on?'

Trailing closely behind Crane, Dorothy felt that she owed Thatcher slightly more information than her friend was offering. 'We did talk about you,' she called back over her shoulder. 'But we didn't think you'd want to get involved.'

'Involved with what?' Thatcher pressed nervously, hurrying after the young girl.

'Well,' Dorothy started. 'It was after I went to see Dr Morgan this morning...'

Her explanation was cut short when she was barged aside by an impatient Crane, who inserted himself between Dorothy and Thatcher. 'Look! The lady said you're not involved, so why don't you just go back to the Zoo and let Janice know you haven't seen us, eh? We'll tell you all about it later, if you can promise to stop being a twat.'

Thatcher stretched out his tall frame and leant forward to address the girl again from above. 'Dorothy, I would be grateful if you could let me know what's going on. Please? I have a funny feeling that whatever this is, it might not be a good idea.'

This time it was Crane's turn to petition Dorothy. 'I told you!' he said. 'I told you he'd only try and stop us! Just tell him he can't come!'

'Come where?' demanded Thatcher. 'What has Crane got you involved in?'

'He's slowing us down...' chided Crane.

There were no quick exits from this conversation, and Dorothy kicked herself for not seeking out her friend earlier and explaining everything when they weren't in such a hurry.

Now she had no choice but to start at the beginning, despite the fact that the Zoo was already sending people out to look for her. She opened her mouth, but Thatcher cut her off before she had a chance to say anything. 'Whatever's going on, Dorothy, do you really believe you'd be better off in the sole charge of this ... *sociopath*?'

'A *what*?' Crane spluttered, squaring up to Thatcher. 'I'll fucking sociopath you, you pissing cock-holster!'

'I'm very sorry you feel that way, Mr Crane, but I have a legitimate concern that you might not be acting in Dorothy's best interests.'

'And I have a legitimate concern about you tucking into the contents of my bollocks!'

Effectively sidelined by her two friends, Dorothy felt her frustration building. This was so obviously not the right moment for this debate. If she didn't step in quickly, no one was going anywhere. 'We haven't got time for this!' she announced to the bickering couple, not even trying to hide the desperation in her voice. 'We can't wait around until you've had your fight!' Crane shot a smug smile up at Thatcher, but Dorothy wasn't finished. She gazed earnestly at her tall friend. 'Are you going to do what I ask you to do? Whatever I ask?'

'No fucking way!' Crane hollered, his smirk vanishing as he spun around to confront the girl. 'He's not coming! End of!'

'We don't have enough time to figure this out properly,' Dorothy explained carefully, before turning back to Thatcher. 'Whatever I ask you to do?'

Thatcher shrugged and nodded. 'Of course. Now can someone please tell me what's going on?'

'Swear to do it, then. Swear it to God,' Dorothy insisted.

Her friend raised his right hand to his shoulder. 'My solemn oath,' he pledged to Dorothy, who continued to stare at him, her eyebrows raised expectantly. 'Yes, I swear it to God,' he finally conceded, leaving himself no wriggle room or scope for misunderstanding. 'I promise. Anything you ask me.'

'Why are you letting him come?' Crane intervened. 'He's going to spoil everything!'

'To help,' Dorothy said. 'To help with the plan. Come on!' With that, she hurried off in the direction of the Zoo, turning her back on Thatcher's disquiet and Crane's whining. Following closely behind her, Parsley barged his way between the two antagonists, who in turn fell into step at the rear of the party.

There would be a better opportunity to fill Thatcher in on the details of the plan, Dorothy recognised that, and no doubt he would then have plenty of suggestions that Crane would shoot down on principle. But not now. Not until they were away from the Zoo and far from the uncertain agenda of her jailers. Behind her, the squabbling continued.

'I rather expect you have some explaining to do,' Thatcher declared, already sounding more relaxed.

'Fuck off,' Crane answered gruffly.

'Just what have you set in motion, Mr Crane?' the other man pressed. 'You'll have to tell me sooner or later. Do I need to go and collect my meds?'

'No. No pills, no medicine. Dorothy's first rule.'

'Well, how long are we going to be, then?' Thatcher persisted. 'I will have to go and grab my pills at some point. Are we going to be out more than an hour?'

'Your shout, douche-boy,' Crane muttered. 'Go back to the ward. Fine with me. I didn't make the law.'

'You are being deliberately evasive, Mr Crane,' Thatcher admonished good-naturedly. 'Maybe I'll have more success if I seek an explanation from Dorothy.'

'Fine,' sulked Crane. 'She's the only one that knows where the car is anyway.'

From somewhere behind her, Dorothy heard a pair of shoes scuff noisily to a halt on the tarmac. She twisted around to see what the delay was this time. At the back of the group, Thatcher had stopped dead in his tracks and was clutching his rosary necklace, the blood draining from his face. '*Car?*' he croaked.

WEDNESDAY, 18TH AUGUST

No Place Like Home

*S*played out under the dishevelled sheets and blankets that covered her bed, and adrift amongst the debris of eleven other women, Dorothy's eyes flicked open.

And when Dorothy's eyes opened in the mornings, she was definitely awake. Aware and alert, energetic and enthused. Primed for whatever that day had planned for her. This was how it always used to be when she was a child, but it was a skill she had only rediscovered over the past few months.

Of course, in her younger days she would waken in a state of high anxiety: a pervasive dread that could take advantage of the tiniest cracks in her sleeping cycle and quickly fill them with the worries of a day to come. In those days, she would have to sneak out of the house when everyone else was asleep and go walking – to try and fill her brain up with an ever-expanding scheme of the roads and estates around where she grew up, to exhaust her and distract her until she had no choice but to pass out instead of dwelling on the future.

But these days she could ride over the bumps in her sleep

patterns. If she woke up, and it wasn't time to be awake, she would just turn over with a smile and fall back under without a misgiving. But if it was time to be awake, she was all in.

Around her, she could hear the rest of Poppy ward stirring. Conspiratorial whispering between roommates, footsteps slapping against the floor tiles, traumatised moans from Glinda on the far side of the room. Fresh laughter and old arguments. With a frisson of anticipation at the possibilities of the new day, Dorothy sat up and expertly disconnected herself from the half-full drip bag that ran down to the cannula in her arm.

A bright square of daylight forced its way around the edges of the pull-down blind, with the promise of cloudless skies beyond. Today, Dorothy would celebrate the tenacity of summer by wearing her rainbow-coloured leggings and the softest T-shirt she could find in her pile of clean clothes. Failing that, there was always the larger pile of not-quite-dirty-enough-yet clothes, which would almost certainly yield results. Climbing out of the City Green nightgown, she rummaged through the jumble on top of her bedside cabinet for items of underwear before turning to the collection of clothing strewn across her bed and hanging from the metal frame.

Wednesdays were always fun. Wednesdays brought with them a sense of the unexpected, and opportunities for adventures that other days just couldn't match. But before she could begin this particular Wednesday, she had to go and find Henry.

∽

THE STENCH in Appletree ward was especially ripe that morning, and Dorothy could already imagine the orderlies bickering about whose turn it was to deal with the mess. Once upon a time the smell had made her physically retch, although only when she stopped to think about what she was actually inhaling. Henry had once reminded her that he had to spend every night in the company of such unpleasant odours, and he reckoned his lungs must have a permanent patina of other people's shit and piss spread over their internal surfaces. Just the thought of Henry being forced to breathe in poo had made Dorothy laugh so hard that she inadvertently released a little urine into her trousers. The thought that everyone now had to inhale her piss as well had made her laugh harder still, until she found she had emptied her entire bladder onto Henry's bed.

Although Appletree ward was already buzzing with activity and conversation, there were always a couple of occupants who resisted the daily call to arms in favour of a more gradual transition to consciousness. Underneath a crude wire disc and an arrangement of dead pigeon feathers, Henry's blond curls poked out from beneath his blankets as he clung vainly to the last throes of slumber. Dorothy bounded over to him, past naked Mervyn as he stumbled around the room in a frightened haze, stepping over Noah's prone form while he searched the floor for something really small, and stopping across the way from big Bill Thatcher, who must have just returned from a jog, as he was hunched over a chair wiping beads of sweat from his red face with an old T-shirt. Without slowing down, she vaulted across the line of bizarre *objets d'art* that hung from the end of Henry's metal bed frame and staggered up the bed on her knees until she straddled his sleeping form.

'It's the morning!' she sang.

Beneath her, Henry's head slowly twisted around, his dormant face emerging from underneath the tight curls and covers. One eye cracked open to register the scene above. 'Christ, girl!' he berated her sluggishly. 'It's the middle of the fucking night...'

'It's 7:30!' Dorothy continued, impervious to his censure. 'Up time!'

Henry sat bolt upright in his bed, aghast. 'What?' he demanded desperately. 'Already? Why didn't you say something sooner?' His shocked expression collapsed beneath a massive beaming smile. 'It's the middle of the fucking morning!' His tongue pounced from his mouth to gently flick the tip of Dorothy's nose. She squealed in delight and returned fire, and before too long the couple were taking turns to trade affectionate licks. Eventually, Henry withdrew from the fray and dabbed his nose dry on a lock of Dorothy's hair before adopting his stern look again. 'Shame on you! Keeping me waiting like that, Princess,' he reprimanded her fondly.

In the Zoo, no one really talked about their age, so while Dorothy knew that Henry was a bit older than she was, she wasn't really sure by how much. That said, he wasn't close to being as old as Thatcher (who was practically ancient), and he was probably even younger than Crane. What made it hard to know for sure was Henry's inability to grow any facial hair thicker than gossamer: that, and his relentless efforts to avoid doing anything that might resemble adult behaviour. He was on a permanent quest to find the humour in everything. Although this made him a hopeless liability during group therapy sessions, his jovial outlook was so infectious that it helped defuse almost any problematic situation. While this made the counselling work of the doctors less productive, it certainly made it easier. A deep network of crow's feet stretched backwards from Henry's eyes – the inevitable price paid for a lifetime of laughing – until they were buried under his golden ringlets.

'Hey!' Thatcher called amiably from the opposite berth. 'Knock it off, you two.'

Having mopped up most of his perspiration, Thatcher was

sat on the end of his bed, wrestling with his trainers. Every day he went running in the same tracksuit, regardless of the temperature outside, and it was now so old and ragged that it looked like it might have been bought for him while he was still a school boy. With his long grey hair flopping over his crimson face in a hot, sticky mess, his morning jog was not the best opportunity for vanity anyway. He did, however, get through running shoes pretty quickly – his current pair were absolutely filthy beneath layers of spattered mud, in sharp contrast with the pristine white trainers that adorned Dorothy's feet.

Dorothy turned back to her boyfriend. 'Who's the sweaty man?' she demanded loudly. 'That sweaty old man over there?'

'Hopeless case, I'm afraid,' Henry confided with a shake of his head. 'Completely institutionalised. I only hope he doesn't bring everyone else down.'

With a satisfied groan, Thatcher prised a trainer from one of his gargantuan feet. When the trapped odour wafted its way across the aisle, Henry's eyes bulged in horror. He leant past Dorothy to address his roommate directly, with a look of disbelief that almost bordered on respect. 'Dude!' he exclaimed. 'Is that you? Did a mouse drag something dead into your shoe? And then die in there as well? And then shit itself for good measure?'

Thatcher raised the trainer to his face and took a playful sniff. 'Oh, it's really not that bad,' he countered, before offering it over. 'Maybe you just need to savour it up close?'

'If you bring that any closer, I'm gonna scream "rape",' Henry retorted.

With a smile, Thatcher dropped the offending trainer to the floor and made a start on his other foot. 'Well, I would certainly counsel against doing that,' he said. 'Just imagine what kind of reprobate you might be saddled with as a neighbour were I to be forced to—'

His sentence was cut short by a pillow hitting him on the side of his face, flung with genuine animosity by the occupant of the next bed along. With his head tightly wrapped beneath a second pillow, Crane's muffled voice interrupted their exchange. 'For fuck's sake! Just shut up and let me get some sleep!'

'Wow!' remarked Henry with a grin. 'Who shoved that stick up your arse this morning? You're not even out of the wrong side of bed yet.'

Thatcher smiled, before turning his attention to Crane. 'And a very good morning to you, Mr Crane.' He smirked. 'Did you turn over onto your catheter again?'

Henry barked out a laugh. Taking a cue from her boyfriend, Dorothy also burst into a fit of chuckles. Apparently unhappy at being on the receiving end of the conversation, Crane sat up in bed with an angry expression on his face, which he directed towards Thatcher. 'No,' he answered, making no attempt to join in with the good-natured chatter. 'I'd be fine if you hadn't kept me awake all night lollypopping everyone's dicks while they were asleep.' He called across the room towards the petrified man, still naked and looking lost. 'Oi, Mervyn! Merv! Dry it off and put it away, would you? You're going to get the Snatcher going again.'

Although Mervyn chose to ignore his advice, the bubble of friendly banter had been popped. Thatcher shook his head sadly at his neighbour. 'Mr Crane,' he scolded. 'Why do you do that? Why do you feel this compulsion to aggravate?'

'Yeah? Well, why do you wake up every morning the same twat you were when you went to sleep?' Crane snapped.

A familiar disagreement was starting up, and Dorothy didn't really want to have to witness this particular instalment of their long-standing feud. As if reading her mind, Henry pulled an exaggerated expression of concern before whispering to her, 'Remember, we're here to observe only. Keep the interactions to a minimum. We don't want to alter the course of human history. And we certainly don't want to have to deal with all this silliness.'

In a single move, he swung his legs out from under the covers and stood up on the far side of the bed, next to the metal stand for his IV bag and his over-stocked bedside cabinet. For the first time that morning, Dorothy saw his left arm: rung after rung of healed scars stretched like a ladder up the inside of his forearm from a period of fastidious self-cutting, climbing towards his cannula implant. As her boyfriend started to pick through a pile of clothes, tidily folded and stacked on the chair next to his bed, Dorothy recognised a familiar chemical fragrance: part ammonia, part burning plastic. It was the same smell she had to endure every day when she unclipped herself from her own IV.

Henry had been on the Programme for exactly the same length of time as Dorothy; in fact, the depth of their friendship was in no small part down to the hours they had been thrown together for all the associated group sessions. And, like Dorothy, every night Henry had to plumb himself up to a drip bag of clear fluid, covered in Almiratech logos and disclaimers and indecipherable handwritten scribbles. But somehow the tang of the Programme medication in that corner of Appletree ward seemed more intense, closer to a spill than a squirt. It had been like that all week. Dorothy wondered how Henry had suddenly got so bad at connecting the drip to the valve in his arm. That said, the smell was still preferable to the assault from Thatcher's trainers.

Having selected something to wear, Henry adopted his stern face again and drew a circle in the air with a finger, encouraging Dorothy to turn around and give him some privacy. She obliged with a giggle. As soon as her back was turned, Henry tugged at the plastic tubing that attached his arm to the hanging drip bag, which came free with disconcerting ease. The connector had been wedged under the cannula rather than hooked up to it – Henry was not taking his medicine, and he was going to some trouble to hide his subterfuge.

'Ooh la la – your multicoloured arse is bringing out the Frenchman in me today,' he called across to Dorothy's back as he dexterously swapped out his undergarments beneath his City Green nightshirt. 'I feel like kissing you on both cheeks.' He pulled on a pair of jeans. 'You'd have to promise not to blow me one back, though.' With a dramatic shuffle, Henry appeared fully clothed from underneath his nightwear, bounced across his unmade bed, and scooped Dorothy up over one shoulder. She shrieked delightedly and kicked her legs as if being carried off against her will, causing Henry to grin even harder. 'Princess!' he proclaimed to the buttock perched next to his ear. 'Stop your protestations! I'm here to rescue you from all this madness!' His deception complete, he hoisted the squealing girl out of Appletree ward, past his roommates and their variously chaotic starts to the day, and out to see what new adventures the Zoo had in store for them.

∽

BY THE TIME Dorothy had collected a big pile of buttered toast, the rest of her friends were sat at their usual table in the canteen, busy not talking to each other. It wasn't unusual to find Thatcher eating his breakfast in a sulk, but rarer were the mornings when Crane had also been rankled into silence. Some unfriendly words had clearly been exchanged. Parsley was installed between them, keeping his own counsel. Thankfully, Henry appeared to be happy to do most of the talking.

'And it all gets burned away at night,' he was explaining to the others. 'The trick is to figure out how to stay asleep for long enough. Crazy thing, sleep. Amazing. Way better than doctors or pills. Your brain packages up all the bad karma, sticks it in a dream, and then – get this – most of the time you *don't even remember* having that dream!'

'I like my pills,' Crane muttered into his cup of tea.

'No, you don't,' Henry reassured him. 'If you did, you wouldn't need to wake up so grumpy.'

'Fuck off,' Crane countered. 'I haven't seen you handing back your meds.'

'Ah, well, I'm a different case, you see. I'm doing it for science.' Henry tapped the side of his nose conspiratorially. 'I'm trying to mess with their stats.'

'Bullshit. You're shovelling the same shit as the rest of us,' Crane declared. 'Least I can fit my meds in my pocket. You're gonna have fun carrying a drip bag around for the rest of your life.' He launched into a passable impression of Henry's excitable babble. 'Oh, I'm sorry, do you mind if I just hang this up? I'm actually fucking insane, you realise?'

'Mr Crane, can you please be mindful of Dorothy?' Thatcher interjected, scowling. 'You need to think about how comments like that make her feel.'

Crane rolled his eyes, but Henry jumped back in before the other men could derail the conversation with another argument. 'Oh, no, no, no! You so don't get it – you don't understand how medical trials work, Señor Cranium. Some people get the shiny new medicine, so the scientists can measure all the side effects and figure out whether it's making them better or not. But half of the people get a bag full of water. Or something that looks like medicine. And that's me. I'm in the control group.' He was talking quickly, flapping his hands, shaking his empty mug. And the longer he went on, the more worried Dorothy was becoming. It wasn't even Henry's unusually fidgety delivery that was troubling her – she was more concerned with why her boyfriend hadn't told her his theories about the Programme earlier. If there was something wrong with their medication, or something that might get in the way of the future they had planned, she had a right to know.

'But that's OK,' Henry continued. 'Because I'm literally doing all the same things the Programme meds do, but just with loads of sleep. And then when Dr West comes down to count everyone at the end of the trial, they'll see that somehow I got better on my own without their medicine, and it's going to drive them mad trying to figure it out! *Skål!*' Henry raised his mug in a triumphant toast to himself, and took a long chug. He looked genuinely distressed to find it empty.

'Does that mean I'm on the fake medicine too?' Dorothy asked. 'It smells the same as yours.'

'No, I'm sure you're getting a taste of the good stuff,' Henry reassured her. 'They just make up the placebo medicine so it looks and smells exactly like the real one. If people figure out which group they're in, it can break the experiment. I mean, you feel different since the Programme started, right?'

Dorothy nodded suspiciously. 'Yeah. Don't you?'

Henry's face broke into a broad grin. 'Sure! Yeah – I feel loads different. But that's all down to you, Princess! That's not Almiratech. I've been given enough meds in my life to know how they make me feel. And I don't feel anything with the Programme. Not a thing. Nothing bad, no side effects, nothing particularly good either. I should be feeling really focused, or like I don't give a toss, or just jumbled up, maybe. Muddy.' He took another swig from his empty cup before carrying on. 'Anyway, I don't. I mean, I feel OK, most of the time, but I still feel bad when things go wrong. It hasn't made me any less sensitive. Hasn't stopped me from feeling unhappy. I've just got a better perspective, that's all. And it's entirely your fault, lady. I'm building my own positivity on my own terms. These bags of placebo are a distraction.' He smiled again at his audience.

Dorothy glanced around the table at her fellow diners for their reactions, but it didn't look like anyone else had been paying much attention. Thatcher was picking at his toast, still brooding over the insult that had been delivered before she'd sat down, and Crane always liked to look aloof and bored when he wasn't in charge of the conversation. Only Parsley seemed interested in what their friend had to say, even if this morning Henry was proving harder to follow than usual. And while Dorothy liked the idea that she was solely responsible for her boyfriend's improved mindset, anything that changed their narrative made her apprehensive. The Programme was an important part of the journey that she and Henry were on together, after all.

'How will you know?' she demanded. 'Can you go and ask Dr Morgan or Dr West, or do you have to wait till the end of the trial before you find out?'

'Just gonna keep getting the sleep, Princess. Deal with all my shit that way. Carry on feeling fine. There's nothing to say we have to stick with the Programme if it's not working.'

It didn't sound like a particularly satisfactory answer, and she turned again to her friends for a ruling.

'Sure. Whatever,' Crane replied dismissively, glancing up from his forced ennui. 'Take it to group therapy. I'm sure they'll have something to say.'

∾

Group discussions and counselling sessions were held one floor down and on the other side of the building. Within the Zoo, the place was referred to as the Old Theatre, but it was just another large multipurpose room – a bit like the day room, only quieter and darker. No one could remember the last time the space had been used for a performance of anything, although two heavy black curtains still hung from the ceiling on either side of a raised dais, gathering dust. Sitting in a semicircle in the centre of the room, Dorothy, Henry and the other five patients on the Programme leant in eagerly to join the discussion, caged on all sides by stacks of chairs and motivational posters.

Wednesday morning counselling sessions could be touch and go. Every other week, the hospital seemed to operate without most of the orderlies until sometime in the afternoon. The missing staff members could usually be found lying across a row of chairs at the back of the TV room, or sleeping on piles of laundry. It wasn't uncommon for Dr Morgan to roll in too hungover to properly conduct the meeting, and he seemed to have arrived in a fairly pliable state that particular morning. It only took a couple of targeted pleasantries to probe his temperance, and with this came the opportunity to steer the conversation off into more interesting directions before Morgan could start gathering feedback on the progress of the study.

'Did your date with that woman from the internet go OK?' Dorothy asked, pre-empting the ambush. 'The one on Saturday night?'

Dr Morgan's love life was at the very top of the list of diversionary debate topics, not least because it seemed as if the doctor had actually come to value the insights of the Programme participants. Helping to get Morgan paired off had become everyone's business, even if it was mainly to avoid being forced to pick away at their own issues three times a week.

'Oh!' Morgan replied, looking taken aback. 'Didn't I tell you about that?'

And so began the midweek discussions of the Almiratech Seven. On a good Wednesday (or on a bad one following a heavy Tuesday night), it was sometimes possible for the participants to hijack the whole two hours of the group session – a practice they would have felt less comfortable about pursuing if they didn't all believe that these meetings were a complete waste of their time. By this stage of the Programme they were all responsive, calm, considered, and Dr Morgan's blueprint of revisiting traumatic events from their pasts just felt embarrassing, as if they were telling tales about people they no longer recognised. Since emerging from his introverted shell at the start of the Programme, Henry had risen to become their de facto spokesperson, but today he seemed strangely terse, in sharp contrast to his animated lecture at the breakfast table. He and Dorothy sat in the middle of the pack holding hands, although his annoying flapping had yet to taper off. Dorothy found herself crushing down quite hard on his twitching fingers whenever they threatened to become too spirited, but if she was hurting him he didn't show it. Today, Henry was letting the other patients have a go at coaxing information out of their physician.

'So, how did you leave it after dinner?' asked Nikko, a relatively new recruit to the Programme, known around the Zoo for his unfeasibly long arms.

'I'm not sure,' Morgan replied. 'We didn't really talk about it. I suppose I'll just have to call her and see whether she wants to meet up again.'

'Text!' came the cry from the patients.

'Yes – sorry! I'll text her later. Quite right.'

'Gotta keep it casual, boss,' Nikko added. 'Don't want to scare her off just yet.'

After a debate on the appropriate length of time to wait before contacting someone again following a semi-successful date, Morgan eventually attempted to drag the conversation back on track. He pulled off one of his pairs of glasses and cast a bloodshot gaze across his group as he set about cleaning the lenses with his shirt. 'So ... how is everyone else? Henry? We haven't heard much from you this morning.'

'Variable four, becoming southerly five to seven. Occasionally rough,' responded Henry defensively. 'Precipitation later.'

Dr Morgan stifled a laugh, but everyone else stared blankly at the young man, who threw up his arms and waved them wildly in the air. 'What?' he demanded. 'Stop looking at me like I'm not mad!'

Seated on the other side of Henry, Lizzie-the-twin snorted with mirth. She was slightly older than Dorothy, and had been billeted in the Zoo along with her identical twin sister, to whom she neither looked nor spoke. Although Henry had never given her cause to feel jealous, Dorothy always felt a stab of resentment whenever one of the freaky same-women cosied up too close to her boyfriend.

'Yeah – mad. Like you're not mad,' Lizzie interjected. 'Like the new girl in the day room yesterday. Fruit loopy.'

The Old Theatre burst into laughter, with the notable exception of Dr Morgan. Political incorrectness was another tactic frequently employed by the inmates to draw the doctor away from his insistence on painful introspection and, sure enough, he immediately adopted his most professional expression. 'You know very well that we don't use that kind of prejudicial language, Lizzie.'

'What's the issue, Doc?' her twin enquired innocently. 'I

saw her too. Properly batshit mental bananas. She one of yours?'

A young orderly struggled through the doors facing the semi-circle of tittering attendees and quietly shuffled towards the group, emerging from stage left to approach Dr Morgan from behind. The doctor looked up to address his sniggering patients with a conspiratorial grin. 'I admitted her, yes. We generally find it works best if we let the loonies in.'

A wave of unexpected laughter almost buried Dorothy's next question. 'But she'll get better?' she asked. 'Is she going to come on the Programme?'

'She's the wrong kind of batshit mental bananas, I'm afraid,' Morgan answered, giving a twisted smile, before some sixth sense prompted him to glance over his shoulder. When he found himself staring directly into the grey midriff of the swaying orderly, who stood only a couple of feet away, the doctor's smirk vanished. Hilarity consumed the rest of the room. Only the orderly fought to maintain a straight face as Morgan tried to backtrack. 'No, actually ... you see, I didn't mean...'

'Just to let Dorothy know her aunt is here,' the orderly reported. 'Day room.'

'Oh, OK!' Dorothy replied. 'She's here today. Thanks.'

Dr Morgan extended the man a curt nod and returned to his giggling charges. Listening to the orderly's thundering footsteps as he exited the Old Theatre made Dorothy wonder how he'd managed to sneak up on the doctor in the first place. Dr Morgan clamped down on the bridge of his nose while he waited for the laughing to stop, composing himself for the final push. 'Right. Well. Thank you. Thank you all for the heads-up,' he said amiably. 'Anyway, unless anyone needs anything, we can probably just close the session. Before I say something even more inappropriate.' Without waiting for an answer, he began to stand up.

Henry cut him off. 'Yeah. Doc? I've got a question for you. Mainly for you. Or, for everyone, really.'

The doctor relaxed onto his chair again and gestured for Henry to continue.

'OK. Cool. Thanks. Cool. So, I suppose all I want to know is how would we know ... how could we tell if the medicine wasn't doing anything?'

'I'm sorry, Henry, I'm not sure I understand,' Dr Morgan replied uncertainly. 'Are you saying that your medication isn't working for you?'

Henry threw up his wobbly hands to ward off his doctor's concerns. 'No, I feel great. I feel fine,' he declared. 'Super fine. Really. I just wondered whether it was actually the drugs that were making us better. How would you know that? How could you tell? I mean, what if we're just getting better on our own? From being here? Being with each other? Talking about stuff. Hanging out. What if that was the real reason?'

Dr Morgan beamed with unconcealed pride. 'Absolutely, Henry! You're completely right! The Programme is so much more than just the medicine in the IV bags. It's also these group sessions, it's our one-on-ones. It's all of you supporting each other. And I know you do support each other – thank you, every one of you. As for how much the medicine itself is contributing – well, we won't actually know until the end of the trial. When they get all the results in from the other hospitals too.' The enthusiasm on his face suddenly switched to puzzlement. 'Sorry ... why did you ask that?'

'No reason, Doc. Just wondering. Just curious,' Henry reassured him. 'Nothing wrong with curiosity. Unless you're a cat, I guess.'

'No, I suppose not.' Dr Morgan sounded hesitant.

There must have been something in Henry's question that sat uneasily with their doctor, something that left him looking slightly rattled. Dr Morgan scanned the receptive faces of his patients before leaning forward to address the group. 'Listen, everyone,' he announced. 'I know I don't say it enough, but ... well, I'm blown away. I'm so proud of you all, how everybody is reacting to the Programme. These are important times, and I hope you all realise that you're playing crucial roles in something that could turn out to be really meaningful.' His voice cracked, and Dorothy wondered whether he'd be able to make it to the end of the session without shedding a tear. He continued, 'So, I just wanted to say ... thank you! Thank you all for being better.'

Dr Morgan stood up with a heartfelt smile on his face, and let his appreciation wash across his charges. He nodded at them one last time before shuffling off to his darkened office. One by one the patients exited the Old Theatre until only Dorothy and Henry remained, still holding hands, still basking in the afterglow of their doctor's praise.

'Do you want to go? Go back upstairs?' Dorothy asked, when it became clear that Henry wasn't in a hurry to head anywhere else.

Her boyfriend turned towards her, glowing with an indeterminate aura. He opened his mouth and roared a drawn-out 'Miaow' that reverberated around the room.

If Henry was being funny today, it wasn't in the way he normally was, and Dorothy felt a little annoyed with herself for not getting the joke. He had, however, calmed down considerably since the beginning of the group therapy session, and that was a promising sign. She stood up and pulled on Henry's hand, attempting to coerce him onto his feet. 'My aunt is here,' she explained. 'Do you want to come and talk to my Aunt Ruby?'

But Henry stayed seated, shaking his head in small twitches. 'No. Nope. Thank you, no,' he murmured decisively. 'I think they're coming back. I better go and listen to what they have to say.'

'Who? Talk to who?'

'You know: old friends, family...' Henry tailed off, looking distracted. It didn't sound like he was trying to be funny, and Dorothy was struggling to keep up with his strange logic. Her boyfriend picked up his thread again, addressing no one in particular. 'Some of them aren't here. I mean, I know they're not here. Some of them are already dead. Some of them aren't even using their own faces.' A glimpse of paralysing anguish surfaced before he caught himself and fixed his unconvincing grin back in place.

'You want to go and talk with *dead* people?' Dorothy demanded, incredulous. 'Really dead people?'

Henry's gaze drifted off again. Dorothy imagined that he was busy thinking up an amusing response to her ridiculous question, but it soon became clear that he was already preoccupied with something else entirely.

'Henry?' she interrupted. 'Are you talking to a dead person right now?'

Her boyfriend gave her an encouraging half-smile. 'Lunchtime,' he promised. 'Later. Go find your aunt.' He raised her hand to his lips and brushed a light kiss over her knuckles before pressing a nostril onto her wrist and riding it all the way up to her elbow. Where Henry would normally have rounded off such childish behaviour with a bout of contagious hysterics, today he simply rose from his chair and sauntered across the Old Theatre towards the door, leaving Dorothy alone and perturbed, and with a thin trail of snot stretching up her forearm.

THE ZOO

~

UNTAMED SUNSHINE FLOODED in through the three big windows in the day room, bathing the space in a lustrous silver glow that brought inspiration and optimism into the Zoo. Although the room was busy, Ruby had found herself a spot off to one side, where she was smiling nervously and doing her best to avoid making eye contact with patients and staff members alike.

Seeing her aunt still triggered an attack of butterflies, even after all this time, despite the fact that Dorothy was actually quite looking forward to catching up with her. She tried to cast her mind back to when Ruby had last visited. It had been a few months, certainly. It might even have been before the start of the Programme. Although there had been a time when Dorothy would have liked nothing better than to never see her former foster-parent again, ever since she had moved into the Zoo there had been a dramatic improvement in her aunt's attitude. Freed from the responsibility for raising Dorothy into a functional and happy member of society, Ruby had relaxed almost overnight, giving both women the chance to reappraise their relationship. Over the years this had matured into an unconventional friendship that neither of them had expected. Dorothy bounded over to Ruby, calling out her name, and the older woman stood up to welcome her. She wrapped her aunt in an enormous hug.

After allowing herself to be enveloped, Ruby gently pushed Dorothy backwards and into her own space. 'Hello, my lover!' she effused. 'Let me have a little look at you!' She clutched Dorothy's shoulders and held her at arm's length while she cast her gaze up and down, before delivering her verdict. 'Plum! Proper plum, my dear!'

'I am proper plum, Auntie. Proper plum!'

Ruby steered the girl towards a nearby seat. 'Well, it's a fine treat for us all to see you so full of bounce, my lovely,' she said. 'Why don't you take a moment and tell your Aunt Ruby all about it? Let me know how those brain bugs are getting on.'

'They're gone!' Dorothy proclaimed excitedly. 'Maybe even since I last saw you. I got better!'

'Well, that's just marvellous!' gushed Ruby as she relaxed back into her chair. 'And they've put a lick of paint in here since my last visit as well.'

Dorothy leant forward in her seat. She had a whole speech ready to unload on her aunt, one half of a conversation that she had been practising by herself. She was not about to let it be waylaid by a discussion on the room's decor. 'No, I am better. Really,' she explained earnestly. 'Dr Morgan thinks we're all getting better, all of us on the Programme.'

Ruby reached over and laid a hand on top of Dorothy's, patting it affectionately. The girl immediately pulled her arm away, irked. Her aunt never listened to her when she had something important to say. Dorothy continued, 'And Dr Morgan says if I stay OK, then they're going to think about letting me go. I can leave the Zoo! They want to put me in a community hostel to start with.' A frown appeared across Ruby's brow, but Dorothy persevered with her prepared rhetoric. 'But I'll get a room – a room to myself! And I can find a job. And then when Henry gets out, we're going to get married. He might even get out of here before me.'

'Dotty-girl, I'm so glad you're feeling happy,' her aunt ventured in her most supportive tones. 'But, well, we've spoken about this before, haven't we?'

'No!' Dorothy cried out instinctively, before acknowledging to herself that there might be a credibility gap that she needed to bridge. 'Well, yes. I suppose. But this time it's different. Really different. Dr Morgan is blown away, that's what he said.'

Dorothy braced herself for the point of the discussion, trying to avoid getting side-tracked by Ruby's premature judgements. 'So, anyway, Henry and I were thinking. If we're going to get married, it'd be really nice – I mean, it's probably the law, actually – but it would be good if my father could come as well. To the church.'

'Oh, Dotty!' Ruby lamented. 'This one again? We can't go talking this same conversation into a circle every time.'

Dorothy scrunched up her face. 'Please?' she whined. 'Please, Aunt Ruby? If you just let me know where he lives, I can write the invitation myself. I won't tell him where I got the address from. Please?'

'Not this old chitchat, precious girl,' the older woman implored. 'Even if I thought it good for you, I'd not have a start in finding him. You know this, my lovely – I've told you all this before. There's been plenty of tellings, truth be told.'

'But you do! You do know! It's in your file room!' Dorothy pleaded.

'Oh, Dotty! It goes in the ears fine enough, but somehow it gets all chewed up in the middle!' Ruby shook her long-suffering head. 'Anyway, I want to know some more about this Harry fellow of yours.'

Hearing her boyfriend's name misremembered hit Dorothy like a punch to the gut – as much a total surprise as it was a reminder of everything she already knew. Her aunt was determined not to listen to what she had to say. Dorothy flopped back in her chair, in a sudden sulk. 'In your ears, you mean,' she muttered sullenly.

'Dorothy Gale!' Ruby rolled her eyes. 'Will you kindly put a stop to all this crotchety nonsense, please? Even if I'd been told where he lived when he had you fostered, it was all when you were just a little tiddler. Most likely, he would have taken himself off to somewhere new by now in any case.'

'But he didn't want to!' Dorothy insisted, hoping that petulance would succeed where practised argumentation had faltered. 'He wanted to stay there forever. It was The Woman who wanted to go somewhere else.'

Ruby looked at her former ward, a confused expression on her face. 'What woman, Dotty?' she asked. 'There was never no woman that I was ever told about.'

'The woman that made him give me away,' Dorothy clarified, sitting forward in her seat again. It was a long time ago, but it didn't help her cause if her aunt couldn't even remember the important details.

'Well, I never knew about no woman, Dotty-girl. Only your father. And there's no way of reckoning what he was thinking all that way back when.' Ruby sighed. 'I've come a long way here to say a pleasant hello to you, my precious thing, not to have cross words. And you'll not be believing who I bumped into last week. Just in the town. Go on! Take a guess.'

Dorothy leapt to her feet, scraping her chair across the tiled floor. 'That's not right! That's not right at all!' she blared, wagging an accusatory finger at her aunt. 'Your memories are wrong! If you'd listened to my father, you'd know the truth. But you didn't! You don't listen to me and you didn't listen to him!'

'That's quite enough, Dotty!' Ruby glanced self-consciously at the nearby patients and visitors, before returning to the conversation. 'Of course I listen to you. I listen to all the things you have to tell me, whether I want to hear them or not. Now, sit yourself back down and find your calm, young lady.'

'It's Henry! It's Henry, not Harry! See? You never, ever listen!' Dorothy growled her knockout blow. 'You're the only person that can help me, the only person that can make my wedding day as happy as it can get. And until then, you've got nothing to say to me. Nothing at all.'

Her rehearsed reasoning completed, Dorothy turned and

marched away, hoping to get through the day room doors and out of earshot before Ruby had a chance to recover her poise. Although the irritation she felt was real, Dorothy was also aware that she had just been afforded a rare opportunity to storm away from an argument having had the final word. She granted herself one last look over her shoulder before leaving the room, a decisive goodbye to the forlorn figure slumped on her own in the corner.

Outside, Dorothy scurried down the corridor and through a set of fire doors, moving deeper into the Zoo and out of range of her aunt's dishonesty. Only when she was convinced that she was in the clear did she come to a halt, turning instead to stare at a blank green wall. Although her brow was still creased and she was noisily blowing and sucking air through her nostrils, she wasn't sure whether she was experiencing genuine outrage or if it was all just part of a subconscious strategy to manipulate Ruby's emotions. Or whether there was even any merit in trying to differentiate between the two.

Thankfully, she knew a foolproof cure for anger. With her legs rigidly locked at the knee, Dorothy folded herself over at the waist, slowly reaching down to touch her immaculate shoes, then further still, until she managed to place her palms on the floor between her feet. With a nimble hop she kicked her legs above her head, tucking in her chin and leaning forward just before her heels collided with the wall, easing into a perfect handstand. Her loose T-shirt tumbled down to drape itself across her face, exposing the white bra underneath. Dorothy closed her eyes to focus on her breathing. 'Find a smile from a frown when you turn it upside down,' she muttered indignantly to herself as her face slowly turned crimson, repeating the mantra, building up speed until all meaning was lost in the rhythm of the words.

When the process was complete, Dorothy kicked her feet

away from the wall and gracefully landed back on the floor. She stood upright immediately to better savour the momentary dizziness, reeling gently on the spot as any residual displeasure dissolved into the head-rush. She giggled quietly as she let herself be distracted from her annoyance by the familiar sounds of the Zoo: the hum of distant conversation and laughter; a triumphant cheer from someone winning a game in the day room; a fleeting scream from one of the treatment rooms.

Dorothy waited a moment longer to let the grogginess pass. 'Oh – macaroni day,' she purred, and gambolled off to reconnect with the soothing routines of an institutional Wednesday.

∽

OVER A PLATE PILED high with cheesy pasta, Dorothy had taken it on herself to propose the subject of lunchtime debate. Opposite her, Crane picked at his food, making no attempt to hide his boredom with the conversation. Next to him, Thatcher leant in with a smile, encouraging, questioning, doing everything he could to prolong the discussion. Parsley sat where he always sat. Having already ploughed his way through lunch in three unchewed mouthfuls, the colossus was patiently waiting for Crane to abandon his meal. On the other side of Dorothy, an empty chair anticipated Henry's arrival, and the surreal tangents that his presence inevitably brought to the repartee.

'But what do you imagine you'll want to do for a job?' Thatcher quizzed her. 'I don't believe that you'd be happy just hanging around in your house all day, every day. You may as well stay in the Zoo if you want to do that.'

'We might have a farm,' Dorothy replied without hesitation. 'Like my father's farm, but really near the city. That's loads of things to do. Or I could be one of those people on TV that tells everybody what the weather is later.'

'Gonna need a diploma to do that,' Crane pouted. 'Next idea.'

A frown etched a series of deep wrinkles into Thatcher's brow, and he glared down at the younger man. 'You really shouldn't be so dismissive, Mr Crane. I have every faith that Dorothy can achieve whatever she puts her mind to. And if that involves going to university first, I'm sure she will prove more than capable.' He directed a reassuring smile towards the girl.

'What do you know about going to university, jizz-lips?' Crane retaliated, straightening from his slouch at the prospect of some verbal jousting. 'Or are you just saying what you think Dorothy wants to hear? I mean, it sounds like you're trying to fuck her.'

'Good God, man!' Thatcher exploded, spraying balls of cheesy spittle across the table. 'Mr Crane – that is quite enough!' He turned towards Dorothy, looking aghast. 'I am really very sorry that you had to hear that, Dorothy.'

With a deft flick, Crane launched a piece of pasta towards his tall companion, which missed its target by some margin. 'Yeah?' he declared, rising to Thatcher's challenge. 'Well, we're all getting a bit fed up with the shit you talk sometimes. Don't pretend you're ever getting out of here. Hopefully you'll be dead soon, and we can all finally get a bit of peace and quiet.'

As Thatcher's jaw dropped, Dorothy realised that her part of the conversation was over. Her friend had just been goaded into playing a round of Crane's game, and the younger man was already bobbing restlessly as he waited for Thatcher's reaction. When it finally came, there was a palpable resentment in his tone.

'You are unbelievable!' Thatcher announced slowly as he

twisted the beads on his rosary necklace. 'I am so glad I never had the misfortune to encounter you when I was in one of my darker moments of self-loathing.'

'Shame. Downer Snatcher sounds like way better company than the twat we're forced to suffer now.'

Thatcher's eyes welled up with tears. 'Oh, you really wouldn't have wanted to meet me in a former life,' he quietly assured his antagonist. 'Trust me.'

'Ooh! Don't cry!' Crane mocked him playfully. 'Maybe I'd have let former Thatcher brown me out in exchange for a pill or two. He'd have liked that. Did he learn how to do that at university?'

Sitting at the other side of the table, Dorothy watched this latest skirmish in her friends' long-standing campaign play out with its predictable bile and venom. In all the time she had known them, she had never understood why Crane singled Thatcher out for all this abuse; however, neither had she figured out why Thatcher always rose to the bait. This was usually the moment in an argument when Henry would step in to defuse the tension, like the time he swallowed a whole sausage without chewing it after making his friends beat out a drum-roll on the table. Or the time when he stood on his chair and encouraged the other diners to bring over their scraps as part of an experiment to see how much food Parsley could eat in one sitting. Even on a quiet day, Henry could usually be relied on to cram vegetables into his ears and nose. But without him there, Crane's opprobrium was allowed to spew forth, unchecked. Dorothy rose unnoticed from her chair to hunt down her missing boyfriend while the exchange opposite continued. On the seat next to her, Parsley moved to stand; she placed a hand on his shoulder and gently pressed him back into his seat as he hummed a quick melody to himself.

The last thing she heard as she shuffled away from the table was one of Thatcher's comebacks, delivered with all the poignancy of someone who had just taken every one of his adversary's slanders to heart. 'Oh, Mr Crane,' he spluttered. 'Sometimes I wonder if Dorothy is going to miss you at all.'

∾

SINCE THE MAJORITY of the Zoo's inhabitants were clustered in the dining room, it didn't take Dorothy long to sweep the building. She found Henry in Appletree ward, lying on his unmade bed, silently considering the crowded ceiling. She cavorted across the empty room. Henry turned to scrutinise her as she approached, a lazy smile forming on his lips.

'Why aren't you eating?' Dorothy asked as she drew alongside his bed. 'It's macaroni day. You like macaroni day.'

Henry patted the mattress next to him, and Dorothy eagerly perched on his bed. He gazed up at her with a beatific expression, which Dorothy returned with an uncertain smile of her own. 'Did you want a cuddle?' she suggested.

Her boyfriend raised his head from the pillow in acknowledgement. Dorothy shuffled herself under his shoulders to cradle his head on her lap, her feet swinging off the side of the bed.

'Shame on you, Princess,' he mumbled. 'Keeping me waiting like that.'

'Did you see your dead friends?' she enquired.

Henry closed his eyes and his smile deepened. 'They went away,' he whispered.

'Oh. They didn't stay long,' Dorothy joked, hoping he'd scared them off for good. She leant forward to brush the tips of her hair across her boyfriend's face, and he let out an appreciative sigh. In any case, she had news of her own. 'So, my aunt didn't want to tell me where my father lives. I told her we were getting married, and I told her how happy Dr Morgan is with us, but she still didn't want to help. Even though she knows where he is. And she didn't even get your name right. She doesn't listen to anyone.'

Henry gently rocked his head from side to side sympathetically, flicking his nose against a strand of Dorothy's hair. She continued, 'But it doesn't matter, because we can go and find him before we get married. Aunt Ruby can't stop us when they let us out of here. When we won't need the drips and the medicine, because the Programme will be finished and we'll be better. Like we are now.'

'No drips. No Programme,' Henry drawled in agreement. 'We make each other better.'

Dorothy kicked her legs excitedly. 'We are! We are making each other better!'

A drop of blood shook free from where it was pooling on the bed frame, inching down the metal tubing and dripping onto one of Dorothy's pristine white trainers. With the path cleared, more of the viscous fluid followed along the same track; a second drop chased the first onto her shoe, quickly becoming a steady patter and then an unbroken trickle. 'When we get married,' she continued, unaware of the horror show beneath her, 'and we have a house, can we have one with an upstairs that no one is allowed to go to except us?'

With every breath, Henry's body relaxed further into Dorothy's embrace, his face becoming steadily more serene. She stroked the silly curls on the side of his head as she indulged her fantasies of their planned life together. The reservoir of blood dribbled off the bed frame and splashed untidily onto the floor, where it formed a shallow pool. Above it all, a single sloppy tear exposed ripped arteries in Henry's wrist. Their contents ran down his fingers like a melting waxwork, feeding the growing puddle beneath.

Henry inhaled deeply. He opened his eyes a crack to look into the face of the woman in whose arms he lay. 'Princess,' he whispered, letting the word slip from his throat as he slowly released his breath. 'Don't keep me waiting too long.'

His eyes closed, his smile widened, and the two of them sat a while in silence to contemplate their future together, and a time beyond the Zoo.

ACKNOWLEDGEMENTS

The book was written in part during the pandemic, providing a welcome distraction while the apocalypse raged outside. *The Zoo* has proven to be as important in safe-guarding my lockdown mental health as all the Zoom calls with my family or the Aretha Franklin back-catalogue, and inevitably some of this has crept into the themes of the book. While I was hoping that the events of the last couple of years would make us all 20% kinder than we were at the start of the pandemic, my characters have obstinately refused to listen.

There are a couple of really useful online resources to help writers turn their ill-formed scribblings into finished novels: *Jericho Writers* and the *Alliance of Independent Authors* (*ALLi*). A big thank you to Eleanor Hawken and Holly Seddon of *Jericho Writers* for their insightful and comprehensive developmental editing notes, and to Jane Hammett (from the *ALLi* database) for her meticulous proofing. I also found Richie Cumberlidge of *More Visual* from the *ALLi* catalogue, designer of this fabulous cover.

I owe my heartfelt gratitude and apologies in equal measure to my über-patient beta readers, all of whom had to deal with borderline unreadable drafts way too early in the process. To the diplomatically alphabetical Dale, Daren, Eve, Gail, Julie, Leif, Lindsey, Lisa and Vod – thank you, sorry, and you did make it better. The lesson for next time is to get the professionals involved first to sweep the manuscript for mines, and only then presume to exhaust the goodwill of my friends.

And finally, a special thank you to Lucilla, Jacqui, Dave and the Mog. They know why.

Back ~~ground~~ wards telling fits perfectly with how so much is reversed.

- Like Happy Ending - ~~B~~ Oz says her story will have a happy ending which to her is not returning to Kanzas but going on her journey and not coming back -

Wicked witch of the West not wicked; companions not brave intelligent or kind

Witches
Ruby (at East Close)
West

Told in reverse - fits with this story as it is as going back

Each chapter begins with waking

Printed in Great Britain
by Amazon